D0438316

bowker's *bonfire*

Also by Tony Caxton

Murder in a Quiet Place

bowker's *bonfire*

July 1/01

tony caxton

st. martin's press
new york

A THOMAS DUNNE BOOK.
An imprint of St. Martin's Press

BOWKER'S BONFIRE Copyright © 1996 by Tony Caxton. All rights
reserved. Printed in the United States of America. No part of this book
may be used or reproduced in any manner whatsoever without written
permission except in the case of brief quotations embodied in critical
articles or reviews. For information, address St. Martin's Press, 175 Fifth
Avenue, New York, N.Y. 10010.

Library of Congress Cataloging-in-Publication Data

Caxton, Tony.
    Bowker's bonfire / by Tony Caxton.
        p.   cm.
    "A Thomas Dunne book."
    ISBN 0-312-13936-5
    I. Title.
    PR6053.A94B69   1996   95-33691
    823'.914—dc20   CIP

First Edition: March 1996
10 9 8 7 6 5 4 3 2 1

bowker's *bonfire*

1. .... *minching lane*

They came out of nowhere, two men in dark blue boilersuits and black ski masks, each carrying a five-gallon can of petrol. They walked quickly and quietly along Minching Lane and stopped at a small shop with an old-fashioned painted sign: *R. Matthews, Newspapers, Tobacco, Confectionery.*

The clock of St Bardolph's Church struck three, a deep, clear musical chime above the sleeping town. One masked man nodded to the other and pointed farther down the street. The other nodded back to show he understood his instructions and moved off.

Matthews' shop door was wood-panelled for the bottom half and glass-panelled at the top. A cardboard sign that dangled inside said: *Sorry, we're closed.* Through the glass could be seen a long counter with displays of chocolate bars and chewing gum. On the facing wall were racks for newspapers and magazines.

The man outside unscrewed the cap of his petrol can and fixed a short rubber tube to it. He put the tube through the letter slot in the door and tipped the can. He could hear the petrol splashing down on the shop floor and smell the fumes.

Both sides of Minching Lane were terraces of old houses, with a parade of shops at one end, facing each other across the road and the parked cars. Above the shops there were apartments for the shopkeepers and their families. Minching Lane was run-down and old-fashioned, and the day couldn't be far off when the town council demolished the entire street and rebuilt it.

Matthews' shop was second from the end. There was an alley at the back to give access for delivery vans—the second man took this route to reach the back door.

There was no letter flap to pour petrol through, but he'd known that in advance. And it was dark here at the back without the street lamps. He'd expected that, too. It was an old wooden door but it had a modern lock to keep thieves out.

He hadn't come to break in. He lifted his heavy can head-high to tip petrol down the door and held his breath. He poured half the can, felt petrol lapping around his feet, and swore while he stepped back and set the can down on the doorstep. The screw-top was off. He waited and listened.

In the apartment over the shop, Ronnie Matthews was asleep in bed with his wife Doreen. And in the next room their two little girls were asleep. The younger, Diana, was cuddling her teddy bear. Janice, who was two years older, had a blonde Barbie doll on the pillow beside her.

At the front of the shop, a full can of petrol had been poured in through the letter flap. The man in the ski mask fed one end of a thick string through and down inside. He shrank close in to the side of the building when he heard a car in the distance, surprised that anyone was out at three in the morning in this small town.

All was quiet again. He took a box of matches from his pocket and struck one. A last look around before he held the match to the petrol-soaked string. When he saw blue flame running up it, he turned and ran. He'd taken seven steps when Minching Lane was lit up by the glare of five gallons of petrol igniting.

At the back, the other man heard the roaring of fire. This was the signal he was waiting for. He had the matchbox ready in his hand. He moved a long way back before he struck a match, pushed it into the box, and skimmed the flaring mass at the door.

Tongues of flame licked up, higher than the door, right up to the windows above, where the family lived, and over the bedroom windows, waking up Ronnie Matthews. The room was bright as day. He sat up fast and shook Doreen's shoulder.

'The shop's on fire,' he shouted, fear in his voice. 'Get the kids up quick—I'll see if we can get down the stairs.'

Detective Inspector Bowker hunched over the steering wheel as he drove into Bedlow-on-Thames. No regulation car would accept his bulk neatly or conveniently. Six-feet-six in his socks and wide as a barn door—his seat was pushed all the way back, his head brushed the car roof, his knees doubled up under the wheel. His shoulders took up more than half the car and left hardly enough space for Detective Sergeant Jack Knight beside him.

'Been here before?' Bowker asked.

Knight had been transferred from the industrial Midlands three months earlier and was not much interested in the scenic charms of the Thames valley, only in doing his job well enough to make sure of promotion.

'No reason to,' he said, 'and not much chance either, the way you keep me busy.'

'It's not a bad little town.' Bowker ignored the jibe. 'I've brought my wife and kids here once or twice for a picnic in a rowboat on the river.'

'Nice family outing,' said Knight, unmarried and unattracted to the pleasures of domesticity.

'This road in is called Gallowgate. In the old days, they used to hang sheep stealers and other criminals on a wooden gallows along here—in front of a cheering crowd.'

'That's a bit bloody thick,' Knight said, 'hanging people for stealing a sheep! I thought it was only highwaymen they strung up—the old-style muggers on horseback who waved their pistols at stagecoaches and shouted *Stand and deliver!*'

'Them too,' Bowker agreed sombrely, 'but that was more on the main roads to London, where passengers had money and valuables worth stealing.'

'Makes sense,' Knight said.

'After they'd hanged the highwaymen, they coated them with tar and left them swinging in the breeze until they rotted and bits dropped off. As a warning to other villains.'

'They never did!' Knight was astonished.

'Pity they don't do that now; it would save you and me a pile of trouble. You see that plaque on the big marker stone by the road? That's where Bedlow gallows stood. The local council put a plaque there so tourists would have something to take a photo of. It tells you that the last person they hanged here was Amos Dinwiddy in 1832, if I remember correctly.'

'What did he do, steal the Mayor's gold watch?'

'According to the plaque, he murdered a young girl he'd got in the family way and buried her body in a ditch.'

'Crime doesn't change much,' said Knight. 'That chap on trial two weeks ago when you gave evidence throttled his girlfriend to death and dropped the body down a manhole. Couldn't find a handy ditch, I suppose. Knocked down to manslaughter, and he got off with three years when his lawyer said she'd laughed at him for being useless in bed.'

'See what I mean?' said Bowker. 'Time off for good behaviour and he'll be on the streets in eighteen months—another killer who got away with it. When he strangles another girl, he's got a ready-made excuse; she laughed at him.'

Knight was wondering why Bowker was being so talkative today. By nature, the Inspector was not a gregarious man; chattiness was not his style. He was black-haired and as swarthy as a gypsy; massive and menacing, uncertain of temper.

Behind his back, other coppers nicknamed Denis Bowker 'The Mad Mangler' because of his resemblance to a popular TV wrestler. It wasn't just his looks, his natural air of ferocity had a lot to do with it.

'What's that?' Knight asked. 'Another tourist sight?' Over to the right were the ruins of an old stone building. The roof had gone and the walls were broken, but the empty window spaces had arched pointed tops of the type seen in old churches.

'Ruined abbey,' Bowker said, still surprisingly genial. 'The Benedictine monks built it five hundred years ago. They're the mob who make that green liqueur that tastes like cough medicine and costs more than good Scotch whisky. The abbey went derelict after King Henry the Eighth ran them off the property and sold their farmland because he was hard up.'

'Doesn't sound legal to me,' Knight commented.

'Nor to me. I'd call it stealing, but he got away with it. The town spends money on the ruins now for lawns and flower beds to make it interesting to visitors.'

'I don't suppose it was called stealing in the old days when kings helped themselves to other folk's property,' Knight said. 'There weren't any police in those days, anyway.'

They drove under a Victorian brick railway bridge and were in High Street, broad and busy with traffic. The left-hand side of the street was almost entirely taken up by a shopping mall, the other side was end-to-end banks and building-society branches—and antique shops with displays of dubious Georgian furniture.

At the bottom end of the street they drove over the old stone bridge across the Thames. Knight was lulled by Bowker's unusual affability into asking a question better left unspoken.

'This job we're here on,' he said rashly, 'are we supposed to take it seriously or have we been sent on a wild-goose chase to save somebody's face?'

The glare he got would have sent any lesser man into terminal shock.

'We're investigating a serious case of murder!' said Bowker, his tone grating as an iron nail scratching down a marble tombstone. 'Four murders to be exact; two of them were children. So don't ask me bloody silly questions. We're here to find out who was the evil bastard who did it and get the handcuffs on him.'

'Right,' said Knight, retreating frantically. 'What I mean is what's our chance of catching him after all this time?'

'Bugger all chance.' Bowker scowled blackly. 'Not now that the local coppers have prodded about for three months and found nothing. That doesn't mean we're not going to try our damnedest—even if I have to punch heads till somebody confesses.'

Knight was never sure if Bowker was joking or serious when he threatened grievous bodily violence. When he was first assigned to the Inspector, he'd said good-bye to his chance of promotion. A copper associated with the unpredictable Bowker couldn't fail to acquire some ugly black marks on his record.

He revised this view after three murder cases with the morose Inspector. Bowker solved his cases. Being associated with a perfect record of success couldn't hurt Knight's prospects—

that was how he saw it now—though he still flinched sometimes at Bowker's methods.

'The first case I was ever on with you,' he said, 'that bimbo who had her head smashed in on her hearth rug—I asked if your investigations were all as bloody complicated as that one. And you said they give you only the complicated ones. I wasn't sure you were being serious, but I know better now. Cases don't come harder than this—it's been buggered up by experts before they gave it to us.'

'So what do you want, another transfer?' Bowker snarled.

On the right, with a view over the river, stood a very modern town hall, all tinted glass and coloured panels, like something on a fairground. Next to it was the police station. Bowker drove into the station yard and parked his dusty car in the only space available.

It was clearly marked *Superintendent Billings,* in large white letters. Jack Knight started to grin at the thought of official rage and aggravation when the Superintendent came back to find his slot taken. But Bowker was always ready to offend anyone he considered pompous, without fear or favour, meter maid or Chief Constable.

The man they had come to see was waiting for them in a second floor office, Detective Inspector Harry Mason. He was fiftyish, thin brown hair and a bald spot in the middle. He wasn't at all pleased to see Bowker. An awkward moment, being taken off a case because you've failed, Knight thought.

Mason stood up to shake hands in a surly manner. He was wearing a blue-and-red striped tie with a brown suit, a combination not pleasing to the eye, in Jack Knight's opinion.

'I won't pretend I'm pleased to see you.' Mason stared hard at Bowker. 'I've put in an official complaint about being taken off the case before I've had enough time to clear it up.'

'And I'd do exactly the same if it was me,' Bowker agreed. 'I didn't ask for this job; it's something I've been told to do.'

'Well, then,' Mason said grudgingly, 'you've read the update. The files are all in order—it'll take the best part of a week to read your way through them.'

A pained look on Bowker's face told Knight that if files had to be read, it wouldn't be the Inspector who did it. His hatred of paperwork was a legend among his colleagues.

'I'll get around to that later,' he said, convincing nobody. 'For now just give me a rundown of the facts.'

There was a file on Mason's desk, but he didn't need to refer to it. The hard facts were so few, he had them in his head.

'April twelfth this year, a small shop burned down in Minching Lane. I'll show you where that is on the street map in a minute. A neighbour heard a noise and phoned in the alarm. By the time the Fire Brigade put the blaze out the shop and living quarters above were only a shell. They found four bodies in the ruins; Ronald Matthews the shopkeeper, his wife Doreen, the two daughters, Janice and Diana, one nine years old and the other seven.'

'Burned well, did it, this shop?' Bowker asked bleakly.

'It's a wonder the whole bloody terrace didn't go up in smoke that night. They've had to move the people out of the premises on either side because they reckon it's still unsafe. Matthews' floors collapsed in the fire, and the bodies were burnt so badly they couldn't be identified. We asked around the local dentists until we found the one with their dental charts.'

Knight fidgeted, uncomfortable with the implications.

'They've been buried,' Mason said with ghoulish satisfaction. 'The pathologist said there was no point in keeping them in the freezer after he'd done the postmortem.'

'Let's hope they died fast of breathing smoke before the fire got to them,' said Bowker.

Mason ignored that. It was no part of his job to consider

the sufferings of crime victims. But Bowker's good mood had drained away at the prospect of what lay ahead. Murder upset him, which was an unprofessional response he kept to himself. And the murder of children was guaranteed to upset him badly.

'A clear case of arson,' Mason said. 'You could smell petrol even after the premises were burnt right out. We found an empty five-gallon can by the shop door and another can that had burst open by the back door.'

'Two villains, then.' Bowker had a murderous look on his face. 'You've got some evil bastards here in Bedlow, Inspector, to do a thing like that.'

'They're no worse here than anywhere else,' said Mason, as if defending his local malefactors.

There was a look of utter disbelief on Bowker's face. Jack Knight thought it sensible to slip a question in quickly before the enraged Inspector commented offensively on Mason's attitude to wrongdoing.

'It was a tobacco and newspaper shop,' he said. 'Did Matthews rent out videos as well?'

'He did, in small way,' said Mason. 'It's all in the files. I know what you're thinking; was he into porn videos? Hard porn, the illegal stuff. They're very dodgy people in that trade, and if Matthews upset a supplier, it could be a motive.'

'Just a suggestion,' Knight said.

'It's been thoroughly investigated, Sergeant. There's nothing in it. The only porn distributor around here is Dougie Ronson, a nasty piece of work we've run in more than once. We stick him in front of the magistrates, his lawyer does his stuff, and they fine Dougie a hundred pounds—the case never gets as far as a Crown Court. We burn all his stock we can find, and the next day he's back in business.'

'Clean as a virgin's conscience, was he?' Knight asked.

'I personally gave him a very hard time over the fire,'

Mason said thinly. 'I scared him half to death. But I couldn't prove anything, and it's my belief he had nothing to do with it.'

'An obvious thing to do after a fire like that would be check on the landlord.' Bowker came to Knight's rescue. 'When you own a clapped-out building in a good position, you off-load the tenants and rebuild. There's millions in it for a sharp and active property developer.'

'Nearly the first thing I did,' said Mason, shaking his head, 'but the entire street belongs to the town. The council bought it at the same time they sold the old town hall to a developer to put the shopping mall on the site. I expect they'll want to knock Minching Lane down one day and redevelop, but I can't see the Town Planning Office doing an arson job.'

'That's why you've got a modern town hall and police station, is it?' Bowker scratched his square chin. 'I wondered who paid for all that tinted glass.'

'What about drugs?' Knight asked, feeling better now that Bowker was supporting him and anxious to let the Inspector know he was using his brain. 'Do you get much trouble with dope here? If a big distributor gets annoyed he'll sometimes make an example of the prat concerned to remind the others who's boss.'

'You're going over old ground, sonny,' Mason said. 'It's all been looked into. Our local drug barons are the Burton brothers, Wayne and Gary—we know very well what they get up to but we've never managed to get them for it. Not yet, that is.'

Bowker's thick black eyebrows crawled up his forehead, but he said nothing.

'The uniforms pick up five or six teenagers a week stoned out of their minds, and we charge them with possession. None of them will ever admit who they buy from. So we raid the Burton house and the garage they own—the raids are so regular, it's like a milk round. We never find any drugs, not even pot. If Matthews' shop was an outlet, the evidence went up in flames. I've found nothing that connects Matthews with the Burton brothers.'

'Forensic fished nothing out of the ashes?' Bowker wore an intimidating scowl. It was well known that he distrusted Forensic and all its findings.

'If you'd seen the site, you wouldn't even ask me,' Mason said dismissively. 'Look at the photos in the file. All the fire left was a big black bloody mess of ashes and cinders.'

'It's because a whole family was murdered, kids and all, that we're talking drugs and porn and organized crime,' Bowker said mildly, determined to remain calm. 'Murder on that scale seems too excessive for a grudge by a neighbour who's annoyed because the Matthews family had a cat that peed on his garden—or some such quarrel. But little feuds over the garden wall can blow up into unbelievable mayhem sometimes.'

'The Matthews family didn't have a garden,' Mason said. 'None of the shops have; it's a delivery area. And if there was a cat, there's no bones been found.'

Bloody hell, Jack Knight was thinking, he's a real plodder is Inspector Mason. No wonder he's got nowhere with the case.

Mason went on, 'But I know what you mean, and I agree. Just before Easter we had two schoolkids beat an old woman to death because they kicked their football over a fence into her garden and she wouldn't give it back. They'll never be convicted, more's the pity, because they're both under twelve.'

There was a low rumble from Bowker, but he made no comment.

'You can be certain I had a good look at Matthews' neighbours and friends and family,' Mason went on, 'all in the files. But I didn't find anything.'

'No, and I've got a grisly feeling there's nothing *to* find,' said Bowker, sounding very depressed by what he'd heard. 'April twelfth you said, and today is July sixth. Three months with all the men and resources you need, and nothing turns up. That tells me that chummy covered his tracks so bloody well that we may never find him.'

'That's a hell of a way to take over an investigation.' Mason sounded aggrieved. 'I'm still keen to carry on, even if you're not. I can crack it, given enough time. This is my town, I'm not having criminals get away with murder.'

Poor old devil, Jack Knight thought. He's got no idea of what Bowker's like when he gets going. One sniff of a crime, and he's like a bloody great mastiff howling for blood. But how could he know? Poor old Mason—he's stuck in a small town with not many years to go to his retirement. He's fed up because he'd like to clear up the case, and it's been taken off him. He'll be no help to us.

Bowker astonished him by pulling a police notebook out of his pocket and sliding it across the desk to Mason. He'd never seen Bowker with a notebook before; his Sergeant was expected to get everything down in writing. And it was very evidently a new and totally unused notebook. Knight would give odds of a hundred-to-one that Chief Superintendent Horrocks had told Bowker to start following proper procedure.

And he'd give the same odds that Bowker's compliance wouldn't last a week.

Bowker said to Mason, 'Before we leave you, I'll take it as a favour if you write down the names of your best five suspects for me.'

'They're all in the files, with notes and full transcripts of interviews with them.'

'Very commendable,' said Bowker with a wintry grin. 'I can't spare my Sergeant for a week to slog through your files. Jot a few names down for me, and I'll be on my way.'

Mason shrugged and pulled a ballpoint from his inside pocket. He wrote carefully on the blank first page of Bowker's notebook and pushed it back across the desk.

'There's six for you, not five.' He pursed his lips contemptuously. 'I've interrogated every one of them, and you'll find tapes and full transcripts on file. I've put Ronson and the Burtons on the list because they're full-time criminals, and that makes them professional suspects for any serious crime committed in Bedlow. The other four had personal contacts with Matthews. So far I've not been able to turn up anything to link them directly with the fire.'

Bowker's calculation made that made seven, not six, but Mason obviously counted the two Burton brothers as one suspect.

'Arnold Hinksey,' he read. 'Moira Druce, Billy Swanson, Shane Hambleton, Lloyd Davies. So who are they?'

'Hinksey was Matthews' best pal; they went fishing together a lot. I don't trust him, and neither will you after you meet him. Mrs Druce was Matthews's bit on the side, though she denied it. But I established it beyond doubt. Might be a motive there.'

'Not usually a woman's crime, burning a house down, front and back together,' said Knight.

'Nobody's suggesting she did it personally, Sergeant,' Mason snapped. 'It took two people to set the fire. If it was anybody on that list, they'd have needed an accomplice.'

'Except the Burton brothers,' Bowker suggested.

'True,' Mason conceded. 'Where was I? Yes, Billy Swanson has a record. We've run him in a couple of times for thieving, and I can see no reason for Matthews to know him unless they had some sort of crooked arrangement between them.'

'You mean Matthews might have been fencing for Swanson?'

'It's a possibility to consider,' Mason said. 'But again, if there was anything on the premises, it went up in the blaze. And Shane Hambleton's up to no good, if you ask me, though I can't just put my finger on it. He works at the boatyard down by the bridge. The other name on the list you have to be careful with. Lloyd Davies—he's a lawyer.'

'What sort?' Bowker asked, sounding keen. 'Buying your

house and collecting on auntie's will? That sort of lawyer?'

'He's the clever bugger who gets Ronson off with a fine every time for possession and distribution of obscene publications.'

'And he was a contact of Matthews?'

'Often seen drinking together in the Crown and Anchor— that's a pub in River Street. Needless to say, I didn't get far asking him questions.'

'Slippery bastards, lawyers—nobody ever gets far with them.' And Bowker tucked the notebook into his inside pocket.

Mason said, 'My Superintendent wants to meet you before you make a start. Introduce you to the murder squad, give you a local briefing. But he's at a conference all morning. Something to do with sensitive policing.'

'That would be Superintendent Billings?'

Mason nodded.

'Sensitive policing, I can see how that would take precedence over multiple murder,' Bowker said with heavy derision. Mason pretended not to notice.

'He's free this afternoon. He asked me to tell you he can see you at three. Something else you ought to know about, although I'm sure he'll tell you about it himself. We've been having a lot of aggravation with the local paper over the case.'

'How so?' Bowker asked.

'It's only a local rag that comes out once a week. Nothing to it, really—houses for sale and secondhand car ads. Not all that much news, except how the local cricket team's getting on. And the Mayor's speech when he officially opened the new public convenience on the riverside walk. Local stuff like that. Only now it's taking a big interest in the Matthews murder, probably because he ran a newspaper shop.'

'Sounds fair enough to me,' Bowker said, mystified.

Mason opened the middle drawer of his desk and brought out a folded newspaper.

'Front page.' He passed it across.

'IF THE POLICE CAN'T, THE BEDLOW HERALD CAN,' Bowker read out to Knight. 'Bloody hellfire, I don't believe this! It says here they've hired a private investigator from London to track down the killer—look at this!'

He gave the newspaper to Knight, his big shoulders hunched as if about to throw a despised crook over a very high wall. There on the front page was a photo of a middle-aged man with a hard look and loose jowls. Under it was a caption identifying him as *Frederick Morten, a leading London private investigator.*

In the story alongside was the rousing saga of how the *Bedlow Herald* out of sheer civic pride and duty because the police had failed miserably to arrest anyone for the savage and shocking killings of a well-liked and respected local family had decided to hire the services of a top London enquiry agent to solve the mystery.

'How long has this clown been on the job?' Bowker demanded.

'Less than a week, since the paper came out last Friday. Soon as it was published, Superintendent Billings went there to talk to the editor in person. Bentley his name is. He didn't want to listen to reason, and this Morten arrived the same day, and he's around and about the town all day long, poking about and asking questions. And he's offering money for information.'

'What the hell did you do to upset the editor enough for him to dream up a damn-fool idea like this?'

'Nothing,' Mason insisted, 'nothing at all. It's some sort of stunt to boost their circulation. The Superintendent is furious about it, being made out to look incompetent. I expect he wants to put you right about the paper in his local briefing.'

Bowker grunted, a noise like a big bear stirring in its cave, ready to lurch out and claw anyone in the way.

'What's the form on Morten?' he growled. 'You must have run a check.'

'Nothing worth knowing about,' Mason said. 'A couple of fines for speeding in his car—that's all.'

'An enquiry agent who's never been in trouble? Pull my other leg! Private detectives are about as lily-white as security guards, and they're mostly recruited outside prison gates when they shamble out into the light of day after serving their time.'

'That's all we've got on him,' Mason insisted, tight-lipped.

'We'll be on our way.' Bowker rose to his full height in one long smooth motion, a performance that impressed Knight every time. 'One last thing—where's a good place for lunch?'

'The canteen upstairs, of course.'

'I know all about canteen food,' Bowker said dismally. 'Irish stew on Mondays, boiled beef and carrots Tuesdays, sausage and mash Wednesdays, cottage pie Thursdays, fish and chips Fridays. Canteen food is the reason why coppers get soft and unhealthy. When the Assistant Chief Constable nips across to Bedlow for a visit, where does your Superintendent take him?'

'The White Hart Hotel, halfway down High Street. It takes you a couple of hours to have a meal there. When you're in a hurry there's a handy pub on this side of the river, not far from the bridge. The Black Dog, it's called. They do a good thick cheese-and-pickle sandwich, and the beer's good.'

Handy for the police station, Bowker thought. Sure to be full of coppers going off duty. Useful for picking up inside gossip. I'll send Jack Knight there for a drink in a day or two.

'White Hart?' he said. 'Right, then, we'll put up there while we're in Bedlow. That suit you, Sergeant Knight?'

'As long as you sign the expenses claim,' Knight said.

2. *crown and anchor*

Denis Bowker left his disreputable car in the Superintendent's personal parking space while he took Knight for a stroll around Bedlow-on-Thames. They stopped for a moment halfway across the bridge. It was a fine warm sunny morning, and the light glinted off the water as boats passed by. Even on a weekday, pleasure boats chugged past on outboard motors, and a few hired rowboats headed for the bridge and the upper river.

'That's Batty's boatyard down there.' Bowker pointed a thick forefinger. 'Shane Hambleton must work there, though I'll be jiggered if I know why Mason thinks he's involved. You might have to read through his bloody files to find out, if the worst comes to the worst. I've rented boats from that yard to take my family rowing, so I suppose I must have seen him— though I can't remember anybody who looks like a Shane.'

'What does a Shane look like?' Knight asked.

'Cropped hair, like a lifer in Dartmoor,' Bowker said without a moment's hesitation. 'A thin gold earring and a silly tattoo on his arm or somewhere it can be seen—*Death or Glory*, or *Love and Hate* or some such piffle. You can spot Shanes a mile off.'

Knight let it go at that. He was finding it hard to visualise the massive Inspector in a casual shirt and trousers hauling on the oars of a boat, wife with picnic hamper at the tiller lines and a couple of kids chattering away to Daddy.

Must be two of him, Knight thought. He's two separate people, like the fairy-tales lawyers dream up to get mass murderers off when we nab them. Split personality, all that drivel. *My client is a devoted husband and father, m'lud, he goes to church twice on Sunday and raises hundreds of pounds for charity for elderly cripples in his spare time. But there's a psychic complication, members of the jury—there's this other personality that takes over now and then, only my client doesn't know about it himself and has no recollection of these ghastly deeds after the event, and I've got a paid-for psychiatrist here to prove it. . . .*

Bowker moved on. He wasn't in a hurry, but his great legs were covering the ground at a speed that had Knight trotting to keep up with him.

'Where are we going, sir?' he asked. He hardly ever said *sir* to Bowker, now they'd got to know each other. When he did, it was a sign he was complaining.

'To see the scene of the crime, of course. Where the hell did you think we were going—to a pub to get drunk?'

There was irritation in Bowker's voice. Knight asked no more. After the discussion with Mason, there was a lot to be irritated about. Even the sunniest of dispositions would be soured by the tale of woe Mason produced, and nobody in their right mind ever thought of Denis Bowker as having a cheerful outlook.

Minching Lane wasn't hard to find; it ran parallel with High Street. All the windows of Matthews' shop were boarded up where the glass had shattered in the heat of the fire. The brickwork was black and sooty. The shops on either side were closed and shuttered: Bedlow Deluxe Launderette and Elsie's Knitting Wool and Patterns.

Structurally unsound, Inspector Mason had said. There was the usual graffiti scrawled on the hardboarding over the hole where Matthews' shop window had been, most of it by kids crowing over their sexual explorations. *PK did Tina Rollins. Bet Turner is a slag.* There were outline representations of prize parts, wildly out of proportion. And in among the dross a more adult message caught Bowker's eye: *Move heaven and earth to save the life of Chairman Gonzalo.*

'Who's Gonzalo?' he asked, his forehead wrinkled. 'Pop star, footballer, one of those bloody stand-up satiric comics?'

'How the hell should I know?' Knight said in surprise. 'Some sort of foreign politician, I should think. And he's sure to be a Marxist—they always are if their name gets put up on a wall. And *chairman,* a dead giveaway that is. Usually it's just *chair* because the wild women object to everything with *man* in it, but maybe he's from a South American banana country where women are still worth less than donkeys.'

Bowker shook his head doubtfully and led the way to the back of the terrace. It was the same story here: boarded-up windows and smoke-blackened brick, broken slates fallen from the roof.

'Are we looking for clues?' Knight asked. He expected to be growled at for that, but Bowker limited himself to a hard look.

'As there are no victims to be looked at anymore, it's useful to get some idea of the nastiness of the crime,' he said. 'What kind of wicked bastard sets fire to a house with two people and their children fast asleep on the top floor? Tell me, because that's who we're looking for.'

'*Two* of the bastards,' Knight said. 'One did the front door, one did the back. How about turning over Inspector Mason's drug barons for a start? The Burton brothers—there's two of *them*. And they run a garage, so no mystery where the petrol and cans came from.'

'Life's never that easy. I thought you knew that.'

'Surprising really,' Knight said. 'Two jokers with big petrol cans strolling around the town at night and nobody sees them.'

'Doesn't surprise me. In this sort of town they're all in bed by ten-thirty. Even the disco shuts up at eleven.' Bowker turned away from the blackened debris to head back to the life and bustle of the High Street.

'I've just noticed something.' Knight sounded pleased, 'That sign across the road on the shopping mall, the reason why they named it the Benedict Shopping Mall. It's for St Benedict and the ruined old abbey—am I right?'

'They'll promote you to Inspector if you go on detecting like that,' said Bowker. 'We'll walk through the mall to the road at the back—it runs down to the river, where the public carpark is. The Crown and Anchor pub is along there.'

'Where, according to Inspector Mason, the deceased used to have meetings with the local crooked lawyer, name of Davies,' Knight said, proving that he'd memorised the names and places.

'I wonder who his informer was,' Bowker pondered aloud. 'Most people keep their mouths shut about tricky lawyers.'

'Most likely a barmaid with a grudge. Do you think they sell that drink your Benedict monks brew? I've never tasted it.'

'They're sure to have it. But you won't like it, it's a drink for genteel tarts, like creme de menthe.'

'Never had that either,' said Knight. 'Am I missing something in life? Genteel tarts—I like the sound of that, though

I've not met one, only the usual scrubbers you see standing about on street corners in miniskirts.'

The shopping mall was not crowded at that time of day, mostly women pushing baby carriages or with small children skipping in their wake. Two security guards in dark blue uniforms ambled to and fro with no visible sense of purpose.

'What do you think they'd do if a smash-and-grab artist put a brick through the jeweller's window?' Bowker asked glumly.

'The young one's brain-dead,' said Knight. 'Look at his eyes; you can see nobody's at home. Not bright enough to be a bouncer at a disco, so they hired him for this job. Any sign of trouble, and he'll stand there gaping and wondering what to do.'

'The older one would know what to do,' Bowker said. 'He'd run for his life.'

The Crown and Anchor was a pleasant old pub with wooden beams and white plaster on the front. It had a garden between it and the pavement, with benches and tables set out for customers to sit with a pint of ale and a snack and watch little boats go by on the Thames. Bowker walked straight through the garden into the pub. It was cool and shady after the sunshine outside. The walls were panelled with dark wood, and there were framed prints of prize cattle.

Knight fetched two pints from the bar. He was disgusted to see there was no barmaid, only a youngish short-haired man in a T-shirt and a long white apron tied around his waist. He took Knight's money with a winning smile and got a hard stare back.

'Don't know what pubs are coming to,' Knight complained as he sat down beside Bowker at the corner table he'd chosen.

'You mean you miss the spit and sawdust and the scruffy

men in cloth caps swearing and kicking each other?' Bowker asked.

'There are three pretty girls outside in thin summer dresses, sitting with a drink in the garden,' Knight said reproachfully.

Bowker ignored the comment.

'If the lawyer met the deceased here for purposes we ought to know about, they didn't sit outside where every Tom, Dick, and Larry going past could see them together. They'd be in here, and I wanted to have a look.'

'You've got a down on lawyers,' Knight said with a grin.

Bowker sank half his pint in a long swallow. The only killer who had ever escaped him was a lawyer. It still rankled.

Knight went on, 'Seriously, though, we'd be making a better use of our time sitting outside and chatting up those girls and forget about the investigation. From what that prat Mason told us, it's a washout.'

'*Inspector* Mason,' Bowker said swiftly. 'A prat he may be, but he's your superior officer, and don't you forget it. Let's have a little respect for rank.'

'Sorry, sir, no disrespect meant. What did you make of it all when he laid it out for us?'

'He dumped a truckload of Mary Ellen on us,' Bowker said with gloom and despondency. 'He's done the bloody lot, that man. He's queered the pitch. He's warned every miserable soul in any way connected to the victims. If they hadn't got a watertight alibi before he interviewed them, they have now, every last one. I'm buggered if I know where to begin.'

'Maybe the Superintendent will be able to give us a lead when we see him,' Knight suggested without much hope.

'He'll be able to put me right on sensitive policing. I think that means not twisting suspects' arms up behind their backs to make them confess. I know about that already.'

'You want me to read through the files Inspector Mason was on about? Might take some time, it sounds as if he taped everyone he talked to, including the Mayor's speechwriter.'

'No point.' Bowker emptied his glass. 'He said himself there's nothing there of any use. I'll take his word for it and spare you a lot of boring reading. You know why we're here, why he's been taken off the investigation?'

'The newspaper,' Knight said at once. 'It sticks out a mile. The paper hiring a private eye's given a lot of senior coppers the hot flushes. Not just the respected Superintendent Billings in Bedlow. Thick brown clag has spread across to our bosses, and they're doing some sweating and heavy breathing. So's the Chief Constable, I bet. They'll give poor old Mason, sorry, Inspector Mason, the soldier's farewell before the year's out. It'll be a nice early retirement on medical grounds and a commendation for twenty-five years' undistinguished service.'

'You're a cynical and sarcastic sod,' said Bowker. 'Why I put up with you I do not know. And don't call Morten a private eye—we're not in bloody Los Angeles.'

'What am I supposed to call him?'

'He's an enquiry agent. He's paid to go ferreting in dustbins for evidence of adultery. He chases after people who go missing because they owe money.'

'Fifty-to-one he's an ex-copper,' Knight offered.

'I'd be a mug to take that bet—it's a brassbound certainty he was a copper till he was slung out.'

'Might have retired on pension and want to keep busy.'

'Don't you believe it. The ones who retire on pension go into private security with big companies. Morten's a wrong'un—must be to work for a newspaper making a mockery of the local police.'

Knight nodded in agreement.

'Something else bothers me,' Bowker said. 'Nobody is run in for committing a crime in this town, except a few snivelling teenagers on pot. The villains we heard about from DI Mason are still at it; drugs and porn and God knows what else. He says he knows what they're up to, it's just that he can never find the evidence to convict them. This place is Sin City.'

'You wouldn't think it when you walk about the town, it's all antique shops and tourist traps and visitors hiring row-boats on the river,' Knight said with a cheerful smile. 'I used to think it was in big cities where you found all the truly nasty people doing evil things. Since being out in the sticks with you, I've had my eyes opened. Talk about bloody rural depravity!'

'People are the same everywhere, Jack. They're capable of any atrocity when it comes to old-fashioned lust and hatred and making a lot of money quick.'

Only rarely did he use Knight's first name, and then always in circumstances that could reasonably be described as unofficial.

'Let's have another pint of ale and a meat pie,' he suggested with untypical amiability. 'We've got the Superintendent to see this afternoon, and then we can get down to some real work. Over the pie and ale I'll tell you about the first case I had after I was made Inspector, the only case that's ever shocked me.'

'Not the rich old lady and the lawyer who did her in—you've told me that one. More than once.'

'No, no,' Bowker said with an impatient grin. 'Listen and you might learn something useful. It was a missing-woman case, a nineteen-year-old college student. She was an American, over here at the art college. She went hiking on her own up the Thames valley on her summer vacation.'

'Bloody hell!' Knight said sadly. 'Another victim waiting for a crime to happen. Why do they do it?'

'The parents flew over from Minneapolis and kicked up a fuss, as you'd expect, and I was told to get results quick. So I had a check through records of missing persons in the area, and damned if there weren't eleven women reported missing in the past five years. There were others missing as well, but I concentrated on females under twenty-one. Eleven of them, that told me something.'

'This is going to turn into a very nasty story,' said Knight. 'I can see it all now. You collared a serial rapist and killer—am I right?'

'That wouldn't have shocked me. Sickened me, yes, but shock is something else. What I turned up was a married couple owning a bed-and-breakfast place, a pretty house with wisteria growing up the walls and yellow sunflowers five feet tall in the garden—you could have won photographic competitions with that house. Every time a girl on her own stayed the night there, hiking or maybe boating up the river, this charming couple crept into her room to knock her unconscious when she was sleeping and lug her down to the cellar.'

'Bloody hell! They did girls in for a few quid they'd have on them, and maybe a credit card?'

'Wasn't money they wanted,' Bowker said blackly. 'Down in the cellar they'd rigged an old kitchen table with straps and steel chains. They stripped the girls naked and—'

'I don't think I want to hear about it,' Knight said hastily. 'You'll put me right off my meat pie.'

'We dug seven bodies up out of the cellar floor,' Bowker said gloomily. 'Never found the other four.'

'I remember that case now; I read about it in the newspapers. It was the year I joined the police.'

'That why you joined the Force, Jack? To capture sick-minded slithery bastards who like to torture young women?'

'No, it was for the uniform. I fancied myself in blue driving a car with a siren and a flashing light on top. Like you see on TV, hundred-mile-an-hour chases with mobsters shooting shotguns at me. But I was promoted Detective Constable after a few years, and that was the end of the uniform and the siren.'

'You're having me on!' Bowker said suspiciously.

* * *

Superintendent Billings was in uniform when they met him that afternoon, a hand-tailored uniform with shining silver buttons on the front and his insignia on the shoulders. Bowker gave Knight an evil grin, as if to say, *now there's a uniform for you!* The man wearing the uniform was about forty-five, sleek and so executive that he was almost an inspiration to behold. He wasn't Bowker's sort of copper at all.

'I'll be straight with you,' he said, at which Bowker groaned inwardly, knowing the words usually meant the opposite. 'When I took the decision that we need more than our local resources to bring the Matthews investigation to a satisfactory conclusion, I requested the services of a Chief Inspector. Then there could be no ambiguity of command with Inspector Mason.'

Bowker's face darkened ominously at the implications of what Billings was saying.

'But,' the Superintendent went on, 'it seems someone has seen fit to take no notice of my carefully-thought-out request, and I am sent an officer of the same rank as Mason. I foresee certain difficulties of command. Mason has longer service than you and will naturally be reluctant to take orders from you.'

'There's no problem.' Bowker's tone made it obvious that he hated the Superintendent on sight.

'I'm relieved to hear that. Are you telling me that you have no objection to working under Inspector Mason's orders?'

'We're at cross-purposes,' Bowker said with a scowl. 'I meant there'll be no problem because DI Mason won't be on the case.'

'That's not acceptable; he's done all the work on it.'

'He's done three months' work that's led nowhere,' Bowker said in a voice like a gale straight from the North Pole icecap, 'I came here to take over and retrieve what can be retrieved. That won't be much, from what I've seen so far.'

The changing expressions on Billings' face made it simple to track his thinking. He wanted someone arrested and locked up in a cell to get the newspaper off his back. Otherwise his chances of ever making Chief Superintendent were zero. If possible, he'd save his own man's reputation by keeping him on the case to the end—whether he'd bungled it or not. But he'd sacrifice Mason without too much agony if that would save his own neck.

He wanted to reprimand Bowker for his offensive attitude, but Bowker was his only hope of finding the murderers. So that was out. He was silent for five seconds, his fingernails drumming on his well-polished desk. A sideways twist of his mouth showed that he reached a conclusion. If Bowker was in sole charge and got nowhere, the fiasco could be blamed on him alone. Billings would be in the clear.

'Very well, Inspector,' he said, 'the case is yours as of now. I shall assign Inspector Mason to other duties. The murder is not the only crime outstanding on our books.'

'So I've heard,' Bowker said sourly. He knew how the minds of senior officers worked. There was no mystery about what had gone through Billings' head.

'Good. I've got your murder team on standby; I'll take you to meet them now. The enquiry has been stepped down after so long, as you'd expect, but you have four of the original sixteen who worked on the case. Good coppers, all of them, I can vouch for that.'

Bowker's expression made it all too obvious he wouldn't buy a used car if Billings vouched for it—flash uniform and buttons or not. 'Before we do, can I have your thoughts on the persecution you're getting from the local paper? I've read the article about an enquiry agent from London being hired.'

For once Bowker had managed to use an acceptable word, though only from a sense of general solidarity, not from sympathy with the Superintendent. Billings certainly saw the newspaper action as persecution, but it was not a topic he wanted to talk about. It reflected badly on his handling of the situation.

'Lot of bloody nonsense.' He tried to sound sincere, a state of mind that didn't come easily to him. 'I'd advise you not to pay much attention to anything they print in the local rag. If you find the person responsible for the Matthews murders, the editor's nose will be put right out of joint. I shall demand that he publish a full apology.'

Knight decided it was time he said something. So far he'd been quiet, and he wasn't convinced the Superintendent was aware of his existence.

'The editor's got his knife into you, sir?' he asked with excessive innocence.

The Superintendent glared at him. 'I am not aware of any reason why the editor should choose to launch a vendetta against the Police Service or me personally,' he said witheringly.

Jack Knight didn't wither easily.

'That's all right then, sir,' he said sunnily. 'We'll put him down as a nutter and take no notice of what he prints.'

On Bowker's face a look of utter contempt had appeared at the words Police Service instead of the old-fashioned *Police Force*. Must be some bloody silly claptrap Billings had picked up from his sensitive-policing course.

Superintendent Billings wanted no more. Bad enough to have to put up with dumb insolence from Bowker, he wasn't going to take it from a damned sergeant as well. He stood up smartly and said he'd take them to meet the murder squad.

The Incident Room was up on the top floor. All the members of the squad were there, pretending to be busy. It was familiar to Bowker; the layout of desks and phones and computer screens. There were big photos pinned up on a wall of the burnt-out shop premises. And four photos of shapeless black-charred lumps that might be the remains of the Matthews family.

What was lacking was a sense of urgency. The investigation was at a dead end. Nothing was happening.

The team stood up when Billings entered the room, two men and a woman in plainclothes and a constable in uniform who looked well over forty. They stared curiously at Bowker, impressed by the size of him and by his lowering air of menace.

'Pay attention,' Billings said unnecessarily. 'I want you to meet Inspector Bowker, who is taking over the Matthews enquiry. And Sergeant Wright.'

'Knight, sir.' Jack Knight spoke up for himself.

'Eh? Oh, yes. Well, Inspector, here is your team; DS Trimmer, DC Hagen, DC Cote. And PC Purley. I'll leave you to make their acquaintance and give them their orders. My door is always open to you, if there's a problem or anything you want to talk over with me. Just drop in, anytime.'

Bowker nodded sombrely, a nod that might have signified tacit gratitude, but more likely the opposite.

'Sit down,' he said to the team before Billings was even out of the door. He perched himself on a corner of a desk and faced the four.

According to Billings, they were all good coppers. The senior man, Detective Sergeant Trimmer, was about Knight's age. He was stocky and looked tough, but not bright. He was wearing a hairy grey tweed sports jacket.

Detective Constable Hagen was about twenty-five and he had a sunny smile—not that he had anything to smile about. Unless he hadn't yet realized his career was mired in the clag.

The woman, Detective Constable Cote, was in her late twenties and attractive in a hard-faced way. She wore a long-sleeved blouse tucked into a grey skirt and she wasn't smiling. She knew what the score was.

The uniformed PC Purley was just that—a uniform. When Mason's murder enquiry ran out of steam the best coppers had been taken off it and assigned to other cases. Billings had left only the expendables on the Matthews case.

What the bloody hell am I going to do with this lot? Bowker asked himself. By the look of them, they couldn't catch a bag-snatcher at a nudists' convention.

'Listen to me, you miserable and unloved coppers,' he said in a voice that made the windows rattle, 'we're going to discover the vicious bastard who set fire to Matthews' paper shop and burned him and his wife and kids to death. I don't want to hear you've been at it three months and got nowhere. It's different now.'

'Why is it different, sir?' DS Trimmer asked, sounding as if he genuinely didn't know.

'Because I'm bloody well in charge!' Bowker informed him in a snarl that would strip the bark off an oak tree. 'Understand me well, Sergeant—I cannot bear low-life criminals who do their nasty crimes and go home giggling because they think we're too stupid to capture them. I won't have it! It gives me the colic, being sniggered at by lawbreakers.'

The Bedlow murder squad eyed him thoughtfully.

'Today is July sixth, in case you haven't looked at your calendar this morning. And the date I want you to write down in your notebooks is July twenty-second. That's a Friday, and it's just over two weeks from now. Got that?'

When no one moved he raised his voice to a roar that reminded Knight of a movie he'd seen on TV late at night. *The Beast from 20,000 Fathoms,* all scales and claws, rising out of the sea and bellowing as it waded ashore to trample New York City to rubble and plaster.

'I said write it down—July twenty-second!'

There was a scramble for pencils and notebooks.

'That is the date by which we will have the arson murderer in a cell down in the basement helping us with our enquiries.'

He saw the look of incomprehension on their faces and grinned ferociously at them.

'The reason we're working to that day is because the next day is Saturday, July twenty-third. That is the date when I take my wife and two children on holiday to sunny Spain for a fortnight. We have to check in at Gatwick Airport by eight-thirty that morning. Do I make myself clear?'

'Sir,' said DC Shirley Cote, greatly daring, 'none of us here has had a day off for three months, since this enquiry started. Not that anybody's grumbling, but without sounding pessimistic, I can't see you going on holiday in two weeks from now, sir.'

'You're a bold woman, Constable,' Bowker said, his grin acid. 'I like that. But I've never broken a solemn promise to my wife and kids yet, and I don't mean to start now. By Friday, July twenty-second, I want this child-killer gnawing his knuckles behind bars, like the animal he is.'

'Or she is,' Shirley Cote said, taking her life in her hands.

Billy Swanson lived on a housing development just off Five Acre Meadow Road, Bowker was informed by DS Trimmer. The estate was knocked up on the cheap by the town council thirty years before, to provide homes for Bedlow's poor and hapless.

'Breeding ground for crime, sir,' Trimmer said with a mournful shake of his head. 'Glue sniffing and pot, crack and thieving, vandalising, stealing radios from parked cars, smashing public phones, bag-snatching, gang rape. That's just the school kids. From school they go straight on the dole and graduate to heroin and coke. Nighttime they go burgling the better houses on this side of the river.'

Bowker stared at the sergeant in astonishment.

'The women are just as bad,' Trimmer went on. 'In the club

by the time they're fifteen. Shoplifting as a daytime job and on the game after dark. None of them pay any rent, they claim free housing as unmarried mothers,'

'Bloody hell!' Bowker said to this saga of urban delinquency. 'If it's that bad I'm surprised Superintendent Billings hasn't called the Royal Marines in to sort the estate out.'

Trimmer was a stolid man; he didn't realise the Inspector was making fun of him.

'Ah, if only we could, sir!' he said, a wistful gleam in his eyes, 'but it needs a State of Emergency order before the armed forces can get involved. And it wouldn't do any good. Up on the estate, they'd steal the guns from them.'

'There must be some good 'uns among them,' Bowker suggested.

'If there are, I've yet to meet them. Even the Salvation Army won't go hymn singing on the estate for fear of being mugged by skinheads.'

'Only one thing for it then.' Bowker kept a straight face. 'You need one of these TV preachers in a flash suit and a hairdo like Elvis Presley to go in there live with a megaphone and terrorise them with hellfire and damnation.'

Trimmer gave the suggestion his serious consideration before turning it down.

'It wouldn't work, sir. We'd have to give him 'round-the-clock protection, and we don't have the spare manpower available.'

Bowker had heard enough about the shabbier side of Bedlow and let the joke die. He asked about Billy Swanson.

'You want my opinion sir, you'll be wasting your time talking to him. He's just a small-time crook we've put behind bars four times for thieving, housebreaking, car stealing, and receiving and handling stolen goods. We pulled him in for questioning because one of the jobs he did was the Matthews shop.'

Bowker was puzzled.

'DI Mason told me he thought Matthews might have been fencing for Swanson,' he said.

'Doesn't stop Billy trying to thieve from him, sir. Billy and his brother had a van up to the back of the shop one night and were loading cartons of cigarettes when a neighbour who couldn't sleep spotted them.'

'Billy did time for that?'

'With his record, he was lucky not to get five years. But you know what goes on these days. There's a secret government order to courts to keep thieves out of jail because it costs too much money. Billy and his brother got twelve months each.'

'He's a vengeful thief, is he?

'He's a nasty little crook, sly and evil. DI Mason thought it possible he tried to get his own back. But if you ask me, he's a nonstarter as fireraiser. He's not up to it.'

'You can be sure about that, can you?'

'Early on in the investigation, DI Mason grilled Billy for the best part of twenty-four hours. He'd have given up and confessed if he'd been involved in it. We've got reams and reams of transcript of what he said and none of it's worth a twopenny damn.'

'I believe you, Sergeant. But the first rule of detection is to grab any known crooks by the particulars and squeeze till their eyes water. How about the brother?'

'Couldn't have been involved, sir. He's doing another stretch for stealing a vanload of shoes.'

'Were you in on the questioning of Billy?'

'Yes, sir, we ran the questioning in shifts, DI Mason and me. First him for an hour and then me for an hour while he went for a rest and a smoke. Then him again. And so on like that for all one day and the best part of the night.'

Bowker scowled. 'There had to be two of you present all the time. So who else was in on the questioning of Billy?'

'DC Hagen sat through the whole performance to keep an eye on the tape recorder.'

'So Billy has fond memories of you and DI Mason and DC Hagen. I want to make a fresh start, so I'll take DC Cote with me, if she knows Billy by sight. I want you to go with my sergeant and show him where all the other main suspects live. Not to disturb them or kick doors in, just show him where they live so that he can take me to any of them when I'm ready for them. Their usual haunts as well as their homes, understand? Pubs, clubs, strip joints, massage parlours, snooker halls, whatever.'

DS Trimmer stared at Bowker as if he'd taken sudden leave of his senses.

'Massage parlours and strip clubs!' he said. 'You won't find any of those in Bedlow.'

'Maybe not, but you've got porn and drugs here, according to DI Mason,' Bowker said in a dangerously rumbling tone, 'and two names on the suspect list are connected with them.'

'When you say "suspects," who do you mean?' Trimmer asked, his forehead wrinkled in speculation.

'Inspector Mason gave me a list of names. Knight's got a copy of it you can work from when you show him around the town.'

'Oh, them!' Trimmer hardly disguised his disbelief. 'You mean the people we've cleared already. Wouldn't it be better to make a start somewhere else?'

'I like to do things my way,' Bowker growled at him.

'Right, sir.' Trimmer evidently wasn't impressed by the arrangement. 'I'll take your sergeant around while you take Cote to find Billy Swanson. What about Hagen—what do you want him to be doing?'

'He can make me a list of every filling station for ten miles around Bedlow. The petrol had to come from somewhere local. And a list of all private pumps, like transport companies have, and places where boats get their petrol—boatyards and so on.'

'There'll be hundreds of them!'

Bowker's face turned black with suppressed rage at this first suggestion of obstruction.

'What of it?' he snarled. 'Get it done!'

Bowker had DC Cote drive his car because she knew where to go and he didn't. He waited while she slid the seat a yard forward to get her feet to the pedals and adjusted the mirrors and steering wheel to suit her.

'None of that two-wheel cornering flat out,' he told her in a tone so serious that she couldn't tell whether or not he was pulling her leg. 'This is my own car, and I don't want it wrecked before I can afford to buy another.'

As Bowker had guessed when he heard the name of the housing estate, it wasn't far from the ruins of the old abbey. There was a road off Gallowgate, on the opposite side—Five Acre Meadow Road, leading into Abbotsbury Estate.

The name was encouraging, but the estate was a dismal straggle of roads of semi-detached houses, all down-at-heel and frowsty. The kerbs were lined with parked cars; scratched and dented old hulks, the sort that changed hands for £80 with 90,000 miles on the clock and bald tyres. Neglected front gardens were littered with rusting bicycles and baby carriages, broken plastic toys and flattened beer cans.

'The times I've brought my family to Bedlow for a day out and never seen this!' Bowker said glumly. 'If day-trippers ever got lost and wandered into this estate, they'd run away screaming—if they weren't mugged and raped first.'

'A patrol car drives around the estate every two hours,' said Shirley Cote. 'You see the rattle-trap cars parked outside the houses; sometimes a brand new one appears. As sure as clockwork, whoever lives there has done a robbery. We get a search warrant and go in quick. You'd be amazed how much crime we clear up by regular observation of new cars on the estate.'

'All very well,' Bowker said sourly, 'it's never hard to pick up small-time thieves. Not that it does any good; they do a few months in jail and come out and go stealing again the same day. There's no question of right and wrong for them; they take what they can and never give it another thought. What about the real nasties, the ones peddling drugs and porn? How do you go about catching them?'

'That's over my head, sir, I just take orders. There's not a lot of mystery about who our local villains are: Dougie Ronson and the Burtons. But we can never make it stick.'

Bowker snorted derisively.

Shirley Cote knew her way around the estate's tangle of look-alike roads. She pulled up by a house totally indistinguishable from a hundred others.

'Twenty-seven Sheep Walk Road,' she announced. 'Billy Swanson's home.'

'Sheep Walk!' Bowker said in deep disgust. 'Who thinks up these bloody names? It's more like Dustbin Road.'

'It was all right once. I grew up on this estate two streets away. People were prouder of where they lived then. There used to be roses growing in most of the front gardens, and the women would red-raddle their doorsteps to make them look smart. It's gone down in the world in the last ten years. Nobody cares now.'

Bowker looked at her thoughtfully. 'What was your dad, a copper?'

'No, he's worked on the railway all his life. Still does.'

'Come on, then, let's go and talk to Billy Swanson.'

The garden gate was off its hinges. Bowker led the way up the cracked concrete path to the front door and rapped—so loud it reverberated through the house, drowning the blare of a TV they could hear inside. A shouted dialogue followed. First a woman's voice: *See who the hell that is at the door, Jason!* Then a male voice: *Bloody well go and see yourself!*

'Jason is the oldest son,' DC Cote explained. 'He's on twelve months' probation for molesting young girls.'

'How old is he?'

'About sixteen. Not old enough yet for proper sentencing.'

Bowker grinned mirthlessly and thundered at the door again.

It was opened by a woman of forty in a T-shirt and faded jeans that did nothing useful for her bulging shape. She took a quick step backward when she laid eyes on the massive Bowker looming up on her doorstep.

'Who the bloody hell are you?' she greeted him. 'The rent's been paid.'

Bowker showed her his warrant card for a tenth of a second.

'Detective Inspector Bowker,' he announced himself in a voice that would curdle milk. 'I'm here to talk to Billy Swanson.'

'Too bloody bad—your luck's right out, sunshine,' Mrs Swanson said spitefully. 'He went out hours ago and didn't say where he was going or when he's coming back. So you can sod off.'

'I know where he'll be.' Shirley Cote slid into view around Bowker's bulk. 'If he's not here he'll be in the pub.'

'Then you know more than I do,' Mrs Swanson said nastily. And while she was shutting the door on them, she added, 'Go and find him if you're so bloody clever. And take your tame gorilla with you.'

Bowker stood glowering, teeth bared and a foot raised to kick the flimsy door off its hinges. DC Cote moved away from him. She didn't want to be in the danger zone when he detonated. After a second, he burst out laughing, a sound like distant thunder.

'Long time since anybody's dared call me that to my face,' he said. 'I'll give her best this time—scruffy old eyesore that she is. So where's the pub Billy drinks in?'

'We passed it coming here, I'll show you.'

It was not a pleasant old pub, like the Crown and Anchor down by the river. It had been built as a part of the housing estate, and it looked like the houses themselves, only bigger. It stood back from the road and had a painted sign hanging in front.

'*The Three Jolly Monks?*' Bowker said in staggered disbelief. 'I've been in mortuaries that look jollier than this.'

There were not many drinkers inside. A trio of eighteen-year-olds played a pinball machine noisily. A man in a blue boilersuit sat alone by a window with an empty glass and a newspaper folded open to the horse-racing runners and odds for that day. A man wearing no jacket but with a sleeveless knitted pullover stood at the bar talking to a well-built barmaid with a look of terminal boredom on her face.

'Which one's Billy Swanson?' Bowker asked Shirley Cote.

'The one by the window reading a newspaper.'

'In a boilersuit? Don't tell me he's got a job!'

'Not Billy. He's never done a hand's-turn of work in his life. He wears the boilersuit to look like a plumber or glazier when he lurks at back doors of houses on the steal.'

Bowker stared balefully around the dismal pub, visibly hating it. A few strides took him to the table by the window. While Billy Swanson was gaping at the sudden threat to his well-being, Bowker had his elbow in a viselike grip and hoisted him to his feet. Higher still, and Billy was on tiptoes,

'I want a word with you,' Bowker growled, trotting his victim unwillingly across the murky room and out the door.

'What the bloody hell are you playing at?' Billy squawked. 'You'll break my bloody arm!'

Bowker ran him across the pavement to his car, shoved him into the back, and climbed in after him. Billy found himself squashed uncomfortably against the side by Bowker's breadth of shoulder. DC Cote got in behind the wheel.

'I know you,' Billy accused her, able to focus on her for the first time. 'You're the filth. I've seen you before.'

'Drive around the estate while I talk to Billy. Keep on going till I tell you to stop,' Bowker said. 'Any screaming you hear, ignore it. Billy's manners would make his old mother ashamed of him, but he's going to learn better.'

'What's going on?' Billy demanded, 'I've got my rights.'

He was a thick-bodied man of about forty, his brownish hair thin and missing at the front, eyes shifty, long pointed nose. A bit like a weasel, Bowker thought.

'My name's Bowker and I'm a Detective Inspector. Have you got that, Billy? I've taken over the investigation into the murder of the Matthews family last April.'

'I don't know anything about it, I told that to Mr Mason when he questioned me. You ask him—he'll tell you I had nothing to do with it.'

'Inspector Mason is far too soft on riffraff like you, Billy. He listens to your lies and sometimes he believes them. I'm not like that at all. I'm a natural-born disbeliever. And I'm not a good listener.'

'I don't care what you are,' Billy said, suddenly brave, 'I'm in the clear—it's been proved. So you stop this car and let me out, or I'll put a complaint in about you.'

'I've been complained about by better men than you, Billy. It just bounces off. Let me tell you why I'm using valuable police time consorting with dregs like you.'

'I don't give a bugger,' Billy protested. 'Let me out of this car! I don't have to talk to you.'

'I don't want you to talk to me. I want you to listen for two minutes, that's all. This is your first, last, and only warning that I'm going to run you in for the Matthews murders. Four of them dead, Billy; that makes it serious. And two of them little girls. I reckon the softest-headed judge will send you away for twenty-five years. You'll be eligible to claim your old-age pension when you get out of jail.'

'You know bloody well I didn't do it,' Billy said truculently.

'I don't know anything of the sort, but what's that got to do with it? You were involved, I know that for certain. You know who tipped the petrol in the door and who wanted it done. As it happens, I've got two weeks to clear the case up—that's all. If I can't have the actual villains, you'll do instead. As long as somebody gets a life sentence, the process of justice is served. Understand?'

'You can't get away with that.' Billy was crushed harder into the corner of the car by Bowker's oppressive shoulder, 'I'm not letting you stitch me up for something I didn't do.'

'Face it, Billy, everybody's a victim these days. Why should you be any different? If you read the front of your newspaper as well as the racing pages at the back, you'd know what I'm on about.'

'What do you mean?'

'One in five of the population are victims of society because they never bothered to learn to read and write at school,' Bowker said solemnly. 'Three out of five married women are raped regularly by their husbands. Four out of five children under ten are abused by Satanists twice a week.'

As he reeled off the numbers, he held up fingers near Billy's beaky nose by way of illustration, fingers that were strong and big enough to squash a cricket ball flat.

'Seven out of ten rabble like you live below the poverty line because of an incurable medical aversion against work. Nine out of ten doing time in prison are totally innocent, framed by the police. You'd know about victims if you listened to the news on TV. It's your turn to be a victim and suffer, Billy. Don't tell me I can't violate your civil rights; you don't know what I can do. But you're bloody well going to find out.'

'I'm definitely going to complain about you,' Billy insisted.

'Did you read about that postman a few weeks ago, the one who enticed young boys into his flat to do cruel and illegal things to them? He strangled them to death afterward and drove their bodies about in his Post Office van looking for a good place to dump them. Kemper, his name was.'

'It was on the local news,' Billy said. 'I remember seeing it at the time. Vicious bugger, he must have been.'

'He came to a bad end,' Bowker told him gleefully. 'He dodged out when he saw uniforms coming up the street to run him in, and he gave them the slip in the dark. He wasn't much of a runner, though, and they trapped him on a bridge—like the bridge you've got over the Thames in Bedlow. The evil sod fell right over the parapet into the water. I was in charge of that case, I watched Kemper fall in the river, and I had to laugh.'

'You wicked bastard, you pushed him in!'

'Mind your mouth, Billy—I'm telling you this story for your own good. Have you any idea why he didn't swim to the bank and climb out? It wasn't in the newspapers, the best bit. Both his arms got broken as he went over the side. He splashed about in the Thames screaming for help till he went down the third time. Before we rowed out in a boat to rescue him, he drowned.'

'I don't want to hear about it,' Billy muttered.

'Why should I care what *you* want? I hate and despise crooks. In particular I loathe and detest the scum who hurt children. I spend hours thinking of ways to make their lives miserable. Do you think I sent a wreath to Kemper's funeral?'

'It's nothing to do with me,' Billy said doggedly.

'You had a hand in burning two little girls to death. Deny it till you're black in the face, if you like, you're still a liar. I'm going to make you pay for that, Billy—really pay, not just a year or two in jail.'

'It wasn't me, I tell you!'

'Stop the car anywhere here, Constable,' Bowker said to Cote. 'Off you go, Billy. I'm glad we had this little talk to set you straight. You've got a week before you're run in. And this time it won't be Inspector Mason playing pat-a-cake with you—it'll be me. And I've been reprimanded more times for being rough on suspects than you've had hot dinners.'

The car had stopped. Bowker got out, dragging Billy after him by a grip on the collar of his boilersuit. He unwound himself to his full height, dwarfing Billy and glaring down at him with a black scowl on his face.

'Don't forget Kemper the postman and what I said about people who hurt kids. A life sentence must seem like a seaside holiday compared with what happened to that evil bastard. I wouldn't be sorry if you had a nasty fatal accident while re-sisting arrest, Billy. It would save me giving evidence against you in Court.'

'You wouldn't dare!' Billy said, but he sounded shaken.

Bowker got into the front of the car, his hand clamped around Billy's wrist in a bone-breaking grip. Billy didn't even try to pull away. He just stood on the pavement with a look of anguish and terror on his face.

'Before you leave us, Billy, ten minutes ago you were rude to Detective Constable Cote. You called her the *filth*. That's very offensive. Apologise to her.'

'I'm sorry, Miss!' he gasped.

'Not *Miss*, Billy, she's not a schoolteacher. She's Detective Constable Cote. Remember that because the next time you see her will be when I run you in and she puts the cuffs on your wrists behind your back.'

He let go of Billy's wrist, slammed the car door and told DC Cote to drive back to the police station.

'What you told him about Kemper, sir, was any of it true?' She sounded troubled.

'True Kemper did it? Yes. The last body was still in his van in a mailbag. True he ran before we got the cuffs on him. True he drowned. He jumped off the bridge unaided. It was his choice to die rather than go to jail—maybe he'd heard what the other convicts do to child molesters. Maybe he was trying to escape—how do I know?'

'There are some gruesome tales of what they do to people like him inside,' Cote agreed.

'One of the uniforms wanted to dive in and rescue him, but I told him not to. It was too dark to see anything, and I didn't want a dead copper on my hands. We found a boat eventually and rowed out to look for him, but he was dead and drowned by then.'

'What about the broken arms?'

'I made that up to entertain Billy,' Bowker said sunnily.

'You scared him—he didn't shout obscene words after us when we drove off. What makes you sure he started the fire?'

'How do I know if he did or didn't?' Bowker growled, back to his usual pugnacity. 'He doesn't look up to serious crime to me—but you never know. They say Dr Crippen was a mild little man before he did his wife in. Maggots like Billy get to hear about things we don't. You have to tread on them to squeeze it out.'

'Inspector Mason got nothing out of him.'

'He didn't go about it the right way,' Bowker observed.

When they reached the police station, Knight and Trimmer were still out on a guided tour of the town villains. Alec Hagen was at work with a stack of directories, listing filling stations.

'There's somebody to see you, sir,' he said. 'He's down-stairs waiting, name's Vereker. He's been before.'

'What's he want?' Bowker asked suspiciously, seeing the look on Hagen's face—and on Shirley Cote's. If it wasn't amusement, it was something very much like it.

'It's about his wife,' said Hagen. 'Joanne Vereker. She's missing.'

'What's that to do with me?'

'She went missing on the night of the Matthews fire. He asked for DI Mason because he's seen him before. The DI told him that you're in charge of the investigation now.'

Bowker picked up the nearest phone and asked for DI Mason. He was told that he'd gone home. Bowker's eyebrows came down into a black line of rage and disbelief. Then he bawled at the operator to put him through to Mason's home. Meanwhile he gave Hagen his glare of pure hatred.

'The DI said nothing to me about a missing woman when we were talking about the case, nor did the Superintendent. So tell me the connection between her and the fire, Hagen.'

'Don't know, sir. Have to wait for DS Trimmer to get back and explain it.'

'What do *you* know about it?' Bowker asked Shirley Cote.

'Vereker reported her as a missing person. We've got a report with details of her age and appearance, the usual stuff.'

'DI Mason,' said a voice in Bowker's ear. 'What is it?'

'Tell me about Vereker's wife,' said Bowker, not bothering to name himself, 'What's he doing here?'

'Ah yes, him,' Mason sounded shifty. 'Might be linked to the murder enquiry; it's all in the files. There's something dodgy about the way his wife vanished the night of the fire.'

'Was he one of your suspects?' Bowker demanded. His instinct told him he was being set up.

'Nothing very solid, but I couldn't rule him out. You'll find it all written up in the files.'

'Oh, sod the files!' Bowker muttered, banging the phone down.

'Find the missing-person report and come with me,' he said to Shirley Cote. 'I'll talk to this distressed husband. Hagen, get on with that list. I want it today, not next Friday.'

He had Vereker taken to one of the interview rooms, bleak and cheerless, as they are, blank walls, no windows, no clock, just a Formica-topped table and four chairs.

Donald Vereker was a fair-haired man of thirty. He was wearing an expensive sharp suit and several thousand pounds worth of gold wristwatch. He was in a bad temper.

'I've been kept waiting over an hour,' he said loudly, 'It is simply intolerable.'

Bowker stared at him hard and sat down at the table without a word. He'd met a lot of Verekers before in his work, men with a high opinion of their own importance to the world.

'I've been told you've taken over the enquiry from Mason. Who are you?' Vereker demanded.

'Inspector Bowker, replacing DI Mason. And this is DC Cote. I was out making enquiries; that's why you've had to wait. If—'

'I've met her before,' Vereker interrupted, his tone almost a sneer. He obviously had no regard for the members of the murder squad.

Bowker's face turned dark, his hands clenched into fists the size of footballs. Nobody had a right to be scathing about his team except himself—and nobody had the right to interrupt him when he was speaking.

'I've read the missing-person report,' he said in a roar that would have warned anyone less cocky than Vereker. 'Are you here with any new information about your wife?'

'New information? What the hell are you talking about? I'm here to get action—do you realise it's three months now since she disappeared? And you've found nothing and done nothing. No wonder the local paper's hiring a detective of its own—you're all bloody useless here!'

Bowker said nastily, 'Believe it or believe it not, it's no responsibility of the police to go looking for missing persons. Unless we have reason to think a crime has been committed.'

'Of course a crime's been committed! How stupid can you be? My wife's been murdered—there's no other explanation.'

'Wives go missing for all sorts of reasons. I make allowances for your rudeness in the belief that you're distraught, or else I'd have a few words to say about your attitude, Mr

Vereker. So what makes you think your wife has been murdered?'

'It's obvious to everybody except you.' Vereker was not put down by Bowker's warning. 'She went missing on the night a fire was started in Minching Lane and killed a whole family.'

'Are you telling me your wife started the fire?'

Vereker's face went crimson and his eyes turned up toward the ceiling for a moment. Words were hanging on his tongue—*God save me from stupid policemen*—but he managed not to say them aloud.

'No,' he hissed, 'I'm suggesting she saw something and had to be silenced by whoever is responsible.'

'Why don't you sit down?' Bowker suggested reasonably. 'What did Inspector Mason think about your theory?'

'He said he'd look into it. I don't believe he ever did. When I came back to check on his progress, he said there was nothing in it.'

Vereker seemed slightly mollified that an interest was being shown in his domestic catastrophe. He sat down opposite Bowker, who took the opportunity to look a question at DC Cote, sitting beside him. The corners of her mouth turned down. She shook her head in silent warning before she spoke.

'DI Mason had me make detailed enquiries,' she said. 'I found nothing at all to connect Mrs Vereker with Matthews. And nobody in Minching Lane recognised her photo; not the shopkeepers, nor anybody else living along there.'

Vereker made a snorting noise that signified total disbelief, maybe even derision at police inefficiency.

Bowker gave him the cold eye. 'The arson attack was at three in the morning. Why would your wife be in Minching Lane at that time?'

'How the hell should I know!' Vereker burst out. 'That's for you to investigate. I'm completely fed up and disillusioned by the bumbling attitude of the police in a clear case of murder—I'm going to take it over your heads to higher authority.'

Bowker was experiencing an unfamiliar situation—for once in his life, he was at a disadvantage. He didn't like the feeling.

'Did your enquiries turn up anything useful, Constable?' he asked Cote. 'Anything at all?'

'Nothing, sir. Mrs Vereker had a very comfortable lifestyle; big house, expensive clothes, lots of friends. No reason that I could see for her to leave home.'

'What about another man?' Bowker suggested.

Before Shirley Cote could answer, Vereker was up on his feet, foaming with rage. There was a gleam of gold watch as he waved his arms about like swatting flies.

'How dare you say such a thing!' he shouted. 'It's a slur on her name to even think it, and on mine, too! You're not getting away with these dirty-minded loutish suggestions—I'll get you kicked out of your job!'

Bowker stood up and squared his shoulders, a sight to impress anyone in his right mind. He moved around the table to confront Vereker, less than twelve inches between their noses. Shirley Cote slid out from under the table and across the room, near the closed door. It looked to her as if the Inspector was going to beat Vereker up. One punch will kill Vereker stone dead; he's a only weedy businessman, she thought in alarm.

Not that it came to it. Vereker shrank like a snowman hit by a flamethrower. He flopped into the chair and burst into noisy sobbing, his hands covering his face.

Bowker said nothing for a while, to give him time to recover. The sobs turned to sniffles, Vereker found a handkerchief and dried his face. He was embarrassed, his face flushed. He looked away from Bowker.

'Mr Vereker,' said the Inspector in a tone that was as nearly sympathetic as he could manage, 'personally, I take murder very seriously and make sure murderers are locked up. Left to me, it would be forever, but they don't ask my views on that.

Now, as a sensible man, you well know we have to explore every possibility before we decide to launch a murder investigation.'

'You can rule the idea of a man right out,' Vereker insisted. 'It's not even a possibility.'

'I understand you. And you have to understand that we need to ask that question. The majority of married women who leave home go off with another man; that's plain statistics. But it's true that some disappear because they've been done in.'

'Then I ask you again,' Vereker said miserably, 'what are you doing about my wife?'

'I've been in Bedlow-on-Thames only since ten this morning, and in charge of the murder enquiry since three-thirty this afternoon. There's not been time to do much yet beyond find out who's who. You go on home and leave me to sort things out.'

'Then I can expect positive action within the next twenty-four hours.' Vereker had got over his suffering and was back on form. 'I can promise you there'll be big trouble otherwise.'

Bowker's face twitched ominously, but he kept himself in check—he had formed a deep and abiding loathing of Donald Vereker.

'See Mr Vereker safely off the premises, Constable,' he said to Cote.

Five minutes later, when she rejoined him in the Murder Room, he stared at her accusingly.

'Let's cut out all the Mary Ellen. What's the strength of it, this so-called missing-person farrago?

'You've got all the facts, sir.'

'I'm asking for your opinion.'

'You've seen Vereker, sir. If it was me married to him, I'd do a runner. He thinks he's God's gift but he's just a prat.'

'What does he do for a living?'

'Insurance broker. Got an office in Carter's Road and employs five or six people. Loads of money. His wife had what you might call a lifestyle, but not a life.'

'What sort of insurance—life, cars, houses, TV sets?'

'All of it, including commercial insurance like shops, trucks, and buildings.'

'Minching Lane?' Bowker asked, sounding interested.

'The insurance on all the shops in Minching Lane goes through his office. He's a broker; he takes a commission from insurance companies for putting the business their way. The policy on the Minching Lane shops was written by Cotswold Commercial. They're not paying out till we've completed our enquiries.'

'You did your job well,' Bowker commended her with ferocious geniality, 'but I can't see how it helps. No money for Vereker, the shop burning to the ground. So why is DI Mason lumbering me with Mr Wonderful? Does he suspect Vereker of setting the fire because he thought his wife was in bed with Matthews upstairs, or what?'

DC Cote had her face turned away from Bowker as she tried not to laugh. She was sure that Vereker was DI Mason's revenge for taking his job, and Bowker hadn't tumbled to it yet.

4. .... *cocker park*

Thursday morning found Bowker and Knight on their way to make a surprise call on another suspect on DI Mason's list. It was hot and sunny at nine in the morning, the promise of a perfect summer day. As usual, Knight was driving the car and Bowker was sitting awkwardly beside him, an elbow stuck out of the open window.

Bowker had chosen Ronson the porn baron as his target for the day. No particular reason, he was working his way methodically through the list to meet them all. He was surprised when Knight told him that Ronson had no office in Bedlow-on-Thames—he did what he did from his home.

'He must have a warehouse somewhere,' Bowker was irritated. 'A computer and business records, sales and customers and money transactions, all the paperwork you need for making a fortune.'

'Exactly what I said to DS Trimmer, when he was giving me the guided tour of the local villains,' Knight agreed. 'But he says Ronson doesn't have a warehouse for illegal stuff. He's got the storage place under the railway arches they keep raiding, where he keeps the soft porn. The real nasties are nowhere to be seen, and Trimmer's theory is that Ronson flits the illegals about in a big truck to keep the local coppers guessing.'

'He has to check on the hard porn sometimes, whether it's mobile or not. Nobody trusts their staff without checking up on them, especially crooks. Not in human nature to be too trusting about money.'

'We don't need his stock, except to burn,' Knight suggested. 'If we just found his sales records, we could tip off the tax men and the VAT heavies and they could get him on fraud. That's how the FBI got Al Capone—on tax evasion—did you know that?'

'This isn't bloody Chicago. I want to get him for murder, not tax dodging. They don't even send them to jail for that.'

'If he did the murder,' Knight said carefully.

'That's what we're going to find out. Where in hell are we?'

Knight had driven out of Bedlow, past the ruins of the abbey, and they were on a winding country road, between green hedges.

'Ronson lives miles out,' he explained. 'He bought himself an enormous old mansion. It used to belong to a titled family, but the present lordling went bust at the roulette tables in London and Monte Carlo, according to Trimmer.'

'What else did DS Trimmer tell you?' Bowker was suspicious.

'He can't understand why you're chasing after the names Mason gave you, when they were all cleared early on in the enquiry.'

'Because they're the only bloody suspects we've got. Mason

is a plodder, but he's not stupid. He turned up the possibles, even if he couldn't pin the murders on any of them.'

'There must be some logic in what you're saying, but it's over my head.' Knight received a black look for that.

'Ten-to-one Matthews was an outlet for Ronson's porn mags and videos,' he ventured, undisturbed by the look. 'Very likely all the newspaper shops in town have them under the counter. Ronson has to distribute them somehow, and where else would he go? But even if Matthews wanted out, it hardly seems motive enough for doing four people in.'

'Right,' Bowker grunted. 'It seems to me Matthews couldn't do Ronson any real damage, even if he turned him in. Not while our porn baron has a slick lawyer to get him off with a fine.'

'I don't know if DI Mason had a front-runner for the murders, but John Trimmer thinks Matthews' girlfriend did it: Mrs Druce. He's got this great theory about jealous passion and steamy sex and spurned love turning to blind hatred. So she wiped out the whole family, being a woman scorned. Inspector Mason never took the theory seriously, and Trimmer's going to try it on you. He's seen too many old movies on TV, if you ask me.'

'I didn't ask you,' Bowker said with a sour look on his face. 'But while we're speaking of jealousy and hate, we've inherited a man called Vereker. He turned up yesterday to bully me while you were out with Trimmer.'

'Bully *you?*' Knight said in amazement. 'He's a raving loony. What's he want?'

The road curved around a blind corner to the left, between a pub called The Dun Cow and a thatched cottage. Beyond the bend was a hamlet of six whitewashed houses and a grocery shop with a display of lettuces and carrots in cardboard boxes outside.

'His wife's gone missing,' said Bowker. 'We've got a photo

of her—she's young and glamorous; you'd like her. He's convinced himself she's been done in because she went at the same time as the fire.'

'Oh, him! Trimmer told me about the missing wife but the name didn't connect. Apparently he turns up at least once a week and screams the place down demanding action.'

'So what's Sergeant Trimmer's verdict?'

'He thinks Vereker did his wife in himself and is causing all the aggravation to divert suspicion. Sounds pretty farfetched to me, but you never know.'

'DI Mason didn't agree. He treated it as a missing person and not as a murder,' Bowker pointed out.

'This is between you and me,' Knight said carefully, 'not for repeating to anybody else. Trimmer and the others on the murder squad think DI Mason went deranged sometime back when he found he couldn't crack the Matthews case. They reckon he's done his brain in over it and he's obsessed. He broods about it twenty-four hours a day. Nothing else gets through to him.'

'Is this a leg-pull?' Bowker asked in deep distrust.

'No, it's the truth. If Vereker turned himself in and offered to show Mason where he'd buried the body, the DI would tell him to push off and stop wasting his time.'

'Now we've got bloody psychiatry experts on the squad!' Bowker snorted in derision.

'Take a word of advice, sir,' Knight stressed the *sir* to make his annoyance plain. 'DI Mason is seething about the case being taken away from him. He's gone paranoid about it. He'll trip you up if he can.'

He stopped the car at a pair of black wrought-iron gates nine feet high.

'This is it,' he said, 'Cocker Park, stately home of toffs in days gone by, now the property of local boy made good as a porn dealer.

'The gates are open,' said Bowker. 'What are you waiting for, a printed bloody invitation?'

'DS Trimmer only brought me as far as the gates yesterday. We didn't disturb the lord of the manor. I haven't seen the house, but it'll have to be a bloody palace to live up to the gates.'

'One thing for sure,' Bowker said morosely. 'The perverts of Bedlow didn't pay for all this on their own. Ronson's territory is far bigger than we thought. He must be wholesaling his wares to Oxford and Reading and Maidenhead and Windsor and every town of any size for miles around.'

The private road ran through meadow and woodland, with in the distance the gleam of a lake. Over a flat plank bridge across a stream and then it curved in a well-planned arc, left the trees behind and the house came into sight, a quarter-mile ahead over smooth green parkland.

'Bloody hell!' said Bowker. 'It really *is* a mansion!'

'When I was in uniform, walking the streets of Walsall,' said Jack Knight, 'there was a mad bugger with a straggly beard who marched about the marketplace in a tatty old raincoat six days a week, winter and summer. He had a placard on a pole, one side said THE END IS NIGH in big letters and the other side said THE WAGES OF SIN IS DEATH. I used to pull his leg about it and tell him he ought to change it to ARE instead of IS. And he'd always turn purple and froth at the mouth and say that's how the Bible has it and it can't be altered.'

'Is there a point to this tale, or have you gone geriatric on me?' Bowker asked in exasperation.

'The silly old sod was wrong, him and his Bible. The wages of sin is a bloody fine house, in your own park, and a new Porsche outside the front door,' Knight said with a grin.

The house was a couple of hundred years old, a white frontage with columns, everything gleaming and perfect as if it had been built last week. Bowker counted windows and concluded the house had at least twelve bedrooms. And living quarters for the staff up under the roof.

Knight parked Bowker's tired-looking Honda neatly alongside a scarlet open-topped Porsche and a four-wheel-drive Range Rover.

'No need to ring the bell,' Bowker said glumly. 'They already know they've got visitors.'

'How do you make that out?'

'Ronson's got a security system. Didn't you see the invisible beam between the gateposts when we drove in? Make it hard to raid him after dark, if we wanted to.'

To prove his point, the house door was opened by a man who was almost as big as Bowker himself. He wasn't dressed as a butler, he was in casual trousers and a T-shirt that displayed his hairy arms. He scowled and said nothing. Bowker scowled back and held up his warrant card. The thug with hairy arms wasn't impressed.

'Here to see Mr Ronson,' Bowker said genially.

'He's out.'

'No, he's bloody not. He's in and I'm going to see him. If you give me any grief, I'll run you in for obstruction. What's your name—I've seen your face on WANTED posters.'

'Ellis,' the bouncer conceded grudgingly.

Bowker pushed past him and marched into the house. Ellis came after him, a meaty arm stretched out to grab his shoulder. When he saw the look on Bowker's face, he had second thoughts.

'Mr Ronson's having his breakfast on the terrace,' he grunted disobligingly. 'This way.'

The vast floor of the entrance hall was tiled black and white, and the walls were hung with oil paintings of somebody's famous ancestors in wigs and lace collars. Not the porn baron's, that was for sure; maybe they went with the house. A wide staircase curved upward at one end of the hall—polished mahogany treads inlaid with rosewood marquetry of intricate flower designs.

Ronson had vandalised the classic rear of the house by adding a huge glass conservatory to shelter a round swimming pool. The day was so sunny that the glass sides and top of the conservatory stood open. The pool had a broad surround of azure-blue tiles, an odd contrast with the green grass of the acre or two of lawn beyond. A round white table was set for breakfast. A man sat at it reading a tabloid newspaper.

He wasn't alone. Breakfast-time accessories included no less than three good-looking girls wearing only skimpy bikini briefs and showing off their bountiful endowments. One sat with him at the table nibbling toast and marmalade, another lay full length on a sun bed with her eyes closed, a glass of orange juice near her. She looked hung-over. The third girl was in the pool doing a slow backstroke. None of the girls was a day over eighteen.

'Look who we've got here!' Bowker exclaimed as he and Knight emerged from the house, 'England's answer to Hugh bloody Hefner and his playmates!'

'Hugh who?' Knight asked blankly, staring in amazement at the well-proportioned female bodies on show.

The girls made no effort to conceal their charms when the two policemen approached. Bowker was taken aback by Knight's total ignorance of the pioneer of topless pinups. But it was over thirty years ago.

'How did *they* get in here?' Ronson bawled at his bouncer.

'Charm and bloody tact,' Bowker answered for Ellis.

Ronson was a ginger-haired man in his forties, tough-looking, still lean of belly, maybe from jogging around his park. He was wearing white shorts and a red silk shirt, unbuttoned all the way down, so that the ginger hair on his chest was visible. It was a very repulsive view, and the expression on Bowker's face suggested that he loathed Ronson on sight.

'Detective Inspector Bowker and Detective Sergeant Knight. We want five minutes of your time in connection with our enquiries into the murder of four members of the Matthews family.'

'That's ancient history,' Ronson said, relaxed now he knew it was only the police he was dealing with, not representatives of a rival mob. 'A man named Mason came pestering me. I said all I had to say then.'

'There's two ways of doing this,' Bowker informed him, a glow of malign pleasure in his dark eyes at the prospect of trouble, 'you can answer a few questions nicely here by your pool and be left in peace with your mopsies. Or I can drag you swearing and kicking to Bedlow police station and ask questions there—it's entirely up to you to decide.'

Ronson said with a nasty grin, 'You wouldn't dare, not that I've got anything to hide. Sit down, have a cup of coffee. What do you want to know?'

The girl in the pool swam to the side and put an elbow on the tiling while she smiled at Jack Knight. He smiled back, pleased by the view of her female facilities and wondering if mopsy was a rude word. Women often smiled at him; he was good-looking and well set, clear-eyed, a neat dresser, his brown hair cut tidily but stylishly. He liked the look of the mopsy in the water and was about to ask her name when he heard growling noises from Bowker.

'I'm glad you realise the importance of helping the police in their enquiries,' Bowker said in a tone of pure menace. 'I want to know about your connection with the late Ronnie Matthews.'

'Sorry, can't help you there,' Ronson said with an insincere smile. 'I never met him, didn't know him. If I ever passed him in the street, I wouldn't have known him from Adam.'

'And you wouldn't know the poor bugger now from a burnt-black hamburger. Or his wife and his two little girls.

One was seven years old and the other was nine. Scorched to a black crisp.'

The topless blonde sitting at the breakfast table with Ronson got up and walked quickly to the house. She was looking very sick. The brunette in the pool stopped smiling at Knight, turned away, and did a vigorous crawl to the other side.

'Write that in your notebook, Knight,' Bowker said in a nasty tone. 'Mr Ronson denies ever meeting the deceased or having any contact with him. That's a very clear statement by him.'

'It's got nothing to do with me,' Ronson protested. 'Don't try twisting my words. Besides, you've got no right to barge in and upset Minky saying things like that.'

'Business connection, was it, between you and Matthews? Just a few porno mags and videos for sale under his shop counter?'

'I'd never heard of the man before Mason turned up asking the same stupid questions. Look, Inspector, I'd like to help you if I could. I'm as much against crime as anybody. Crime is bad for business—especially murder. But I don't know anything.'

'You know Lloyd Davies well enough; he's kept you out of jail plenty of times, from what I hear. And the Legal Wonderman knew the dead man well enough to drink with in the Crown and Anchor. So there's a link between you and Matthews.'

'This some sort of joke?' Ronson enquired. 'Since when did a lawyer's clients have to know each other?'

'In my experience, the crooked ones always do. That's why they have the same lawyer.'

'You calling me a crook?' Ronson resented the suggestion.

'Of course you're a crook,' Bowker said in a voice that would start an avalanche down a mountainside. 'Three convictions under the Obscene Publications Act, fined each time. That gives you a criminal record.'

'Ellis, show these coppers out!' Ronson said sharply to his thug. 'And don't let them back in again.'

'Don't be a clod all your life, Ellis.' Bowker grinned like a hangman readying a noose for a neck. 'Your fat-head boss may think you're big enough to see me off the premises, but you know I'll rip your arm off and sling you screaming in that pool if you come one step nearer. Then I'll drag you out by the hair and run you in for assaulting a police officer.'

The bruiser backed away. Ronson changed tune again.

'No offence meant, Inspector. Anything else I can tell you?'

'Tell me about the connection between you and Matthews before he got flame-grilled.' Bowker was relentless.

'I swear to you there wasn't any connection. I never knew the man. You can ask Mason—he went on at me for hours about it.'

Bowker's sideways grin showed Ronson he didn't believe a word of it.

'Never knew the man,' Knight repeated as he wrote it solemnly in his notebook.

'Look, if this is a statement I'm making, I want my lawyer to be here,' Ronson said suddenly.

'Interesting thing about lawyers,' Bowker said, 'they'll tell any lie they can think of to keep you out of jail while you pay them. When they're involved themselves, it works the other way about. To save their own skin, they will make up lies so bloody astounding that you have to laugh. We do the laughing, not the nasty sod whose lawyer's turned on him. The lawyer proves he's only an innocent bystander and you're the villain we're looking for. You get twenty years and he walks free.'

Ronson had a bored look on his face, but it wasn't real.

'He knows all about your business, Mr Lloyd Legal Davies, and when I get around to him, he'll sell you right down the river to save himself,' Bowker said cheerfully. 'We'll be off now, so you can play with the playmates. Don't tire yourself out too much—we'll be back to see you again soon.'

The girl in the pool had gone indoors. The one on the sun bed had fallen asleep with her mouth open. Ellis trailed Bowker and Knight back through the house and slammed the front door behind them loudly.

Driving through the park to the road, Knight was silent for a while, busy with his thoughts. Then he grinned at Bowker. 'What do you think, does he get a leg over all three of those girls?'

'No crime in that, as long as they're over sixteen and willing. If we could get one of those girls to talk to us, it's possible we might hear something to our advantage. Ask your friend Sergeant Trimmer if he knows who they are. Especially Minky—she rushed into the house to sick up when I mentioned little girls grilled to a crisp.'

'I wouldn't mind interrogating her.' Knight had an expression of profound interest on his face. 'I'll have a word with Trimmer about her. Who did you say Ronson was England's answer to?'

'A Yank who turned pompom girls into bare-chested pin-ups and managed to make them look boring. Our local porn baron's doing his bit to keep the old times going, though it looks bloody old-fashioned these days.'

'You stuck your neck out,' Knight said, shaking his head sorrowfully. 'You said things to him that could drop you into trouble if they reached Superintendent Billings' ears.'

'What do you do when you see a wasps' nest?'

'How do I know—I've never seen one.'

'You lob a brick at it,' Bowker told him. 'That stirs them up and gets them buzzing about.'

Bloody strange way to go about detecting, Jack Knight thought to himself. But he didn't say so.

'Who next?' he asked. 'The lawyer?'

'No, not today. We'll give the porn baron plenty of time to get in touch with him and tell him he's been threatened by two police heavies. Davies can simmer for a while and start to fret and worry, but I wouldn't take bets on it. "Lawyer's conscience" is an oxymoron, like "honest drug dealer." We'll go for a chat with the late Ron Matthews' best pal—I've forgotten his name.'

'Arnold Hinksey.' Knight produced the name at once. 'He was a soldier at one time, but he left the army to run an off-licence. He's not the manager for one of the big chains, it's his own.'

'Costs money to do that,' Bowker said ruminatively. 'Did your pal Trimmer have any idea about where Hinksey got it from?'

'No.'

'Any idea why DI Mason had Hinksey on his list?'

Knight shook his head.

'We're working blind,' he complained. 'Are you sure you don't want me to sit down and read through the files?'

'We haven't got time to bugger about with paperwork,' Bowker growled. 'This case has to be cleared up fast for me to take my wife and kids on holiday.'

Hinksey's off-licence was in Old Church Yard, a short cul-de-sac of shops in the shadow of St Bardolph's Church. Only a few minutes' walk from Minching Lane, both policemen noted. The sign, *Trumbold's Fine Wines and Spirits,* up on the front was in old-fashioned gold letters and evidently had been there as long as the shop itself. The small lettering over the door, as required by law, stated that Arnold Makepeace Hinksey was licenced to sell beers, wines, and spirits for consumption off the premises.

The window to the left of the door displayed bottles of cheap red wine imported from unlikely countries: Australia, Bulgaria, Algeria. Bowker's face went dark with disbelief as he read the labels. The window to the right of the door had cans of various imported beers stacked six feet high. *Never seen so much rotgut in all my born days,* Knight heard Bowker muttering to himself.

'Not the place for your connoisseurs,' Knight said helpfully. 'None of your Chateau Plonk for twenty quid a bottle. It's just a teenager drop-in, you can see that—twelve cans of cheap and cheerful lager apiece, and they're ready for anything.'

'Including burning people to death?' Bowker said doubtfully.

At eleven in the morning, there were no customers in the shop. Behind the counter doing nothing much stood a woman in her late twenties, long blonde hair down to her shoulders, a white shirt as well-filled as the proverbial barmaid. Knight's eyes gleamed and he wondered how to get her out from behind the counter, for a look at her rear view. She was wearing tight blue jeans that were a Peeping Tom's delight.

'Mr Hinksey in?' Bowker asked in a remarkably pleasant way. Remarkable for him, that was. She flinched at the sight of him, taking him for a thug come to knock her down and raid the till. Jack Knight stepped forward fast, a friendly smile on his face and his warrant card in his hand.

'I'm Mrs Hinksey,' she said, taking to Knight. 'I'll tell my husband you're here.'

There was a door behind her. She opened it and the two plainclothesmen eyed in fascination her magnificent chest expansion as she drew in a deep breath and called out, '*Arnie!*' There was a short wait before Hinksey came through the door, a tall man of thirty-something in a green polo shirt. His hair was cropped close, army-style, but he had let himself become overweight and soft.

Bowker told him who they were and suggested they should talk somewhere less liable to interruption. Hinksey lifted the flap of his counter to let them through and took them up a flight of stairs behind the door to the flat above. The sitting room was done in cream shades, with oatmeal upholstery on the furniture. It looked comfortable and very clean.

'What's it about?' Hinksey asked.

'I've taken over the enquiry into the death of your late and lamented pal and his family,' Bowker told him with a dark look.

'I hope you have more luck in catching the bastard who did it than the last copper on the job. It's three months now, and he's done nothing.'

'Have no fear,' Bowker assured him with a vicious grin. 'I'll get the bastard. You used to go fishing with Matthews along the Thames, they say. So you had plenty of time to talk to him. Did he ever drop any hint he was in trouble?'

'I've been asked all this before,' Hinksey said, sitting down heavily on an armchair. 'You should talk to the last copper on the job; he'll tell you. Ronnie never had a worry in the world; he was a born optimist. Everybody liked him.'

'Somebody hated the sight of him,' Knight pointed out.

'Set fire to him,' Bowker added. 'Got rid of him for good. So who do *you* think it was, Arnie?'

'No use asking me. I've lain awake at night asking myself who had it in for Ronnie to do that to him.'

There was something deeply unlovable about Arnie Hinksey. It was nothing to put your finger on, but Bowker remembered what DI Mason had said: *I don't trust him and neither will you after you meet him.* And it was the truth, if Hinksey said it was Thursday, Bowker would look at a calendar to make sure.

'If his best pal can't even guess who had it in for him, what chance is there for us?' Bowker said, eyes narrowed. 'What are you hiding from me, Arnie? Did you and Matthews have some sort of illegal activity going together? Porno videos, was it? You get a lot of people through your shop, just like he did—they could buy something else besides a bottle of booze or the daily paper.'

'Not me!' said Hinksey. 'If Ronnie was doing anything like that, he never said a word to me about it.'

'You'll tell me next that you don't know Dougie Ronson.'

'Never heard of him,' Hinksey said quickly. 'Who's he?'

'Write that in your notebook, Knight. Suspect denies he knows Ronson.'

Hinksey bounced up out of his chair, his face red, and took a step toward Bowker.

'What do you mean *suspect?*' he shouted in a rage. 'I'm no bloody suspect!'

Bowker's glare would have stopped a runaway truck downhill. A startled Hinksey stepped backward so fast that he tripped over his own feet and fell into his armchair again.

'You're on my list,' Bowker told him menacingly. 'Think about that when you lie awake at night. Sooner or later, I mean to run you in for withholding information. I don't play by the rules. I'll see you get a jail sentence. Maybe only six months, but it will be the end of your licence to sell liquor. The backer who put up the cash to buy this place for you to run won't like it, will he? He'll do something very painful to you, Arnie.'

Knight realised where Bowker was going. He wasn't thinking of porn at all, but teenagers dropping in to buy six-packs of lager and dope in small bags under the counter. The backers had to be the Burtons, purveyors of pot, crack, coke, and Ecstasy to silly teenagers. If DI Mason suspected it, he hadn't mentioned it. Was it in those bloody files he kept on about?

'I don't know what you mean,' Hinksey muttered.

'I'll come and see you in the hospital when they've shown you how fed up they are,' Bowker said with gloomy pleasure, 'if you can still talk well enough then to make yourself understood. And my sergeant will take down your statement.'

'You can't threaten me!'

'When I threaten you, you'll know you've been threatened. I'm trying to save you more grief and pain than you'd ever think it possible for the human body to bear. And maybe worse than that. Sometimes these beatings go too far and the mark ends up brain damaged, blind and drooling. You'll be no use to me then, or to yourself either.'

Bowker nodded to Knight and they made for the door. Hinksey got up and called them back before they reached the stairs.

'Look, I'll tell you what I know, though it's not much. Maybe Ronnie was dealing in a few naughty videos now and then, but it was nothing to do with me. That's the truth!'

'Did you see any of them?'

Hinksey shuffled his feet and looked down.

'You don't have to be bashful,' Bowker assured him. 'No crime watching them, only if you own them or sell them. When did you have this private viewing?'

'I couldn't tell you exactly when it was,' Hinksey started to look sweaty. 'It was Thursday half-day closing. Doreen— that's Ronnie's missus—took their kids to visit their grannie. So he asked me to their place to watch snooker on TV with him. I took a few cans of lager, and he put this video on the TV instead of the snooker.'

'What was it about?'

'What do you mean? They're all about the same thing.'

'Men, women, straight, gay, lesbo, kids, black, white, group, whipping, torture, indoors, outdoors, British, foreign?'

'Oh, right, I see what you mean,' Hinksey said with a grin, as if a 100-watt lightbulb had been switched on in his brain. 'It was two girls with great big knockers wrestling about on a sort of hairy black rug. They did things to each other—know what I mean?'

'Write that down in your notebook, Sergeant,' Bowker

said. 'A video of women with great big items *doing things to each other*. Did Matthews tell you he was selling videos like that, Arnie?'

'Not exactly, but it's what I understood.' Hinksey seemed happier now that he was helping Bowker with his enquiries. 'He said he'd got plenty more, and he winked.'

'And according to you, he never said where he was getting the videos from, Arnie, even though you were best friends.'

'His business was his business. He didn't ask me about liquor sales, and I didn't ask about his trading. You reckon the videos might have something to do with the fire that killed him, if he crossed somebody over them?'

'I'll let you know when I find out.' Bowker's grin didn't hide his distaste for Hinksey. 'You never mentioned videos to Inspector Mason. Why not, if you're so bloody innocent?'

'He never asked about them, and I wasn't going to tell him on my own. You learn that in the army; never volunteer.'

'Which part of the army had the pleasure of your company?'

'Paratroopers, seven years' service. Why?'

'I like to know who I'm dealing with. I ran a captain in once for murdering his wife for the insurance money. He still called himself "captain" though he'd been out of the army for years. All very military, marching about in medals on Remembrance Day. But when I checked on him, he wasn't a soldier at all; he'd been in the Army Pay Corps. He was a bloody chartered accountant. Where did they send you, anywhere dangerous?'

'Northern Ireland, bloody Belfast. That dangerous enough?'

'I'm impressed. Did you shoot any Paddies there, Arnie?'

'Only the buggers with guns in their hands.'

'It's been nice chatting to you,' said Bowker, a savage grin showing his big square teeth. 'We'll run into each other again before long. After I've asked around about videos.'

Hinksey didn't follow them down the stairs. His wife was

busy in the shop, checking bottles on the shelves with a list in her hand. Jack Knight stood entranced by blue jeans stretched tight over her well-rounded rear view.

'Why don't we question *her?*' he urged.

But Bowker was not a man to be sidetracked. He nodded to Mrs Hinksey as he left, Knight trailing behind him. She nodded back and gave Knight a smile that made his knees tremble.

'She reminds me of that old-time film star,' he said. 'What's her name—Marilyn Monroe.'

'Old-time? Marilyn Monroe?' Bowker was dumbfounded.

'Before my time, anyway. She died before I was born.'

'You're wrong about Mrs Hinksey.' Bowker had recovered. 'That silver-blonde hair and well-developed chest. She looks far more like a different film star, Jayne Mansfield.'

'Who?' Knight asked.

Bowker's car was parked outside the off-licence illegally, on a double yellow line. Old Church Yard was a non-parking zone. A square-built traffic warden in a white shirt and tie and a navy blue serge skirt uniform was writing out a ticket to tuck under the windscreen wiper.

'Don't do that,' Bowker said, sinews standing out in his neck as he coped with his temper. 'We're not tourists, we're here on important police business.'

Knight showed her his warrant card and said they'd been there no more than five minutes.

'Doesn't matter to me how long you've been here,' she said, a flinty smile on her face. 'You're parked on a double yellow. Is it your car or his?'

'Mine,' said Bowker in a voice that would send a normal woman running away shrieking. It had no effect on the meter maid; she handed him the ticket. He tore it to shreds and dropped them on the pavement at her feet.

'Temper!' she said. 'You won't get out of paying it by that, you know, I've got the duplicate in my book.'

By then he was cramming himself into the car. Knight shrugged at her in apology and got into the driver's seat. He drove away very fast, gunning the engine, bringing an even deadlier scowl to Bowker's face.

5.   *batty's boatyard*

On the way back to Bedlow police station Bowker said not
a word, but Knight heard him muttering under his breath that
women like the meter maid who impeded an officer in the
performance of his duty ought to be locked up. And suchlike
menaces.

All the members of the murder squad were in the Incident
Room. Only DC Hagen had anything to do, making the list of
petrol outlets Bowker had asked for. Boring though it was,
Hagen still had a cheerful smile on his face. DS Trimmer was
wearing a blue knitted tie today with his hairy grey sports
coat, Shirley Cote had a primrose yellow shirt tucked into
pale blue slacks. Not a fashion parade, Knight decided, but
plainclothes coppers never seemed to have much interest in
their appearance.

'Gather round,' Bowker snarled, diverting his frustrated

rage over the parking ticket toward his team. 'It's high bloody time you started doing some detecting.'

There was a flurry of activity and fumbling for notebooks as Trimmer, Hagen, Cote, and the uniformed Purley closed in around him. He leaned his backside on the edge of a desk and stared at them bleakly. Jack Knight sat down unobtrusively behind Bowker to watch events.

'Sergeant Trimmer, has Ronson's place been searched lately?'

'Soon after the fire, sir. Inspector Mason got a warrant, and we raided him early one morning.'

'Well?'

'Nice, sir, very nice. Satin sheets on the beds, wall-to-wall thick white carpeting upstairs, a big circular bath you can get two or three people in for a lark. Very tasty nude paintings of young women hanging on the walls, really artistic. But nothing in the way of videos or porn mags. It was just the same as when we raided him before, back end of last year. And nothing at his storage place under the railway arches you could arrest him for—just legal soft-porn stuff.'

'I'm glad you approve of his bloody interior decorating. What else did you do to target him?'

'We confiscated everything we thought was over the top, and we burnt it. He never complained.'

'Starting from now, I want an officer in a car hidden outside the gates of Ronson's palace. I want to know where he goes. Six in the morning till midnight, every day of the week, until I say different. You'll need two officers to share the hours. And if Ronson drives his Porsche, they'll have to be nippy to stay with him—but he shouldn't be able to give them the slip on country roads. I don't want him to know he's being watched.'

'What are we looking for, sir?' Trimmer asked. 'That's a lot of our manpower on one target.'

'Sooner or later he'll lead us to his warehouse.'

'Yes, sir, I see that. But strictly speaking, is it anything to do with the murder enquiry? DI Mason didn't think so.'

Bowker seemed to swell up to an impossible size, his muscles knotted, and a look of stark hatred appeared on his gypsy face.

'I don't want an argument,' he hissed. 'You're working for me now, not DI Mason. Got it?'

'Yes, yes!' Trimmer said hastily. 'Anything else, sir?'

'That little street where Hinksey's off-licence is, there's a charity shop nearly opposite. *Save the Disadvantaged,* some such worthy bloody cause. Got a windowful of secondhand clothes and old milk jugs and rubbish people don't want.'

'I know the place you mean,' Trimmer assured him.

'Those places are run by volunteer ladies with nothing to do while their husbands are playing golf or chasing young girls or whatever they get up to. That means the flat over the shop will be unoccupied. Find out whose permission we need to use it, and put an officer up there to watch Hinksey's premises.'

'Follow him when he goes out, you mean?'

'No, to see who goes in. I want to know how many teenagers go in and out. It's bound to be the same lot regularly, if he's an outlet for dope. And I want photos of their spotty little faces so we can identify them and pick them up when we're ready.'

Sergeant Trimmer knew better than to argue this time, whether he thought drugs had anything to do with the murders or not.

'Cote, you take the shop surveillance,' he ordered, very keen to show Bowker he was a born leader and firmly in control. 'And Hagen, you take the first turn watching Cocker Park. I'll spell you later myself. Purley will man the phones here.'

'Get to it,' Bowker growled, addressing them all. 'Call it in if you see anything interesting I ought to know about.'

Inside two minutes they were on their way, Purley taking over the list making from Hagen.

'Leave that for now and get on to Army Records,' Bowker told him. 'I want to know about Arnold Makepeace Hinksey who says he was in the Parachute Regiment. Everything about him they've got—I want it typed out on a piece of paper when I get back.'

'Get back? Where are we going?' Knight asked him.

'To eat,' said Bowker. 'It's after twelve, and I'm famished.'

'Not the canteen?'

'On a lovely day like this?' Bowker sounded outraged. 'We'll get a cheese-and-pickle sandwich at the pub across the road and sit by the river while we eat it. A healthy outdoor lunch.'

Knight was amazed by Bowker's decision to eat his frugal meal in the open air. But ten minutes later, when they were sitting on a bench on the riverside walk, he understood Bowker's devious thinking. Fifty yards to their right was a boatyard with a sign saying *Batty's Boats*. A bare-chested, bare-legged man in denim shorts was busy on the concrete apron, doing something nautical with a coil of white nylon rope.

'That might be Shane Hambleton,' Knight suggested.

Bowker grunted and bit into his thick cheese sandwich.

'All that Mary Ellen about surveillance,' Knight went on. 'If it's got anything to do with the murder, I'm a Dutchman. You did it because you can't bear to see the team idle. You didn't take what Arnie Hinksey told us seriously, he said it only to get us off his back.'

'I believed it when he said he'd watched a video with his pal Matthews. And yes, he was doing the dirty on his old pal to get us to leave him alone and go chasing the porn baron.

You'd have to be simpleminded not to see through that one.'

'But you've taken him at his word. You've got coppers tailing Ronson.'

'And watching Arnie himself,' Bowker agreed.

'That makes more sense. If he's selling dope as well as booze and cut his pal Matthews in on the act, and then something went sour, well, you have to admit it's a possibility. There are two Burtons and we're looking for two fire lighters.'

'We'll give the surveillance a few days and see what it turns up. They may be good coppers, as Superintendent Billings said, but I don't want them under my feet all day long.'

The Thames sparkled in the July sunshine. Rowboats went past, young men without tie or jacket pulling at oars, girls in thin summer dresses on the stern seats, looking happy. Then a family of small brown ducks spotted the sandwiches and paddled to the bank and waited for crumbs to be thrown to them.

'Nice little town, Bedlow.' Knight flung a piece of crust into the water for the ducks to squabble over. 'Good sort of place to bring up a family, pleasant and quiet. And all that crime going on, including burning people to death. It makes you wonder.'

'Wonder what?' Bowker demanded, black eyebrows rising up his forehead. 'Why people do wicked things? Not much mystery about that, it's because they're evil through and through. You listen to me and don't go reading those softheaded newspapers written by social workers and worse. Ignore all that *Society is Guilty* piffle. Just concentrate on catching rape artists and murderers and let somebody else worry why people do nasty things.'

Knight thought it better to let the subject fade away. He was familiar with Bowker's disagreeable view of humanity and found himself sometimes agreeing and other times not. To cheer up the conversation he asked if Bowker had his book with him, for bedtime reading. He knew the Inspector was a

Charles Dickens fan, though he was baffled why.

Bowker had a complete set of Dickens' novels, given to him by his father on his twelfth birthday. He worked through them, taking the titles in alphabetical order from B for *Barnaby Rudge* down to T for *A Tale of Two Cities*. Each full cycle took him about twelve months. Then he started again and never tired of it.

'Which one are you on now?' Knight asked.

'*Martin Chuzzlewit*—have you read it?'

'No, what's it about?' Knight enquired, certain it would put Bowker in a good humour to talk about his favourite writer. His own knowledge of Dickens was limited to reading *The Pickwick Papers* at school, which he'd thought boring and an old black-and-white movie of *Oliver Twist* on late-night TV. Alec Guinness with two feet of beard, pretending to be a Jewish fence. And a break-and-entry artist who bashed his girlfriend's head in for some weird and unfathomable reason.

'Interesting story for a copper,' Bowker explained with signs of pleasure untypical of him. 'It's a crime story, like most of Charlie Dickens' novels. In fact, you could say he invented the English crime tale. This one's about a young chap called Martin Chuzzlewit—he's in the architecting business but he gets the sack from his job. So he goes to America to make a fresh start, but he loses all his money in a bent land investment company.'

'I thought all land investment outfits were bent—that's how they make their money, isn't it, conning investors? It doesn't sound very interesting to me, if that's all the crime's about.'

'No, the big crime is back home. Martin's got a crooked uncle named Jonas. He marries the boss architect's daughter and then gives her a hard time, which they didn't reckon a crime. But he murders the boss of an insurance company, and that is.'

'You sure this is Charles Dickens?' Knight asked. 'It sounds more like Jeffrey Archer to me. Does Jonas get caught?'

'Just before they arrest him, he does himself in by poison. We had the same thing happen to us with that child-rapist Kemper—except he jumped in the Thames and drowned himself, bloody good riddance.'

'Right!' Knight said. 'Saved us a lot of paperwork.'

'Meantime,' Bowker resumed, 'Martin comes home broke from his trip to the USA. Whereupon his dear old granddad, whose name is Martin as well, tells him he's forgiven him and put him in his will for millions of quid. He marries a nice girl, and they all live happy ever after.'

'No wonder they call it fiction. In real life, Jonas would get off with eighteen months suspended, and Martin would have to get a job driving a cab on permanent night shift.'

'The trouble with you, Jack, is you're a cynic. If you've had enough of that sandwich, we'll go and harass Shane.'

Knight took the hint and flung what was left into the Thames for the quacking ducks. A swan came gliding in hope to the bank, but by then the bread was gone.

The boatyard had a concrete apron sloping down to the river's edge, where a dozen rowboats were tied up, waiting to be hired. There was a large open-ended building with a cabin cruiser inside up on struts to let the bottom be worked on, and a slipway from the building to the water.

At one end of the river frontage, a short pier stuck out, with two pumps on it; one petrol and one diesel. The suntanned man with no shirt thought Bowker and Knight wanted a boat and came to meet them.

'I remember him now,' Bowker told Knight with a crooked grin. 'He's got a different hairdo, but he's a Shane all right.'

The boatman was in his mid-twenties, sturdily built and brown skinned from working in the open. His head was shaved bare back and sides, leaving a thick mat of yellowish hair on top. He had one earring, as big and thick as a curtain-rail ring, looking more like brass than gold.

There were big tattoos on both biceps. A death's head over a Union Jack adorned his right arm, a hissing snake curling about a dagger his left. A prat, Knight decided—looks like a blonde Cherokee in an old John Wayne movie, only not so bright.

'You must be Shane Hambleton.' Bowker stared at him as if he were a convicted serial killer. 'I'm Inspector Bowker and he's Sergeant Knight. We're here in Bedlow to catch the wicked sod who murdered the Matthews family. Why are you a suspect?'

'Me? How do I know?' Shane was visibly shaken by the abrupt question. 'I told Inspector Mason I didn't know anything about it—I was miles away when it happened.'

'I know all about fake alibis, Shane, so don't try it on. Why did Inspector Mason pick you up for questioning? He must have had a bloody good reason.'

'Don't rightly know, he never said. Only thing I can think of is because Arnie Hinksey and me are cousins.'

'I'll be damned if that's not the best reason I've heard yet for running anybody in. *Hinksey's cousin,* you heard him say it, Knight—write it in your notebook. The suspect admits to being Hinksey's cousin. If I had my way, I'd make it a serious offence to be related to Hinksey.'

'Hinksey's *cousin,*' Knight said, writing. 'Your mother's side or your father's?'

'What do you mean?' Shane asked, puzzled. 'What's my mum got to do with it?'

'Never mind that,' Bowker said, 'we understand now why you're a suspect. Tell me why DI Mason decided Cousin Arnie's another. Don't say it's because he's *your* cousin. That's what they call a vicious circle, and the only one allowed to be vicious is me. So give me a good reason, Shane, before I lock you up.'

'I don't know what the hell you're talking about—straight I don't.'

Bowker sighed like a winter gale and tried again patiently. 'Yes, you do. All I'm asking you is why DI Mason grabbed hold of Cousin Arnie for the Matthews murders. Your IQ might be down in the low thirties, Shane, but you know the answer to my question.'

'I'm not thirty yet, I'm only twenty-six.'

'And you've got a nice suntan,' said Bowker. 'I bet the girls go mad when they see your chest and those muscles. Do they tell you that you look like Bruce Willis? Now here's your chance at the big prize—it's Jackpot Time, Shane—what did Arnie do to get his name on our list of murder suspects?'

Shane shook his head dumbly. If he knew anything at all about Hinksey's activities apart from liquor sales, he wasn't going to share the information.

'There goes your chance for a thousand-quid cheque and a long weekend in sunny Las Vegas with Miss World,' said Bowker, 'I'll tell you the answer Shane. Your cousin Arnie is up to some very unlawful dodges in that off-licence of his, and being a good pal of Ronnie Matthews, he wanted to spread some of his luck around. But poor old Ron wasn't as cunning as Arnie, and he made a pig's ear of it.'

Shane's mouth was opening and closing like a goldfish.

'Ronnie offended some very nasty unforgiving people,' Bowker went on. 'One dark night they turned up outside his shop—with big cans of petrol. Ten minutes after that, Ronnie and his wife and kids were frazzled to black skin and grey ash. That was the answer to the Jackpot Question and if you'd said it to me you'd have won this week's Top Prize. Think what you've missed!'

Shane was rocking back and forth on his heels, his mouth open in a complicated mix of disbelief, horror, uncomprehending fear, and other less-identifiable emotions.

'You're bloody mad!' he said eventually. 'Stark staring

mad, saying things like that! I'll have the law on you!'

'I know you're simple, Shane, but there's a limit. As far as you're concerned, the law is me. I'm going to run you in as soon as I've completed my enquiries. You've got guilty knowledge. No point in lying because it's written all over your face and you can't hide it. It's a twenty-year stretch for you, Shane, as an accomplice. You'll be fat and fifty when you come out of clink, you'll look like Oliver Hardy not Bruce Willis. The girls won't be interested in your suntan then.'

And with a terrifying grin Bowker left him, still rocking on his heels.

'You banged his head against the wall a bit bloody hard,' said Knight as they walked back to where the car was parked. 'You're not serious about him being an accomplice to anything. He's not got the brains for it. Street mugging is about his intellectual limit.'

'Even then he'd need somebody with him to make sure he didn't mug a penniless beggar,' Bowker said gloomily. 'I expect him to pass on all that speculation; that's why I said it to him.'

'Who to?'

'Everybody he knows. Same with Cousin Arnie. I don't know who the hell we're looking for, but if we can get chummy stirred up and sweating, he might do something silly and give us a shot at the bull's-eye.'

'The Burton brothers or Ronson, you mean?'

'How the hell do I know what I mean?' Bowker said irritably. 'It's too long after the crime. We're groping about in the dark and coming up with a handful of clag. We've not a cat in hell's chance of collaring chummy; that's the truth of it. But looking on the bright side, we can go and aggravate the dope runners. I might enjoy that.'

They hadn't far to go. Along High Street away from the river, the Burtons' filling station was at the corner of the turn-off into Abbotsbury Estate. On the forecourt stood six petrol pumps in two rows of three; behind them was a workshop combined with an office. Twelve used cars were offered for sale at one end of the forecourt, plastic stickers on their windscreens displaying very optimistic prices.

'Nobody's going to get these villains on tax evasion,' Bowker said as Knight drove in. 'You can forget your Al Capone drama—the Burtons have a legal declarable income. The money they make from drug dealing gets lost from sight somewhere.'

They both got out of the car, and while Knight filled the tank, Bowker drifted across the forecourt to the cars for sale. A man in an ugly purple tracksuit was changing a price sticker. About thirty years old, heavily built, shortish but very solid, a natural thug. He had no neck at all and his dark hair was cropped short as a Devil's Island lifer.

'You'll be one of the Burtons,' Bowker said amiably.

'Who are you?' No-neck asked, staring hard.

'Detective Inspector Bowker, on assignment here in Bedlow.'

'That your car at the pump? I can't give you more than fifty quid for it as scrap; it's ready for the breaker's yard. But to make it up to you I'll sell you this Ford at a very good price. Three years old and had one careful owner, a lovely car, 50,000 miles on the clock and still as good as the day it came off the assembly line.'

Bowker's face turned black with rage at the disparagement of his car. He fell into a semi-crouch, arms out, fingers hooked, transformed into The Mad Mangler in the wrestling ring ready to dismember an opponent. Gary Burton took a step back and balled up his fists, ready to fight. Before the scene deteriorated further, Knight hurried up.

'Which Burton's this, sir?' he asked. 'Wayne or Gary?'

'How the hell do I know?' But at the interruption, Bowker was beginning to subside slowly.

'So which one are you?' Knight addressed himself to the man in the uncouth tracksuit.

'I'm Gary Burton. What do you want?'

'Hah!' said Bowker, loud enough to be heard half a mile off, 'you may well ask! What we want is to catch the wicked persons unknown who murdered the entire Matthews family. And would you believe it, the name "Burton" is right at the top of the list.'

'You need your head testing,' Gary said. 'Me and Wayne's been cleared. We never had anything to do with it.'

Bowker's smile was like a shark showing its teeth just before it bit off a swimmer's arm.

'The times I've heard those words,' he said. ' "It wasn't me, I never had anything to do with it." I wish I had a quid for every time that's been said to me. I'd be able to retire rich and not have to bother myself with lowlife like you, Gary.'

'You watch your mouth, copper. You can't come here and insult me like that. I know my rights.'

'Mr Lloyd Davies looks after your rights for you, does he?'

'What if he does?'

'He's the lawyer for nearly every crook in Bedlow I've spoken to so far. I'd naturally expect him to be yours.'

'Who are you calling a crook?' Gary was becoming aggressive, as Bowker intended he should. But it was counter-productive for Gary to challenge him, as a matter of routine Bowker checked on the record of everyone involved in a murder investigation—and that included clergymen, maiden aunts, and do-gooders.

'I'm calling you a crook, Gary; no point in arguing about it. Three times you've been in court for selling cars with fiddled mileage on the clock. False pretences and intent to deceive, or, in ordinary words, swindling. You're a swindler. Twice you and Wayne have been in court for selling stolen cars with different number plates on them. That makes you a thief.'

'We didn't know they were stolen,' Gary protested. 'We

bought them in good faith in the usual way of business.'

'Pull my other leg, it plays a tune! Without Mr Lloyd Davies, you and brother Wayne would be doing eighteen months in chokey. Where is he, in the office fiddling his tax return? Introduce me, so I have to say it only once.'

'Say what?'

'You'll hear when we're all together. Come on, Gary.'

In the small concrete-floored office, Wayne was adding rows of figures with a calculator. He was a year or two older than Gary and had the same squat no-neck bouncer build. He was wearing a loose shirt outside his trousers, its vivid patterns suggesting the worst excesses of tourists in Hawaii. He looked up from his lists when Bowker, Knight, and Gary crowded into the small space between his desk and the door.

'They're the law,' Gary said with open contempt.

Wayne Burton was staring unblinking at Bowker's bulk and dark expression.

'I guessed that much,' he grunted. 'What do you want from me?'

'To put you behind bars,' Bowker growled back, 'and we've been brought in specially to do the job, Sergeant Knight and me. The local law think you deserve the extra care we can provide. This is a getting-to-know-you call—just so that when a ton of clag gets tipped over you and your baby brother, you'll know who did it. Me.'

'You've got nothing on us.'

'Dream on, Wayne. There's a nasty surprise waiting for you.'

'Anything you want to say to me or Gary, say to our lawyer.'

'I know who he is,' Bowker said. 'I'm here to inform you that your days of hiding behind him are over and done with. Today we turned a big stone over—damned if we didn't find you and Gary crawling underneath.'

'What stone are you talking about?' Wayne tried hard for a note of scorn and derision.

Bowker grinned and shook his head. 'All in good time—after we've checked what the witness says and you're sweating in the Interrogation Room and your lawyer's begging you not to say anything to incriminate yourself. I tell you now, Wayne, I look forward to grilling *you* hour after hour. It won't be so interesting to roust Gary, he's softer than you. He'll collapse after a couple of hours and put his signature on a confession. Then we've got you both dead to rights.'

Wayne said nothing. He shot a look at Gary and then stared at Bowker again, his expression bleak.

'We'll leave you to carry on fiddling the books,' Bowker said amiably. 'Next time we're here it will be to run you in.'

Neither brother followed him and Knight out of the office. As they reached the car Bowker glanced at the numbers displayed on the petrol pump and asked Knight if he'd paid.

'No, I was busy stopping you from clobbering Gary.'

'Then do it now—a fine bloody scandal it would be if we did a flit without paying for the petrol we've had!'

Knight made for the glassed-in booth where a teenage girl sat reading a Jackie Collins paperback romance. There was a blonde blaze bleached in the front of her mouse-brown hair, and she was wearing what looked like a yellow swimsuit. At least, the top part did; the counter concealed what she had below the waist.

She gave Knight a friendly smile as she took his credit card. Girls often did. He smiled back, but it was only politeness; he considered her a no-go area. Mostly because she was plain, but also because she had a Burton look about her: heavy shoulders, too-little neck, built-in blank stare. Being professionally inquisitive, he asked if she was related to the owners.

'They're my uncles,' she said. 'Mum's brothers. I saw you

and your pal go into the office—you doing business with them? My name's Cilla.'

'I think we'll do business with Uncle Wayne and Uncle Gary,' Knight said. His mind was boggling to hear Bowker described as his pal. 'See you again, Cilla.'

'There's a good movie on tonight at the Odeon,' she said with hope in her voice. 'All about a killer who cuts bits off people he kills and cooks them and eats them.'

'Seen it,' Knight said untruthfully. 'Maybe some other time.'

'Come back soon.' Cilla was still optimistic.

'Having a nice chat?' Bowker asked when Knight drove off the forecourt and headed for Bedlow police station, 'trying to pick her up? Bit young for you, isn't she?'

'Bloody hell!' Knight exclaimed, mortified at the suggestion he would consider Cilla a possible. 'She's the Burtons' niece.'

'Is she? It sounds to me as if we've got a dynasty of crooks on our hands here. She didn't seem to be wearing much, I could see you leering through the glass at her innocent young body.'

'Yellow swimsuit,' Knight said. 'Lot of flesh showing, but it didn't look all that tempting. And if she's innocent, then I'm a Chinaman. Anyway, I've been thinking it over, and I've decided I'm in love with Mrs Hinksey.'

'Yes,' Bowker agreed with a certain enthusiasm. 'She's a fine figure of a woman, Arnie's wife. I can understand how your baser instincts would be stirred by the sight of her.'

'You said she looked like Jayne Mansfield, whoever she was.'

'Lovely big blonde woman, shaped like an hourglass, married a weight lifter,' Bowker informed him. 'Made terrible films.'

'That's as maybe. I can't understand for the life of me why a woman with a figure like Mrs Hinksey would marry an unwholesome prat like Arnie. There's no bloody justice in the world.'

'It's taken you long enough to find that out, Jack. Maybe you should give up detecting for a living and go into charity work or counselling. Women are bloody contrary by nature, they never do the obvious. God alone knows why they take up with villains. There could never have been any glamour about Arnie Hinksey.'

'He couldn't have been much better looking when he was in the Paratroops, before he grew that paunch,' Knight agreed, 'and she can't possibly find him attractive now. It must be his money.'

'Jack, Jack—you mustn't let yourself get bitter because the woman you want is hitched to a trashy little crook. After we've put him in clink for dope peddling, you can drive over to Bedlow on your day off and see if she needs consoling. That's if she's not in jug herself for helping Arnie sell prohibited substances to the stupid youth of this nice little town. Her face and body promise a lot, but they don't guarantee law-abiding.'

Inspector Billings' big sleek car was parked in his own named space when they got back to the police station. Bowker grunted in disgust and told Knight to park in the only slot available—it was marked DOG HANDLER—KEEP CLEAR.

'They're out with the hounds running down a fugitive from the chain gang,' Bowker said straight-faced. 'They'll drag him back in leg irons and flog him here in the yard.'

'Or maybe the dog bit a local villain and had to be rushed to a vet for a check-up in case it caught something nasty,' Knight suggested.

'Nice to know we've got trained killer dogs on call,' Bowker said cheerfully. 'We can take them with us if we raid

Ronson's mansion—that'll give his bouncer something to worry about.'

For the rest of the afternoon, they were busy upstairs in the Incident Room. While the rest of the murder team were out doing surveillance, Constable Purley had at last finished the list of petrol outlets. As DS Trimmer had gloomily predicted, there were dozens and dozens of filling stations, marine pumps, bus depots, and commercial transport firms with their own pumps, inside the ten-mile radius Bowker had designated.

'We're looking for a needle in a haystack, and it's a big bloody haystack,' he grumbled. 'The sensible thing would be send a team to ask every one of these if they'd filled two five-gallon cans for anybody in the week before the fire. But we don't have the manpower, and it would be a waste of time. The Burtons have pumps of their own, and if they did it, they're not going to tell us anything.'

He decided he wanted to look at the files DI Mason had seemed so proud of. 'Get them,' he told Purley.

'Any file in particular, sir? There's a hell of a lot. Inspector Mason was very hot on getting everything on paper. Take you days to read what we've got.'

'If any of them had alibis, I'd be interested in seeing them,' Bowker said with a scowl. 'But as the fire was started at three in the morning they'll all claim they were asleep in bed. Alone or accompanied.'

'Well, sir,' Purley said cautiously, not wanting to draw anger and wrath down on his head, 'only one claimed to be in bed when it happened. Mr Lloyd Davies, the lawyer. And seeing that he's divorced, he was sleeping alone. Or says he was.'

'So where were all the others?' Bowker asked in astonishment at finding his supposition so wrong.

'I'll get you the files.'

'Tell me first. You've got a bloody good memory, Constable.'

'As I recall, the two Burton brothers said they were at a big second-hand car auction up in the Midlands and stayed overnight with a pair of Birmingham tarts. Whose address they don't know, being half-sozzled at the time.'

'If we've got the tarts' first names, and the dump where the Burtons claimed they picked them up, they're traceable. But I expect they've been paid to tell us lies.'

'Ronson says he was in London at a business meeting all that day and then a nightclub till about four in the morning, with overseas business contacts.'

'Pornographers from Europe,' Bowker said gloomily. 'Even if we could find them in Amsterdam or Hamburg, they'd swear themselves black and blue to keep their pal Ronson out of trouble.'

'Hinksey and Hambleton said they were together—fishing all night a few miles up the river, above the next lock. The DI had them separated, and they each took an officer to the same spot.'

'All-night fishing,' Bowker snorted in derision. 'It's easily the stupidest alibi I've ever heard. It's as dud as the others. What about Matthews' girlfriend—I've forgotten her name.'

'Druce,' Knight said at once. 'Moira Druce.'

'That's right,' Purley agreed. 'Mrs Druce. She was in Bristol shopping, according to her. She had tea with an old auntie who lives there and took her to the theatre. And drove herself home in the early hours. Give me five minutes and I can put my hands on the files you want.'

'You make them sound as gigantic as the National Archives.'

'We haven't got much paper on Lloyd Davies. He was here only half an hour before DI Mason had to let him go.'

'Interesting in a nasty sort of way.' Bowker shrugged his

massive shoulders, 'I'll get to him later—we're not having bloody lawyers above the law. Bring me the others and let's see how these fake alibis checked out. You in the mood for a laugh, Knight?'

The dining room of the White Hart Hotel was panelled in oak and had a fireplace with a marble mantelpiece. In winter there was a log fire; in summer the fireplace held a display of dried flowers. Over the mantelpiece hung a painting of a hunt in full cry, thirty hounds chasing up a slope toward a wood, into which a bushy-tailed fox was vanishing. Well-fed men in red coats and black top hats were galloping after the pack on big horses.

'Very bloody Old World,' Bowker said, looking around. 'I hope the food's up to it. After a day's work, we've earned our dinner and a good night's sleep.'

The headwaiter himself was Old World enough to be wearing an ancient dinner jacket with a clip-on bow tie.

'We're proud of our cooking, sir,' he said. 'Chef gave up his post at a leading London restaurant to come here.'

That made Bowker scowl, but he refrained from asking why.

'I'm not eating underdone mutton with green glob on dandelion leaves and sunflower seeds because loonies in London think it's trendy,' he declared. 'They need their heads testing.'

The headwaiter kept his face impassive as he flourished two enormous menus bound in maroon leather and tried to hand one to Bowker and the other to Knight. Bowker waved them away.

'None of your precooked deep-frozens,' he rumbled. 'What's on the trolley over there?'

'This evening, sir, roast beef.' The headwaiter was sniffy.

'Sounds good, if it's well done. Scotch salmon to start with, Stilton cheese afterward. Got that?'

The headwaiter's unspoken opinion, as he scribbled away upon his order pad, was that he was dealing with a barbarian who had no appreciation of the delights of gourmet cuisine. The sort of peasant who ought to eat in the OK Burger Bar near the railway station. On the other hand, what could you expect of someone the size and shape of a heavyweight boxer, with a look that would curdle pasteurised milk?

'I'll have the same,' Knight said. It was useless to get into an argument with Bowker over food.

'Wine, sir?' the headwaiter asked scornfully. 'A carafe of the house red, perhaps?'

Bowker gave him so bleak a look it made him drop his pencil.

'Bring me a pint of Guinness in a silver tankard,' he said.

The first time Knight had a meal with the Inspector had been an eye-opener. It was in a pub in Long Slaughter, a village not all that many miles further up the Thames. The death of a young woman took them there, and a nasty sort of murder it turned out to be for Knight's first case with Bowker. The pub landlord had brought them large helpings, course after course, Bowker eating with the voracity of a runaway mechanical digger.

Very likely the portions were less generous at The White Hart, and Knight regarded that as a blessing. Although there was a certain fascination in watching Bowker eat, keeping up with him was risky. Food seemed to turn into more muscle on Bowker's massive frame, but anyone else was sure to double his body weight inside a fortnight, and it would be flab.

'Five down, two to go,' Bowker said thoughtfully while he was waiting for the first course. The dining room had twelve tables, and only three others were occupied.

'Our so-called suspects, you mean? We've still the girlfriend and the lawyer,' Knight agreed, 'which do you want to tackle first in the morning?'

'Lawyer last, I want everyone who knows him to tell him we're snuffling down the trail like a couple of rottweilers. Give him something to sweat about. Don't let me forget tomorrow when we talk to Matthews' girlfriend to ask if she's got a photo. We've no idea what he looked like, everything went up in flames.'

'Doesn't really matter now,' Knight said, 'not since somebody cremated him in his shop. What about that chap with the missing wife—are we going to take him seriously or not?'

A waiter in a short white jacket brought their smoked salmon, Bowker glared in stark disapproval at the inadequate amount on his plate.

'I've been thinking about Vereker,' he said. 'You may call me soft, but I began to feel sorry for the poor silly person.'

Knight nearly swallowed a forkful of salmon the wrong way at the prospect of anyone calling Denis Bowker soft.

'Why?' he asked. 'From what Shirley Cote told me, he's a real pain in the sit-down.'

'Even his own mother wouldn't deny it. But being a prize prat is not against the law. He's been humiliated, and that's hard to cope with—for him it's too much to cope with, so he's dreamed up this farrago about his wife being abducted and killed by the people who started the fire.'

'What you're saying is he needs counselling.'

'I wouldn't wish that on my worst enemy.' Bowker eyed his empty plate mournfully. 'Nobody needs a stranger poking and prying into his personal emotions at a time of distress.'

'You've decided it's a straight case of a fed-up wife doing a moonlight flit? Nothing to do with our enquiry?'

'How the hell do I know? Cote looked into it at the time, and she's no fool. If there'd been any connection with Matthews, I'm sure she'd have found it.'

'On the other hand'—Knight knew Bowker liked him to argue—'no clothes taken as far as Vereker could tell, though I have to agree that doesn't mean much. And no trace of any other man in Joanne Vereker's life, as far as Shirley could make out. No afternoons in motel bedrooms, no strange cars parked outside her house all night when Vereker was away. That's evidence, of a sort.'

Bowker stared at him as if he'd taken leave of his senses.

'You're giving me that Mary Ellen about Sherlock Holmes' dog not barking in the middle of the night,' he said accusingly.

'It wasn't *his* dog, it was somebody else's. Saw it on TV last Christmas. Anyway, you have to agree that when wives bolt, it's usually because there's another man waiting to give them a home and bed.'

'Jack, if the local female freedom fighters heard you talking like that they'd crucify you upside down outside the town hall. There are women who find they're not suited as wives and go off with other women. There's a lot of it about these days. Even in that Midlands hellhole you transferred here from, you must have heard rumours about it.'

'And how!' Knight said ruefully. 'When I was still a uniform, I got clopped on the head with a big placard at a Lesbian Pride protest march. And when I tried to run in the woman who did it, six or seven of her women friends set about me with their fists and boots. I thought I was a goner.'

'Bloody hell, Jack! What happened?'

'We were keeping the peace until a gang of those Say-Yes-for-Jesus clowns tried to break up the lezzie march. Something to do with their religion, maybe. All of a sudden the entire bloody street was one big brawl, with me in the middle of it. About eight people were hitting me at the same time.'

'Nasty,' Bowker said, grinning.

'The mounted police charged the procession from a side street, and by then I was nearly out on my feet. One of them grabbed me by the collar and I was dragged to safety by a bloody horse.'

'All in a day's work for a copper.' Bowker tried hard not to laugh.

A man in a floppy chef's hat and a white apron wheeled the covered trolley to their table. With a dramatic gesture, he slid the dome lid up and over, to reveal a large joint of beef roast to a nice brown. Bowker sniffed appreciatively as slices were carved for him. But his pleased expression turned hostile when he saw the portion on his plate, so hostile that the man in the comic hat hastily carved more. Roast potatoes, brussels sprouts, and sliced parsnips were added in abundance, and eating restarted.

'I was saying,' Bowker remarked when his plate was empty and Knight was still only halfway through his food, 'we can't just assume a boyfriend when a married woman does a vanishing trick—not these days. You haven't met them, Jack—not with your old-fashioned ideas about women—but there's independent women all over, making their own minds up. If they get fed up with hubby, they catch a bus and go. And why not?'

'Old-fashioned, me?' Knight said in outrage.

Bowker was staring across the room, his brow massively furrowed. 'See those two over there—the two men who came in five minutes ago? Got a newspaper on the table between them.'

Knight saw two men in their forties, one in a brown suit, one in a blue suit. The one in blue was almost bald and looked like a Rotarian. The other was glancing from time to time at the two detectives, a gleeful look on his face. Their grins and guffaws suggested a pleasant hour or so in the bar before they'd moved into the dining room.

'Local villains maybe,' Knight said. 'Councillors on the take or businessmen fiddling the accounts.'

Bowker summoned the head waiter with an imperious wave and an evil glare that almost had him down on his knees.'

'Nothing wrong with the food, I hope,' he grovelled.

'The beef was well-done,' Bowker conceded. 'The horse-radish sauce is watery. You can tell the chef to stop buying it from a supermarket and make his own. Those two men over there—do you know who they are?'

The waiter made a turkeylike gobbling noise at the insult to The White Hart's cooking.

'That's Mr Bentley. He owns the local paper—well, his family owns it and he edits it. He comes here for dinner several times a week. *He* appreciates our cooking. The gentleman with him is a guest in the hotel. I don't know his name.'

'But I do.' Bowker's tone suggested that the man in brown was a pervert of the worst kind. 'Cancel the cheese. Charge the meal to my room—202. Come on, Knight.'

Bowker strode through the dining room, Knight in his wake, to where the two men stared up at his approach.

'Evening, gentlemen,' he rumbled. 'My guess is that's a copy of tomorrow's *Bedlow Herald* you've got. Mind if I have a quick look at it?'

Whether they minded or not was of no importance. Bowker picked up the paper from the table and scanned the front page.

'Listen to this, Knight,' he said. 'THE VITAL CLUE THE POLICE REFUSE TO FOLLOW—how about that for a headline? Damned if it isn't the sad saga of the missing Mrs Vereker—we were talking about her not twenty minutes ago. And here's her picture in the paper with half a yard of type denouncing the stupid police for not finding her.'

'You must be Inspector Bowker,' said the balding man in blue with the bifocals. 'I heard you've been brought in to take over the investigation. I'm Bill Bentley, editor of the *Herald*.'

'No need to tell me who this is.' Bowker glared at the man in the brown suit. 'Mr Frederick Morten, I presume, London enquiry agent.'

Bowker was leaning over the table, one hand flat on it and in the other the paper crushed to the size of a golf ball. Knight fully expected to see him lift the table, complete with cutlery and glasses and vase of flowers, and smash it to matchwood. And then beat the two men senseless with a broken-off table leg.

Bowker was enraged, no mistake about it—his dinner had been spoiled. But he restrained himself.

'Did you write this drivel?' he asked Morten with a dreadful grin of hatred.

The enquiry agent shook his head. 'I'm no reporter. It's my job to provide the facts; others do the writing.'

Bowker handed the ball of newspaper to Knight, who rolled it out and smoothed the pages so he could read them.

'You've not done your job, either of you,' Bowker said to the apprehensive pair. 'There's nothing in this story that hasn't been known for months. Mrs Vereker's missing from her home. All the rest of it is Vereker's own fairy tales. It doesn't matter if you waste *your* time; nobody in their right mind expects much from enquiry agents and newspapers. In the police force we have to look for real evidence.'

'*Mrs Vereker's car was found in a local garage by our special investigator, Mr F Morten,*' Knight read from the paper.

'It had not been collected from Abrams Autos after minor repairs and it stood in a corner of the garage yard, only half a mile from the Bedlow police station until careful deduction by our man on the trail discovered it.'

Bowker's expression turned bleaker than ever. Knight knew what was in his mind. He'd been wrong-footed. One up to Morten and the editor, a kick up the backside for the police.

'If I can find her car inside a week, why can't you find Mrs Vereker herself in three months?' Morten challenged him.

'You were a copper yourself once, or I'm a Dutchman. You know the score—this is a free country, and people have the right to go missing if they want to. We take an interest only if there's evidence of a crime. Good night, Mr Bentley. Let me know if your bloodhound finds Mrs Vereker, I'd like a word with her myself.'

'What about?' Morten asked instantly.

'Good night Inspector.' Bentley blinked over the top of his glasses. 'Keep the paper if you want it.'

Outside the hotel on the pavement, Bowker smacked a lamp-post with his open hand, so hard that the concrete column swayed and the light flickered out for a second or two.

'Steady on!' said Knight. 'If you plunge the town into total darkness, there'll be looting of shops and rape in the streets. Superintendent Billings will have you up on charges.'

'That Bentley!' Bowker was fuming. 'He's deliberately making us look idiots with his private-enquiry charlatan. And tomorrow, when that newspaper comes out, everyone's going to believe we're either incompetent or corrupt.'

'That thought crossed my mind, too,' said Knight. 'Not us, the local boys in blue.'

Bowker was too furious to hear him.

'They'll say we've ignored the mysterious disappearance of a local woman—and maybe a murder. It will be on the local radio news, you can bet on it. And if the national press pick it up, we'll be in the clag up to our eyebrows. While those two sit in the hotel swigging good whisky and patting each other's backs—it won't bloody do!'

'I won't say it,' Knight said boldly, 'but DI Mason ought to have turned up that car ages ago. He buggers the case up, and we get the blame.'

'That's what we're here for, I thought you knew.'

'What can we do about Morten?'

'I'm thinking about it,' said Bowker. 'Now the evening's been ruined, we might as well go back to work. Where did you put the car? We can pay our respects to Mrs Druce.'

'Easier to walk. She lives in Penny Lane—only take us five minutes from here.'

'Where's the car?' Bowker repeated.

The White Hart was over two hundred years old. It had been a coaching inn in the days before railways were thought of, and it had an entrance high enough and wide enough for stagecoaches to drive through into a yard. There ostlers changed the horses while the passengers got down for a pint of ale and a hot meal. Nowadays the stone-cobbled yard was a carpark for the hotel's guests.

There was a parking attendant in the yard, as Bowker guessed, a thin oldish man with one arm. The White Hart obviously didn't offer valet parking.

Bowker said to Knight in an aside, 'Give him five quid and find out what car Fred Morten is driving. He's been staying in the hotel nearly a week, so this poor old sod should know.'

He squeezed himself into the passenger side of his own car to wait for Knight.

'Blue Jaguar over there,' Knight informed him. 'There must be more money in private eyeing than I thought. None of your dirty rainmac and cheap bars in mean streets for Fred. It's two years old and I made a note of the number plate, suspecting you might want to know it. Was I right?'

Bowker ignored the question.

'Before we go to Penny Lane,' he said, 'I want to stop at the Bedlow police station to have a word with the duty sergeant.'

Knight shrugged and eased the car out of the hotel yard.

'I know Morten looked as if he'd had a few,' he said, 'and he might have a few more to celebrate making us look bloody fools. Then he'll stagger up to bed in the hotel and sleep it off.'

'No,' said Bowker, 'when I went up to their table I overheard him telling Bentley he'd be back first thing Saturday morning. Tomorrow's Friday. That means he's going somewhere. My guess is that he's going to London to attend to something in his office. Would you say he's in a fit condition to drive a Jaguar?'

'Not tonight. Even in a wheelchair, he'd be a definite menace to life and limb. But you're doing a lot of guessing.'

'We call it "deducting." And we've got to fight fire with fire. Otherwise he'll make us look such bloody idiots that we'll both find ourselves demoted back to uniform and keeping the peace at loony bloody protest marches. Is that what you want?'

'Let's get the bugger!' Knight said.

Penny Lane had been redeveloped sometime in the 1980s, from a street of Victorian terraced brick houses into four five-storey blocks of flats. There were balconies and windows with striped awnings, space between the buildings for communal gardens, with flower beds and lawns and an incomprehensible item of sculpture in metal. It was all clean and well-lit, properly looked after, no scattered litter, no scrawled obscenities or burnt-out cars. The occupants were evidently owners and not tenants.

'What does she do, Mrs Druce?' Bowker asked. 'Do we know?'

'She's a hairdresser. Got her own business in Carter's Road.'

'What about Mr Druce?'

'Long gone, according to DS Trimmer.'

It was not much after nine in the evening but there was not a soul in sight. The four buildings comprising Penny Lane didn't have numbers, they had names instead. Each boasted a neat metal sign standing up from the front area of lawn, announcing which it was: Perdita, Columbina, Rosalinda, Isabella.

'Do you think the developer named them after his daughters?' Knight asked in a puzzled voice. 'Not that you meet girls with names like that. At least, I don't. They're all called "Sue." '

'They sound familiar,' Bowker agreed, 'but I can't think why. Roads and buildings are sometimes named for local heroes, but I doubt if Bedlow has any.'

'There's that sheep stealer they strung up in Gallowgate back in 18-and-something. You could call him a local celebrity.'

'He was a murderer. You can't have a Dinwiddy Place named for a felon who did a young girl in. Not even in these enlightened days, when nobody's guilty and we're all bloody guilty. Though nothing would surprise me,' Bowker said darkly.

'Glad I don't live here,' said Knight. 'Looks nice enough, but I'd feel a right prat giving my address as number 9, Perdita in Penny Lane.'

The building they wanted was Rosalinda, second on the left.

A lift took them to the third floor and Bowker rang the doorbell of Mrs Druce's flat. After a while, the door was opened by a woman in a long pink housecoat. She saw Bowker looming almost as tall as the doorway and almost as wide, his dark gypsy looks and his air of menace—she yelped and slammed the door on him. It was a mistake women often made after dark; they saw his size and jumped to the conclusion he was a demented rapist there to ravage their helpless bodies.

Bowker had his foot in the door to stop it closing and pushed his warrant card round the edge at face height.

'Police,' he announced. 'Open the door, Mrs Druce, we need to talk to you.'

He was trying to sound friendly, although he was vexed by his usual reception. He glared sideways at Knight, who hastily took the grin off his face and looked solemn. To him it was always a big joke when Bowker was taken for an axe murderer by a nervous female.

There was a longish wait, Mrs Druce was taking her time about reading the warrant card under her nose. The photo probably did the trick; it showed Bowker as even more malignant of expression than in the flesh. She opened the door slowly and Bowker smiled at her, not wanting to panic her again. He introduced himself and Knight and asked if it was convenient for them to come in for a few minutes.

The sight of Jack Knight at his side reassured her. She stood back for them to enter and took them into her sitting room. The TV was switched on to BBC world news, the usual account of wars in foreign parts, massacres and genocide, famine and earthquake victims, flood disasters in typhoon areas, oil tankers drifting out of control and spilling millions of gallons of oil into the sea, 300 passengers dead in a crashed airplane in the mountains somewhere abroad. Nothing of urgent significance, Bowker saw in a glance, and turned his back to it. His interest was two people and two little girls brutally murdered.

Moira Druce took the hint and turned off the TV. She settled the policemen side by side on a striped sofa and offered them a drink. Gin was what she had, she said, they could have it with tonic, lemonade, or vermouth. Bowker didn't like gin, so he said they were on duty and couldn't.

She poured herself a large one, took an armchair facing

them, had a swig, and crossed her legs under the frilly housecoat. She did this with a deliberation that had their full attention.

'You gave me a fright!' she accused Bowker. 'I thought—well, I'm not sure what I thought. Are there many policemen your size scaring people?'

It wasn't said in a hostile way at all, and Knight detected an innuendo in her words. Surely she couldn't be flirting with The Mad Mangler!

Bowker bared his big white teeth in a noncommittal grin. 'I know it's late for a social call, but there's a question or two I have to ask.'

'Is it about Ronnie Matthews?' she asked. 'My impression was you'd written the case off as unsolved. Although you don't call it that, do you?'

'No case is ever written off,' Bowker told her, eyebrows down in disapproval. 'Even if it takes years, cases stay open.'

'Like Jack the Ripper, you mean? The case is still open after a hundred years or more.'

Now she was definitely flirting, Knight decided in amazement. And Bowker was pretending not to notice.

'It's three months now since the fire,' she said, 'and if you haven't caught the murderer in that time, you never will.'

She was a big bold woman, Moira Druce, about thirty-five, give or take a year or two. Light brunette with highlights, elaborate hairdo proclaiming her skills, generously rounded body inside her pink housecoat. No mystery why the late Ronnie Matthews was interested in her.

Jack Knight was busy smiling at her. But she had a roving eye for the Inspector, partly subdued by the official nature of the meeting.

'Yes, it's too long,' Bowker agreed. 'I won't make excuses to you because it wasn't my case till now. It's a puzzler. There's no motive. Nobody wanted him dead.'

'Somebody did,' she said sharply. 'Otherwise he'd be alive.'

'No visible motive.' Bowker contained his natural rage with effort. 'How long were you and he good friends?'

'Meaning how long were we sleeping together? I've no reason to hide it now, not with his wife and family gone. About twelve months, it would be. He was a very nice man, Ronnie, loving and kind. And sexy.'

'Who killed him and his family, Mrs Druce?'

'You're asking *me*? You think I haven't asked myself that question over and over again? The Inspector before you had an idea that I did it.'

'Not really,' said Bowker, 'but he had to suspect you because you were close enough to Matthews to have a motive. And you had no one to support your statement that you were driving home in the middle of the night from your auntie's place in Bristol.'

'He made no secret of what he thought,' she said bitterly. 'I burnt the place down and killed Ronnie and his wife and his two little girls because he wouldn't leave her to marry me. As if I ever want to be married again! I've been married once, and that was more than enough. But a nice loving relationship with a man I like and respect, no strings attached, that's all I wanted.'

She fancies Denis Bowker, Knight said to himself—he's right about women being contrary creatures!

'The world is not all that well organised to give people what they want, Mrs Druce,' Bowker said. 'You must have noticed. Who do you believe started the fire?'

'You're the policeman—why ask me?'

'Because you were close to him for twelve months. You learned things about him we can never hope to know.'

'I've never believed it was personal. Ronnie was easygoing—he didn't make enemies. It must have been something to do with business, but he never talked to me about that. So I can't help you much.'

'We've been told he had naughty videos for sale. Did he bring any here for you to watch? You've got a VTR, I see.'

She didn't even blush. She crossed her legs the other way and smiled. She didn't actually wink at Bowker, but the impression was much the same.

'Just a bit of fun,' she said, 'we were both adults. Nothing wrong with a bit of hanky-panky on film to start the mood going—only a giggle, really.'

'What was the description the witness gave us of a video that Matthews showed him?' Bowker asked Knight, straight-faced.

This was a game they played in interviews. Knight turned back through his notebook, pretending to look for the item, building up the suspense.

'Got it,' he said finally. Then, keeping his voice very solemn, he read out: ' *"Two girls with great big knockers wrestling around on a hairy black rug. They did things to each other, know what I mean?"* That last bit was more a comment than a question, the way he said it.'

'I took it to be a leer.' Bowker was equally serious. 'Well, Mrs Druce, did you ever see that one?'

She was laughing openly. 'No, just straightforward sex, men and women.'

'You're sure about that?' Bowker asked. 'Because there is no particular reason for us to be interested, if that's all it was. You can buy videos like that on market stalls. But did he bring tapes of more advanced subjects to watch with you?'

'I don't know what you mean.'

'Yes, you do. Bondage and flogging. Torture and actual bodily injury. Children being abused. The stuff real perverts enjoy.'

'What do you take me for!' she exclaimed, flushed and angry. 'If you think I'd watch anything like that, you must be off your head! All Ronnie ever brought here was normal sex—that's what we liked. Not that we watched videos very often—we were busy with the real thing. And what business is it of yours?'

'I wish it wasn't my business,' Bowker said morosely, 'but it is. Everything is that might have a bearing on Matthews' death. Videos might have a connection—you said as much yourself.'

'If he had anything like that, I never saw it. The few videos he brought here were just normal sex; that's God's own truth.'

'Normal!' Bowker exclaimed. 'What that means today is beyond me! There are porno magazines on sale openly with pictures of people doing things that make me blush. And school kids can walk in and buy them. Do you understand what normal is, Knight?'

'Yes, sir,' Jack Knight said, unperturbed. 'Normal means what I do. With women. Grown-up women who like it. That's normal.'

He couldn't imagine what would make the Inspector blush.

'Thank you for that gem of wisdom.' Bowker glared like a bull elephant ready to charge through a mud-hut village and trample everyone in it flat. 'Well, Mrs Druce, anything to say?'

'I've said it all,' she told him. 'If Ronnie was mixed up in anything like that, I didn't know about it. And I don't want to know about it now. You can put that in your notebook.'

'There's one thing before we go,' Bowker said. 'Do you have a photo of Ronnie Matthews? We've nothing to show around, to see if anybody remembers him being in various places.'

'Is it going to make any difference?' she asked skeptically.

'I'm going to catch the evil bastard who torched the shop and incinerated a whole family,' Bowker said, bleak as the blizzard over the Barents Sea. 'Whether a picture will help me or not, I don't know. But it might.'

'I'll find one for you,' she said. 'I want to see whoever did it rotting behind bars for the rest of his life. And that's too good for him, if I had my way, he'd hang.'

She had an album with photos of family and friends, an oblong book bound in imitation green leather.

'That's Ronnie last summer,' she said sadly, peeling a photo off the page. 'I took it on the balcony here one afternoon.'

Ronnie Matthews perched on the balcony railing, his shirt off and a glass in his hand, smiling into the camera. Late thirties and well built, fair hair, and a boyish grin.

'We'll give you a receipt for it,' Bowker said, and he passed the picture to Knight.

'Got the look of a welterweight about him.' Knight was a boxing fan. 'Did he ever do any fighting?'

'I think he did, in his younger days,' she said, 'well before we got together. Only amateur, though, not the mauling they show on TV. There wasn't a mark on him.'

'Write that in your notebook.' Bowker kept his face straight. 'The witness says, *"Not a mark on him."* '

'You cheeky devil!' said Moira Druce, and she was laughing.

7. ·················· *superintendent billings's office*

Dc Shirley Cote was at her desk in the Incident Room at 8.30 in the morning, typing a report of yesterday's surveillance. Being a conscientious woman, she intended to be in position and ready with her zoom camera when Hinksey opened for business.

'Anything interesting?' Bowker perched on the corner of her desk, his weight threatening to tip it over. She looked at him oddly—he sounded more pleasant than she had heard him before. Like a playful grizzly bear.

'The highlight of the day was when Jason Swanson went in just after six yesterday evening,' she told him, pleased to be able to offer any morsel of information, 'Two lads his own age with him that I can't put names to. They were inside about five minutes and came out carrying a six-pack of lager each.'

'Jason Swanson,' Bowker said thoughtfully. 'Billy's oldest, I remember you said. Doing probation for interfering with little girls.'

'And under-age for buying strong drink,' said Cote, 'though I suppose if we challenged Hinksey about selling liquor to minors, he'd say he'd asked their age and they swore they were over eighteen. But if you ask me, a week or ten days' surveillance will produce enough dodgy sales to have Hinksey's licence taken away.'

'That's something to fall back on. But why does young Swanson trek all the way to the High Street from that miserable bloody housing estate for a can of beer? Ask yourself— there must be half a dozen nearer places selling it.'

'It must be what you thought, sir; the lager's a cover. Jason and his pals get something else from Hinksey.'

'Which raises the next question: where do layabouts like him get the money to buy prohibited substances?'

'Petty theft—it has to be.'

'I expect so.' Bowker shook his head mournfully. 'But leave that for now. Does Moira Druce know you by sight?'

'Don't think so. When DI Mason questioned her about Matthews, I was out making enquiries about Mrs Vereker. Ginny Bampton sat in on the interview—she's a uniformed PC.'

'Good. I want you to get your hair done today. Have it permed or tinted or highlighted or whatever you fancy that's expensive and takes half the day to do and needs the owner's personal and gossipy attention.'

'What do you want me to gossip about?'

'I had a chat with Mrs Druce last night,' Bowker said. 'She's got over the sad demise of her boyfriend Ronnie very well. Life must go on, as they always say, doors close and doors open, hope springs eternal in the human chest, tomorrow is another day, and similar items of homely philosophy. She's a big bold woman with a roving eye, is Moira Druce, she likes men. What she looks for is a nice loving relationship, no strings attached, she said.'

'Sounds fair enough to me.' Cote was puzzled. 'But surely you don't think she started the fire out of spite. I know Sergeant Trimmer thinks so, but nobody else does.'

'He might even be right,' Bowker said mildly. 'Women operate on their own brand of logic. Half the time they don't know why they do the things they do. And the rest of the time there's no bloody reason at all for what they do. So anything's possible.'

Shirley Cote was beginning to go red in the face, it was only the habit of discipline that held her back from acidic comment. Then Bowker grinned at her and to her amazement she saw him as a clumsy Saint Bernard lolloping about. *I must have gone soft in the head,* she said to herself. *He's a wild ape, not a puppy.*

'Anyway,' he said, 'Mrs Druce may have found herself another loving relationship. I'd like to know who with.'

'So you want me to get my hair done and have a girlish gossip and find out who's bringing sunshine into her life? Not that I can see any connection.'

'Probably isn't one. But it could be somebody she knew while she was relating with Matthews. And maybe the two men knew each other or had dealings of some sort. In a small town like Bedlow, there are connections everywhere you look. Like Billy Swanson's delinquent son Jason buys crack or whatever from Arnie Hinksey, who was Matthews' pal to go fishing with and watch porno videos with on dull afternoons. And that selfsame Billy went to chokey for breaking into Matthews' shop. And so on.'

'The music goes 'round and 'round, and it comes out here,' Shirley Cote said with a grin. 'Mrs Druce could be having her new relationship with somebody on our suspect list.'

'Find out for me with tact and finesse. Don't let on you're a copper. But don't deny it if she spots you.'

'With finesse?' Cote's pale eyebrows rose up her forehead as she stared in disbelief at Bowker. 'Very well, finesse it shall be, all the way. I'll walk around to Moira's salon this morning to have the full treatment.'

'Make sure you get a receipt,' Bowker growled.

Jack Knight had been listening with interest. Time for him to say something, he decided, to let the Inspector know he was on the alert and working hard. Mustn't let himself get overlooked amongst these small-town coppers; that wouldn't do his prospect of promotion any good.

'Superintendent Billings was on the phone a minute ago,' said Knight. 'He'd like to see you. He didn't say what about. Meanwhile, we've received Hinksey's crime sheet from Army Records.'

Bowker disliked the thought of jumping at Billings' word and was glad to have a reason to make him wait.

'Tell me Arnie was drummed out of the Paratroops in disgrace, his badges ripped off on the parade ground and the band playing "The Dead March" while they kicked him out of the barracks gate and chucked his dishonourable discharge papers after him,' he begged.

'No such luck,' said Knight, handing over the fax, 'you must be confusing him with Beau Geste and the French Foreign Legion. The fax says he left them of his own free will, he wasn't given the elbow. And you won't like it, but he didn't spend any time in military prison running around a drill square with ninety pounds of rocks on his back.'

'Pity,' said Bowker, deeply disappointed, 'there is something very unlikable about Hinksey. He's the sort who should be put away for years and years, where he can't do any harm.'

'It says he was a full corporal at one time. But he lost that when he shot up a couple of Paddies at a checkpoint in Belfast. On the other hand, the enquiry exonerated him, it says. Sounds bloody wrong to me. Either he was to blame, or he wasn't.'

'We'll get him for something,' Bowker grumbled. 'You've been studying that list of petrol outlets for long enough. Any ideas occur to you? Anything to be followed up?'

'No.' Knight's expression was cheerful, despite a lack of progress with the list. 'For all the good I'm doing, I might as well be reading football league results.'

Bowker scowled at him and went down to see Billings. The Superintendent had the *Bedlow Herald* on his desk, but his mood was elated despite that.

'Sit down, Inspector,' he said, 'I've got some very good news for you. That private enquiry agent was stopped last night by a traffic patrol for erratic driving and breathalysed.'

'Really?' Bowker sounded astonished.

'Our lads found he was well over the legal limit and required him to accompany them to the station. Morten became abusive and, after being warned, he was handcuffed and brought in to be seen by the police surgeon. He remained abusive and non-cooperative, and he was charged with drunken driving, threatening behaviour, resisting arrest. He spent the night in a cell downstairs.'

'Bloody hell!' Bowker was hardly able to believe his luck.

'He's due to appear before the magistrate later this morning. I imagine the case will be held over to let him arrange legal representation, and he'll be released on bail.'

'Ten to one Mr Lloyd Davies, the villain's friend, steps into the scene,' Bowker said. 'That man pops up like the Demon King shooting up through a trapdoor in a Christmas pantomime. Where was Morten when the patrol pulled him over?'

'Just outside the town, on the main road—driving a powerful Jaguar. Very dangerous. In the circumstances, I shall personally congratulate the two officers who spotted him and took action.'

'They deserve our thanks,' said Bowker. 'There's far too much drunk driving and people being mangled up in crashed cars. It's nice to know we're doing our bit to keep death off the road.'

The Superintendent gave him a curious look, not certain if he was being serious or not. He decided to let it go.

'I was thinking of other considerations,' he said. 'The knock to Morten's credibility is very damaging, in my opinion. He'll be found guilty of the drunk charge and fined, no question. And if the threatening-behaviour charge sticks, he's finished with the newspaper. Bentley would never dare use him after that.'

'As you say, it's good news.' Bowker's smile was vicious, 'Some days start off gloomy and dull, and then the sun comes out and you can hear the birds singing in the trees.'

Billings gave him the cold eye.

'When Morten was brought in last night,' he said, sounding as executive as any man has a right to be, 'he made accusations of police persecution. They often do, of course, when they've got themselves into trouble. Any idea of what he was talking about, Inspector?'

'No, sir,' Bowker said firmly—the first time he'd addressed Billings as 'sir.' 'I saw him in The White Hart with Bentley last night. Bentley gave me a copy of today's *Herald*, just to gloat, and Morten was cocky about locating Mrs Vereker's car. Not that I let them annoy me. I stayed calm and professional. After that I went to interview a witness, Mrs Druce.'

'You didn't say anything a lawyer could persuade a magistrate was harassment, Inspector? We don't want trouble from Mr Lloyd Davies when the case comes up.'

'Not a blind word, as God is my witness,' Bowker stated, with utter sincerity in his voice. 'My sergeant was with me and will verify that, if need be. I might even have congratulated Morten on his smart piece of detective work.'

Leadership material though he was, Billings knew when his leg was being pulled. His fingers drummed on his well-polished desk while he stared thoughtfully at Bowker.

'Ah, yes,' he said after a longish pause. 'I understand they'd want to gloat over the story in the paper about the car. One up to them, one down for us. What do you make of it?'

'Mrs Vereker left by train. Or she went on a bus. Or she went in somebody else's car. Hers was being mended, and she couldn't use it. Her husband never gave it a thought after she'd gone.'

'You're taking the same line as DI Mason—that she ran away from her husband?'

'There is no evidence of anything else,' Bowker insisted.

'But suppose Mason was wrong. Should he have taken Vereker's story more seriously?'

'Have you met Vereker?' Bowker scowled.

'No, I haven't. Why do you ask?'

'He's one of the walking wounded. His ego's been amputated by his wife leaving him. There's a great big shotgun hole through his self-esteem, crippled for life, maybe fatal. Any story will do to protect himself from the painful reality.'

'You can't be certain about that. Morten found her car, and if someone finds her dead body in a dustbin next week, we shall be in serious trouble for not starting an investigation earlier.'

'But DI Mason *did* investigate.' Bowker had ceased to call the Superintendent 'sir.' 'There's a bloody big thick file he opened, everything in it including her birth certificate and shoe size. And it leads nowhere, except to the conclusion that she went missing because she wanted to, for reasons unknown.'

'That's all very well,' said Billings, excessively executive, determined to cover himself. 'I want you to take up where Mason left off and pursue the enquiry into the missing woman. We must take into account that the disappearance may have a bearing on the Matthews murder case.'

'In my view, it's no more than coincidence,' Bowker insisted.

'Your view, Inspector, is only a view, and not necessarily the true facts of the situation. In *my* view, there is no such thing as coincidence. We cannot afford to take chances. I want you to treat the disappearance very seriously indeed from now on.'

Bowker went back upstairs in an extremely gritty mood. Knight saw the look on his face and busied himself with the long lists of petrol stations. He had no idea what he was looking for, and he didn't believe Bowker had, either. The truth was the Matthews murder case was a dead end. Nobody was ever going to solve it now, not even Bowker.

'Knight,' said a voice like bottled thunder, 'come here for a minute.'

He went over and sat facing Bowker across the cluttered desk the Inspector was using.

'I have to hand it to you.' Knight tried for a note of cheerful admiration. 'You settled the hash of that private eye. Sherlock Morten was run in late last night, drunk in charge of a motor vehicle. It's all over the station. There's going to be celebration drinks when the day shift goes off, across the road at The Black Dog. We're invited. You're a hero to every copper in this station for tripping Morten up. To add to the merriment and rejoicing, he got stroppy with the traffic patrol, and he's been done for threatening behaviour.'

'The Superintendent told me that,' Bowker said sourly. 'He's as pleased as a puppy dog chasing its tail.'

'We've got Morten off our back, so why aren't you happy? Not what we were sent here to do, but it's definitely a goal for the home team.'

'I'll have to take you off the murder investigation for a day or two. I want you to find Mrs Vereker for me.'

'The plot thickens.' Knight was irrepressible. 'I see it all: the

Superintendent's broken out in a sticky sweat over the car being found, right? He wants us to fake him an alibi.'

'What have I said to you in the past about respect for senior officers?' Bowker asked with a sigh like a forest gale. 'A day may come, God save us all, when they make *you* a senior officer. But not if you sit about on your backside instead of detecting. So go and find Mrs Vereker for me, and don't take long over it. We've a murder to solve—four murders, in fact.'

'Do you think it's worth checking for a boyfriend?'

'DC Cote has been over that. Just go through the routine till you find Mrs Vereker; don't fuss over her bedtime arrangements. She's living somewhere and must be spending money. Most likely she's got a job by now. Get her National Insurance number, talk to the Department of Social Security, check with her bank, talk to the credit-card outfits, see if the tax people know anything of her whereabouts—they'll be after their slice of any money she's earning. Look at electoral rolls; try British Telecom for a new phone number in her name. Ask the Salvation Army, even, if you have to. She might not call herself "Vereker," she might have gone back to her maiden name, Morley. You know the drill.'

'When I find her, what do you want me to do—run her in for wasting police time?'

'I don't want you to do anything, not even speak to her. Find her address and come back here with it. Today's Friday—you can have till Monday midday.'

'Can't be done,' Knight said swiftly. 'Government departments don't work at weekends.'

'Always excuses!' Bowker exclaimed, rolling his eyes upward. 'You can have till Tuesday midday. So get a bloody move on!'

Soon after eleven that morning, Bowker arrived unannounced at Lloyd Davies' office and informed the receptionist he wanted to speak to her boss. If his brooding air of menace terrified her, she concealed it well—she was no stranger to thugs turning up and asking for Davies.

'Your name?' she said.

Bowker laid his warrant card on her desk. She looked up at him with a different expression.

'He's busy all day,' she said. 'Can you come back tomorrow?'

'No,' Bowker said in a voice that made her shrink back in her chair. 'I'm here to see him now. Just tell him.'

'What's it about?' She didn't give up easily, this one.

'None of your business,' he snarled. 'Tell him I'm here.'

Two minutes later, the lawyer bustled out of his inner office, a warm smile on his face and his hand outstretched in greeting. He was short, five-foot-four, dark-haired and thin. He wore heavy spectacles and a pin-striped suit that had cost him a lot of money.

Whatever his private thoughts about a surprise visit from the police, his action plan was to be the very soul of goodwill and civic co-operation.

'My dear Inspector, come on in.' He beamed. 'I'm delighted to meet you at last—I've been hearing about you.'

From the Burtons and from Ronson, Bowker thought darkly, his smile as cheery as a hyena about to bite a tribesman's foot off as a midmorning snack.

'Just a minute,' he said. 'I've got a colleague with me.'

As if on cue, in marched a policewoman in uniform. She was a part of Bowker's ploy to tip the lawyer off-balance. As all his team were out on assignment, he'd borrowed her for the occasion—she was Ginny Bampton, originally on DI Mason's murder squad and taken off when Billings ordered the action to be run down.

WPC Bampton was a big woman, broad and burly; there were hard muscles under her shirt. She had the stoniest stare Bowker had ever seen on a woman, truly intimidating. And ideal for his purpose.

'Ah,' Lloyd Davies said thoughtfully, looking at WPC Bampton. Blue uniforms walking the streets to deter muggers and help old ladies across the road were commendable, but uniforms marching into his office were a very different proposition. Any woman the size of Bampton gave the shortish lawyer feelings of inadequacy.

His inner office was pleasantly furnished; nothing antique or showily expensive, but good quality and well-matched. He waved his visitors to chairs and settled himself behind his desk, and he was still beaming in an effort to remain in control.

This is the clever bugger who gets the local lawbreakers off with a fine, Bowker reminded himself. *Not much to look at, but a mind like a rattrap. Time to walk wary.*

Not that Bowker intended to pit his wits against a lawyer; it wasn't his way. Upset them so they fall over their own feet was his approach; tie their shoelaces together and watch them trip arse over elbow. He sat silent in his chair and stared bleakly, till Davies felt it necessary to start the conversation.

'What can I do for you, Inspector?' he said, most anxious to oblige in every possible way.

'I'm making enquiries into the fire back in April that killed the Matthews family,' said Bowker, knowing that was no surprise to Davies. 'As Matthews' lawyer, you can probably help me.'

'Of course, any way I can,' Davies assured him blithely, 'but I see your colleague has got out a notebook and pen. What is the significance of that?'

'None,' Bowker said genially. 'Force of habit, I imagine. Put your notebook away, Constable.'

She gave him a doubtful look, as if to say, *Don't you realise we're dealing with a slippery crook here?* She glared at Davies even more doubtfully and the unspoken words, *Watch your step, you slimy bastard* were hanging in the air.

Bowker was full of bonhomie. 'By now you've had the time

to sort out the last will and testament of Ronnie Matthews. I'm interested in knowing who benefits.'

'You are aware that dealings between legal advisors and their clients are confidential, Inspector.'

'Not with wills, when there's been a murder, as *you* are aware,' said Bowker.

Lloyd Davies turned his smile of goodwill up to 150 watts. 'Ah, the thing is, Inspector, Matthews didn't make a will. Or if he did, it was lost in the fire. I certainly didn't draw up a will for him, and as I handled his other legal business, that indicates to me that he never made one. A lot of men don't, you know; they see it as an omen of mortality.'

'His *other* legal business.' Bowker was still affable. 'What would that be—the shop lease, transactions like that?'

Davies nodded.

'If there's no will, who benefits? Who's the next of kin?'

'Another problem, Inspector. So far I've been unable to trace any next of kin for either Matthews or his wife.'

It was like pulling teeth, asking a lawyer to answer even a simple question. For a moment Bowker treated himself to a fantasy of holding Davies down flat across his desk with a knee in his throat while he yanked his teeth out with a pair of bloodstained mechanic's pliers. He liked the idea.

'Both of them were orphans, that what you're telling me?' He was refreshed by his brief vision of blood and broken teeth.

'Matthews was taken into care as a small child and brought up in foster homes. As far as I can establish, his mother died of drugs or alcohol dependency ten years ago. His father was never known.'

'Bloody hell!' Bowker exclaimed, appalled to think any child grew up in such circumstances. 'What about Mrs Matthews?'

'Both her parents died in a motorway pile-up in the 1970s. It had a lot of news coverage at the time; you may recall it.

Over seventy vehicles crashed end-to-end in thick fog, twenty or thirty dead.'

'I remember it. Worst road disaster ever in Britain. Made the *Guinness Book of Records*. She had no brothers or sisters?'

'Two brothers who were in the car and died with the parents. A sister who married and emigrated to Australia. She could make a claim. I'm trying to trace her, but it's not easy. All letters and Matthews' address book were destroyed in the fire.'

Ginny Bampton made a throat-clearing noise that suggested she was holding herself back from advising Bowker that anything the shyster was doing was for his own benefit, nobody else's.

'Big country, Australia,' Bowker said in a disbelieving tone. 'All scrub and desert and nothing but kangaroos and blacks on a walkabout chucking boomerangs at each other. Wild colonial boys drunk from getting-up to bedtime. So if you find the long-lost sister, how much cash might she get?'

Lloyd Davies didn't answer. He sat staring at Bowker over his desk with a thoughtful look on his face. He took his spectacles off and polished them with a white handkerchief from his breast pocket. He held them up to the light to check if he'd wiped the dust and smears off. Very obviously he was wondering whether or not to lie to a policeman.

'I can easily get a court order.' Bowker's grin was fiendish. 'What's the point of holding me up for twenty-four hours? No advantage to your client, poor devil—he's dust and ashes now.'

'You misunderstand me, Inspector,' the lawyer said glibly. 'I merely paused to collect my thoughts. I do not have the file in front of me.'

Bowker's patience was paper-thin now. He had been too amiable for too long. His dark complexion flushed darker yet. His thick black eyebrows drew together and met. Ginny

Bampton removed her fixed gorgon stare from Davies for a second to glance at Bowker and caught his mood. Her colourless eyes swivelled back to the lawyer and he twitched in his chair under the full blast of her silent accusation: *liar, shyster, swindler, bilker, cockroach.*

'Some things stick in the mind,' Bowker said nastily. 'So how much?'

Davies looked away from WPC Bampton's glare and got a grip on himself, 'There's insurance on the stock, not on the shop itself,' he ventured. 'Matthews was only a tenant.'

'Magazines, chocolate bars, videos?' Bowker suggested. 'A second-hand ice-cream cabinet? The lot wouldn't add up to more than a few hundred quid. Add in the contents of the flat above, two or three thousand?'

'Quite so.'

'What else?' Bowker demanded, his interest roused by Davies' reluctance to disclose the figures. 'His life insurance?'

'Ah, yes, on my advice Matthews insured his life for £25,000. You must know that the insurance company concerned is deferring payment until the question of the fire is cleared up. Unfairly, in my view. But when crime is involved, insurance companies tend to adopt a very cautious approach.'

'I should bloody well think so! Any other insurance?'

'None.'

'So the total estate of the late Ron Matthews amounts to less than thirty thousand quid?'

'There are investments,' the lawyer said cautiously.

'Like what? What sort of investments does an orphan running a paper shop make? Stocks and shares, Government bonds? Uncut diamonds and gold bars? Old Master paintings?'

'Matthews distrusted all conventional forms of investment. He believed they were fraudulent, even gilt-edged stock. He didn't really trust banks either. He kept the shop accounts down to an absolute minimum—just enough in his bank account to cover his suppliers. He dealt in cash whenever he could, money that never went through any account. At regular intervals, I made him aware of the legal risks of doing this, of course.'

'Naturally,' Bowker agreed, and Ginny Bampton stared harder. 'So what did Ronnie put his spare cash into?'

'The only form of investment he made was property. He thought it safe because he could go and see it. It couldn't be stolen.'

'What sort of property?' Bowker asked through gritted teeth, 'Offices, flats, massage parlours, what?'

'Houses. He owned several houses in the town, all rented out. I did the conveyancing work for him each time he bought one.'

'So you know how many houses he owned. I'd like to know, too.'

'Five,' said Davies. 'Good class property, all of them.'

'Worth what?' Bowker pressed him.

'To get a true value, you'd have to bring in a surveyor.'

'So guess for me.'

Davies went all judicious, pressing his fingertips together and leaning back in his swivel chair. 'In the present state of the housing market, I'd say over four hundred thousand pounds.'

Bowker snorted. WPC Bampton snorted.

'Four hundred thousand quid? From a corner newspaper shop?'

Lloyd Davies said nothing. He cleared his throat gingerly and gazed into the wide blue yonder, total honesty displayed on his face. It was clear enough now why he was reluctant to get into a discussion of his former client's finances.

'Comments are waiting to be made,' Bowker prodded him. 'In my book, four hundred grand is the number four with five zeros after it. That's a bloody lot of newspaper sales and ice-cream cones. And Ronnie was only thirty-something, he couldn't have been in business on his own for more than ten years, at most.'

The lawyer continued to say nothing, fingertips steepling. His 150-watt beam had been switched right off.

'Have you any idea of how Matthews acquired that much money? Any small hint you could drop my way?' Bowker was being openly sarcastic now.

'No, Inspector, I have no knowledge of how he made the money, none at all. He could have won it in a lottery. Or gambling on horses. Or was given it by a grateful customer.'

Davies was lying brazenly. He knew it and Bowker knew it, and Ginny Bampton knew it.

'When he bought a house, how did he pay?' Bowker asked.

'When I let him know that the papers were ready to sign and exchange, he came to my office with the money in a carrier bag. Usually a Safeway bag, from which I deduced Mrs Matthews bought her groceries there regularly.'

'And you and he counted out eighty or ninety thousand in banknotes right here on your desk each time?'

Davies nodded.

'In what—fifties, twenties?'

'I don't really remember,' Davies said vaguely. 'Paper money, that's all I know.'

'Used and dirty ten-pound notes, I bet,' Bowker insisted, 'or maybe even fivers. It takes a lot of those to make up a hundred grand. You'd be here half the day counting them.'

But Davies didn't react. Bowker tried again.

'It never struck you as unusual, buying a house with a bag of dirty old banknotes?'

'Unusual, yes. Illegal, no, Inspector. Several of my clients are eccentric in their ways.'

'Yes, I've met one or two of them,' Bowker said shortly, 'and I expect to meet them again, soon. I'm sure you can tell me who kept Matthews' books for him, for his tax return. An accountant ought to be able to explain his cash flow to me.'

'He used a retired accountant who likes to keep his hand in—he went into the shop every so often to do the accounts. Once a month, I think. I can give you his name—John Hillyard. He lives in Spinsters' Reach. That faces the Thames, starting from the bridge, going upstream.'

Not that he'll be able to tell me anything, Bowker said under his breath. *Otherwise you wouldn't be so bloody quick giving me his name and address.*

'Considering you were a friend of Ronnie Matthews besides his lawyer, you haven't told me a lot about him,' Bowker said, deep suspicion in his tone.

'Whatever gives you that idea, Inspector? We weren't friends in any social sense. The relationship was purely professional.'

It was in Bowker's mind to state there was nothing pure about Davies' profession, but he bit the words back.

'You were seen drinking with him more than once. In that nice old pub facing the river, the Crown and Anchor.'

Davies shook his head. 'I remember running into him there once. He bought me a drink—or did I buy him one? I can't remember—it's some time ago.'

'You were seen together on several occasions.'

'Out of the question. Your informant is mistaken, Inspector.'

Bowker nodded and let it go. He was asking himself why it was so important to Davies to deny any contact with Matthews except legal matters. There was something here to be dug out. But not out of Davies himself—as a lawyer, he was a trained liar. Some other source; maybe one of his clients on the suspect list knew something useful that could be gouged out of him.

Bowker stood up and leaned over to put hands the size of hubcaps on Davies' desk. In his rumpled dark suit, he looked a lot like the Creature from the Black Lagoon—very dangerous and not predictable, with a long-standing grudge against the human race. WPC Bampton also rose to her feet. The look on her face was so accusing that Davies flinched momentarily.

'Good day to you, Mr Davies,' Bowker said in a voice from the depths of the Black Lagoon. 'You have been more useful than you can imagine. Just one last thing before I forget it; is Donald Vereker a client of yours?'

'Yes he is, poor fellow,' Davies said solemnly. 'Bad business that, his wife disappearing.'

Bugger it, Bowker thought. *Another connection to worry about.*

8. .... *windmill lane*

The £400,000 seemed a very respectable motive for doing Ronnie Matthews in. Most murders for profit were done for a lot less. Bowker had arrested perpetrators who had murdered for a pittance—in particular, he remembered a twenty-two-year-old hooligan who got an old woman to open the door by saying he was from the Social Security. Forced his way in and smashed her head against the wall before departing with her savings: £200 in an old Ovaltine tin hidden under her bed.

He got off with a plea of manslaughter. Never meant to cause her any physical harm, according to his lawyer. Did a few years inside and came out to look for other easy victims. *Sometimes I wonder why we bother to catch them,* Bowker said to himself, *but if nobody empties the bins regularly, the country will turn into a plague pit in no time and poison us all.*

There was a private nurse he'd arrested a few years back. She was a pleasant middle-aged woman, hired to look after a doddering old chap with stacks of money and no near family. After a month or two, he wrote her into his will out of gratitude. So then she shot the poor silly old sod full of insulin and killed him, not wanting to wait too long for the inheritance.

When his estate was sorted out after the funeral, there was no fortune in investments. There was just £25 in premium bonds and a £47 overdraft on his bank account. The house didn't belong to him, he'd sold it cheap some years before to an investment firm on condition he stayed there rent-free the rest of his days. He had been living on the proceeds ever since. His life insurance had been cashed in years before and spent. When nursie did him in with her hypo, he had reached the end of the line financially.

The total inheritance amounted to tatty old furniture riddled with woodworm and a car that had stood under a carport on flat tyres since 1975 and wouldn't fetch £20 even as scrap. God was laughing that day, Bowker decided.

Nurse Nightingale with the fatal needle drew a life sentence, which meant she'd do seven years before she was out on licence. Not a lot for snuffing out somebody's life, in Bowker's opinion—he bracketed her with the doorstep thug, both guilty of very nasty crimes and deserving more condign treatment to teach them not to do it again.

That £400,000 was a very tempting amount. Anyone anxious to lay his hands on Ronnie's ill-gotten gains would be deeply motivated. But the problems were obvious. No point doing Ronnie in unless you knew the cash would come to you. And there was nobody obvious in line for it; no heirs and no partners. Or none had emerged in three months since the fire.

Equally unclear, who knew Matthews had that much? He sounded like a closemouthed man in financial matters, very untrusting. Maybe his wife knew about the money, maybe not. Not very likely that Matthews would tell Arnie Hinksey, the pal he went fishing with. Friendship didn't stretch that far. So who might know?

Assuming the cash was made by selling illegal porn videos and magazines, the supplier would know the size of the profits that Matthews was racking up. And assuming that to be Dougie Ronson, the Squire of Cocker Park? An interesting thought, but not one that led anywhere much. Bowker couldn't see a way for Ronson to get his hands on Matthews' estate.

Lloyd Davies the Demon Lawyer knew all about Matthews' money. Suppose, after a few months of bogus searching, he put in a claim on behalf of somebody in the suburbs of Australia, who said she was Mrs Matthews' sister. Who had faked papers to prove it. The Court releases the estate to Davies, representing the claimant. He pays off the Aussie helper with a few thousand quid, pockets the rest, and who's to know? Australia is a long way off.

Too bloody complicated, Bowker thought moodily, too much like a Charlie Dickens story, hidden malice and inheritances that go wrong. Little Nell dying of hardship and malnutrition with dear old Grandpa sobbing at her bedside and the evil hunchback money lender Quilp in slavering pursuit.

No, Bowker reminded himself, what we've got here in Bedlow-on-Thames is a family of four cremated alive in a newspaper shop. Seven suspects without a motive between them. Except for houses to the value of £400,000 we didn't know about until now. And another angle to explore; Ronnie didn't make all that cash selling porn over his shop counter. He had to be into bigger deals—wholesaling for Dougie Ronson to other outlets in the town, maybe.

Ronson knew how much Matthews was making. And he was a client of Lloyd Davies. What about Ronson and Davies hatching an evil plot together to relieve Matthews of his dodgy savings? A wild surmise dawned in Bowker's mind at the idea—could he be lucky enough to run a lawyer in for murder? When that day came, he'd buy drinks for every copper in the station until they fell down drunk and incapable.

The odds were high against it. As a class, lawyers didn't often kill people. Swindle clients out of their money, yes, that went on nonstop, but why bother to do them in if you'd already got their money? Offhand, Bowker could think of only three lawyers who'd been tried for murder, and two of them had poisoned their wives.

The other one got away with it, scot-free, by hiring a witness to provide a fake alibi. He was the one who had eluded Bowker and honed his instinctive dislike of lawyers to a sharp edge.

If it had been doctors, that was a different tale altogether. Doctors did in wives, patients, girlfriends, relatives, friends, and passing strangers for money, love, lust, or hatred—all the normal reasons for killing people. In fact, the statistics said that the professional it was least safe to trust with your life was a medical doctor. And that was disconcerting, if you didn't feel well.

Meanwhile, there was a new line of enquiry: Ronnie Matthews's astonishing rainy-day savings. Which led back to Dougie Ronson the porn baron. Hagen's surveillance hadn't turned up anything useful yet—just a trip in the Porsche to the poshest golf club in the Thames valley. And an all-night session in a Maidenhead nightclub with Minky and another of his playmates, the one who had the hangover by the pool— Terri, her name was, according to Hagen. Lloyd Davies was with them as Ronson's guest for a night of fun and frolic. Which was interesting, in a nasty way.

Dougie must be running his hard-porn business from his mobile phone. Try for an intercept on it? Bowker wondered. But sooner or later, he promised himself, the bastard will have to turn up in person where the stock is kept. And then we've got him.

After leaving Lloyd Davies' office, Bowker sent Ginny

Bampton back to the police station. Write a note for the file of what that lawyer told us, he said. Get on to the Town Hall people who collect the council tax and get me the addresses of the houses Matthews owned. Davies knew the addresses and he could ask him, but he didn't trust the lawyer.

Bampton reminded him she was loaned to him only for the morning. Bowker brought a little sunshine into her life by saying he was requesting she be assigned to the murder squad again.

With Jack Knight off on a needless hunt for Vereker's missing wife and two of his detectives tied up with surveillance, maybe he was shorthanded to follow new lines of enquiry, Bowker said to himself.

To be truthful, that wasn't the reason he wanted Ginny Bampton on his team. He'd been impressed by the waves of sheer vicious hostility she'd blasted at Lloyd Davies. With his own eyes, he'd seen the lawyer flinch in his expensive swivel chair. A talent like Bampton's was wasted walking a beat around the town.

Bowker strolled through the town himself, looking, listening, and thinking, letting all the information he had churn about in his mind, hoping it would sort itself out into some coherent order. He had lunch in The Black Dog, the pub near the police station: cold roast beef, sliced cucumber, and potato salad, with a pint of Old Ruddles best ale. At 1.55 he strode into the Incident Room, ready for anything.

The normally quiet and nothing-happening scene was bedlam. PC Purley was sweating into his uniform and trying to answer four phones at the same time. WPC Ginny Bampton was there at a desk, writing something down. And Superintendent Billings was there, waving his arms and declaiming, though no one was listening.

'Hah!' he barked. 'There you are at last, Inspector! Where the hell have you been?'

'Pursuing my enquiries,' Bowker said bleakly. 'Do you want me for something?'

His tone made the Superintendent pause. But only for a moment before he was off again, though on a less accusing note.

'We've got a sudden death,' he told Bowker. 'It's one of your suspects. Happened about half an hour ago, and the first reports said it was an accident. But now we've got men on the spot they say it looks more like suicide. If he was considerate enough to leave a note, that could clear up the Matthews case nicely. DS Trimmer has gone to the scene. That left nobody here but Purley, so I had to take charge personally.'

'Who's the body?' Bowker ignored the dig.

'Swanson. A thief with a record as long as your arm. Tried to rob Matthews' shop a couple of years back and was caught in the act. Did time for it, along with his brother.'

'I know who Billy Swanson is,' Bowker said stonily. 'A little crook with no more conscience or feeling than a side of mutton. If he's done himself in, I'm a Hottentot.'

'There's an eyewitness, I was told.' Billings glared back at him in an executive manner. 'Shouldn't you be there, Inspector, or do you intend to leave the investigation to DS Trimmer?'

'Where's the body?'

'It's on the railway line, about a mile out of town. Windmill Lane—there's a bridge over the track. Swanson walked in front of a train, from what we know so far.'

'I can show you where that is, Inspector,' Ginny Bampton said quickly. 'You'll never find it on your own.'

'Where's your sergeant?' Billings asked, 'Wright or whatever his name is.'

'It's Knight—and he's pursuing enquiries,' Bowker answered stubbornly. 'Come on, then, Constable. Lead me to Windmill Lane. I hope you've got a strong stomach—Billy's body must be a bit mangled if a train ran over him.'

'Where are the rest of your team?' The Superintendent didn't know when to leave well enough alone. 'Why is there nobody here? Where are Hagen and Cote?'

'Following my orders,' Bowker snarled at him. 'Investigating the Matthews murders.'

WPC Bampton was right about one thing; he'd never have found Windmill Lane on his own. It was a narrow and winding road from nowhere much to nowhere at all, with hedges and fields on both sides. Cows were grazing in some and crops grew in others. The railway bridge was brick-built and humpbacked, just wide enough for a loaded farm cart, not for two cars to pass each other. It was a sturdy relic of great Victorian days of fast steam trains and a reliable regular service.

Two police cars were parked diagonally on the grass verge by the roadside just short of the bridge, the blue light on top of one still flashing. A uniformed constable sat in the other with both doors wide open, talking into his radio, an urgent look on his face. Reporting back, maybe, Bowker thought, but more likely putting in for overtime. He told the uniform to get out of the car and look official in case any civilians came by.

There were two other cars and a scruffy old van, dented sides and red with rust. Unsaleable—you'd have to pay a car breaker good money to haul it away and pulp it. There was an ambulance, doors open at the back, two paramedics sitting inside smoking and waiting to be told whether to go or stay, take the body or leave it.

'That's Swanson's van,' Ginny Bampton told Bowker. 'I'd know it anywhere. I bet it hasn't got a road-tax disc.'

'They don't pay road tax where Billy's gone,' Bowker said. He straightened up to his full six-foot-six to give his back and arms a good stretch after being confined in the car.

There was a gap between the hedge and the bridge and

trampled grass. If there were ever any signs, marks, foot-prints, or other evidence, there wasn't now, Bowker noted in great displeasure. He went through the gap and down a steep bank to where a group of men stood around a canvas screen they had erected to hide what they'd found from public view. In the unlikely event that any public passed along Windmill Lane.

A farm labourer on an old bike with a shot rabbit hanging off the handlebars. That was about the strength of the traffic down this road, Bowker thought—maybe a courting couple after dark. A nice quiet place to die in.

DS Trimmer had a sergeant and three constables with him, all wearing bright yellow crash jackets over their uniforms so that the next train down the line would see them a mile off. As they were nowhere near the track, it didn't seem to matter much. But bobbies loved their symbols of authority—blue lights, sirens, crash jackets—and had to be indulged.

A man with a black leather bag and a frown must be the doctor and a man wearing a white hard hat, as if he was ex-pecting the bridge to fall on his head, might be anybody at all. He, too, wore one of the glaring yellow jackets over his suit. Fifty yards up the line was a railway work gang of six with spades, picks, and crowbars—God knows why they had been sent for.

DS Trimmer told the assembled throng around the canvas screen who Bowker was and stood back to let him have a look at the sad proof of Billy Swanson's passing.

The line ran through a cutting when it came out of the bridge, and the banks were steepish. Billy was lying on his back about halfway up the grassy slope, his mouth open and his eyes open. There was a dried trickle of blood from one nostril, but Bowker could see no injuries, minor or fatal. The scruffy boilersuit had only its normal stains: oil, grime, dirt, and grease, where Billy wiped his hands. No blood soaking through, no sharp ends of white bone sticking out.

Bowker addressed himself to the doctor, who was writing on a pad. A memo to himself, presumably—Billy was well past needing a prescription for medication. There was the faintest whiff of whisky about Dr Thoroughgood; either he lunched in a pub, or he was a determined tippler.

'I expected to find him in bits,' Bowker said. 'Head here and legs over there, buckets of blood soaking in everywhere. That's the usual way of it when they dive under a train. All I can see is a nosebleed.'

'There's not a bone in his body that's not broken,' said the doctor, giving Bowker a curious look. 'Limbs, pelvis, spine, and ribs. If you look closely, you'll see for yourself that he's out of shape.'

'By God!' Bowker exclaimed, down on one knee on the grass to take a closer look, 'You're right—he's gone flattish.'

If the doctor smelled of whisky, Billy fairly reeked of gin— as did the front of his boilersuit.

'So what happened to him?' Bowker asked.

'Not my job to speculate,' the doctor said sharply. Evidently he had taken a dislike to the Inspector. 'I'm here to pronounce him dead, that's all.'

'I can see he's dead because he's not bloody breathing. Right then, doctor, if that's the best you can do, pronounce him dead officially and bugger off—we've got work to do.'

'That chap in the hard hat can tell you what happened,' said Trimmer. 'He works for British Rail. His name's Austin.'

'Doing what? In that get-up he could be a plate-layer! But not wearing a tie like that. It's got little cricket bats on it—he must play for Bedlow in the Sunday League, God help us!'

Trimmer started to repeat Wilfred Austin's explanation of his place in the scheme of things. Bowker listened for a moment and then switched off—he didn't care if he had the assistant sub-divisional manager (health and safety), British Rail south-west region (Bedlow and Babingford section). Or something like that. It wasn't easy to grasp the intricacies of railway bureaucracy. He scowled Trimmer into silence and beckoned the man over.

'Were you here when the train hit Billy?' he asked.

'No, of course not! I was in my office. But I've interviewed the driver briefly and got his initial reaction. A full enquiry is necessary when an incident like this occurs. It's mandatory, part of our operating procedure. Sometimes we even run a public hearing with all parties legally represented and a chairman who eventually produces a written report for publication.'

'We like to have an enquiry ourselves if we find a dead body. It's an old police custom you might have heard of,' Bowker said in a dangerously moderate tone. 'What does your driver say happened?'

'He's in shock, as you might expect. In any proceedings that may transpire, he will be represented by legal counsel provided by his union.'

'I don't care if he's represented by a trained ape appointed by the Little Sisters of the Poor,' Bowker said in exasperation at officialdom. 'What bloody well happened?'

'As I piece together the sequence of events from his account, in the unfortunate circumstances a somewhat incoherent account, Driver Flock was about to put the brakes on for the final five-eighths of a mile into Bedlow station, his next scheduled stop. It's a down gradient all the way from here to Bedlow, you see.'

Bowker was swelling up and turning black with frustration.

'How fast was the train going when it came under that bridge, and was the driver sounding his hooter?' he demanded.

'About sixty miles an hour, no more, and just about to brake. The use of the hooter at the approach to a bridge is wholly at the driver's discretion. I didn't ask him about that.'

'So if Billy Swanson stumbled down here for an urgent pee, in a state of drunkenness, there'd be no hooter to warn him a bloody great train was racing up behind him?'

'Railway lines are really not suitable places for urination, drunk or sober,' Austin assured him earnestly. 'In addition to the safety factor, there is the public-hygiene consideration.'

'You're right,' Bowker agreed. 'No need to stagger down here, he could have done it over the parapet of the bridge. Did your driver actually see him strolling about on the track?'

'Not precisely. What he says is that a figure appeared out of nowhere, less than six feet in front of his moving train. There was no time to take any action whatsoever. The impact threw the trespasser to the right of the train, here on the bank where he's lying now.'

'Trespasser?' Bowker said nastily. 'The victim, you mean?'

'He was a trespasser on railway property,' said Austin, keen to stand up for his employers. 'We cannot be held responsible.'

'Bloody hell! Billy Swanson wasn't an ideal citizen—not by a long chalk. I was expecting to run him in and see him sent to jail for crimes that don't concern you. But the poor bastard is smashed up and dead.' Bowker was indignant. 'A horrible bloody end—and all you care about is turning him into a trespasser! Perhaps you can sue his widow for damages—he must have dented your train a bit when he banged into it.'

Austin heard the warning note and kept silent.

'I suppose your Driver Flock stopped the train and trotted up the bank with his first-aid kit? Gave Billy the kiss of life? Felt his pulse, all that stuff?' Bowker asked sarcastically.

'Not practical, Inspector.' Austin felt safer now on technical grounds. 'With full braking, the train would have been nearer Bedlow than the site of the incident before it came to a standstill. The driver took a decision to drive on normally to the station and alerted the emergency services from there.'

'Listen to me, Mr Assistant-whatever,' Bowker said in a voice that would bring an express train to a total stop inside fifty yards. 'You get on to the station this second and make sure the train driver stays put until I can get there to talk to him. I don't care how shocked he thinks he is. He's a grown man, not a hysterical young girl. I don't want him sloping off to a pub to get drunk, or going home for a cup of tea and a lie-down.'

'They may have taken him to hospital by now for treatment for shock,' Austin said officiously, 'your attitude is surprising, Inspector, I can only describe it as callous.'

'I missed the course on sensitive policing,' Bowker said with a malign grin. 'For your sake, I hope Flock is still having cold compresses put on his forehead at Bedlow. If not, I shall arrest you for hindering a police enquiry. Got me? So start chatting down your mobile phone and give the proper instructions.'

'Well really!' Austin protested, but he did as he was told.

Bowker left him and took DS Trimmer off to the side.

'Stay here and get things buttoned up and the body moved,' he said, 'I'm going back to Bedlow to talk to that train driver. I don't like what I see and I don't like what I've been told. Not real, any of it—just a lot of Mary Ellen.'

'You said yourself Swanson was drunk, sir—you can smell him five yards off. And up in his van there's a story torn out of a newspaper. Looks like the *Bedlow Herald,* and it's old enough for the paper to be turning yellow. It's the report of the Matthews fire. I'd say that's as good as a suicide note. Better, maybe.'

Bowker stared at him in complete incredulity. 'That what you believe? Billy gets drunk and sits mulling over his crimes and feeling remorseful about his wicked and sinful life? He decides he can't go on like this with his conscience torturing him night and day. He drives here in that rattletrap old van and carries on drinking until he's ready for the Big Off. He waits for a train to appear in the distance and reels through the hedge and down the bank and jumps in front of it when it comes out under the bridge? Have I got the story straight, Sergeant?'

Trimmer was huffed. 'You may laugh at me if you please, but something like that is how I read it.'

'We shall know how much gin Billy drank when they cut him up. See if you can get the pathologist to do that today instead of next week. How many empty bottles did you find in his van?'

A curious look spread over Sergeant Trimmer's homely face, as if he'd glanced down and found he was standing knee-deep in hot, wet cow droppings.

'There aren't any bottles in the van,' he said in a croak. 'I hadn't realised till now.'

'And what do you deduce from that, Sergeant?'

'Billy could have finished the bottle before he came out here to think things over.'

'You've smelled him, I've smelled him,' Bowker said. 'I think the postmortem will tell us Billy was blind unconscious drunk. He could no more drive his van here than fly to the moon.'

Trimmer was in a corner and he knew it. He tried once more.

'He could have driven out here swigging at the bottle all the way, sir. And chucked the empty out of the window. A search of the hedges between here and the main road might find it.'

'Put a couple of uniforms on it when you've done here. It's a waste of their time, but we might as well be thorough,' Bowker conceded.

'What do *you* think happened, sir?'

'Somebody wanted Billy dead. A friend, as they say. He got him dead drunk. He loaded him into the van and lugged him out here, where it's quiet and peaceful and nobody comes past to see what you're up to when you murder somebody. Chummy waits for a train, and when it goes under the bridge, he drops poor old Billy over the parapet and he's on his way down when the train hurtles out this side and hits him. It sends him cartwheeling up the bank, smashed up and deader than dead. Chummy has a bloody good laugh and drives away.'

'I can see a catch in your theory,' Trimmer objected. 'You're forgetting that Billy's van is still parked by the bridge. If it all happened the way you said, there'd have to be another vehicle.'

'Which means?'

'Two of them in collusion—one driving Billy's van, the other one driving the escape vehicle.'

'Right, Sergeant. Two people. Just like there were two people to start the fire at Matthews' shop. The same two people.'

'But why? What did Billy Swanson have to do with that?'

'If we knew the reason why Billy was killed,' said Bowker with immense restraint, 'we'd know who to run in for the arson job. It's a bit bloody late now everything's been trampled over, but call in for a scene-of-crime team and see if they can find some useful item. And have a close look at the parapet of the bridge—there ought to be something to show Billy was tipped over it like a sackload of mouldy old taters.'

'Fibres from his boilersuit,' Trimmer said with enthusiasm. 'Something for Forensic to have a go at.'

Bowker decided not to disillusion the sergeant by telling him his views on Forensic—as useful as an inflamed appendix.

'The newspaper cutting masquerading as a suicide note—there might be fingerprints on it,' he said. 'Besides yours, that is. So be careful with it.'

'How was I to know?' Trimmer said. 'The report phoned in was that a chap was hit by a train. British Rail themselves called it an accident, and there was no reason to doubt them.'

Bowker stared at him as if he were certifiably insane. 'They can't even run their trains on time—so what makes you imagine they can tell the difference between accident, suicide, murder, or the invasion of the body snatchers? I want that van of Billy's looked at with a microscope—prints on the steering wheel for a start. Billy didn't drive it, I'm sure of that. And the floor's to be gone over for any sign Billy was brought here lying down blind drunk and sicking up. I'm off to talk to that train driver before he starts remembering things he never saw. According to Superintendent Billings, he's our eyewitness, God knows to what.'

On the drive back to Bedlow, Bowker had instructions for WPC Ginny Bampton that gladdened her heart.

'While I'm busy at the train station, I want you to go to the Abbotsbury Estate and inform Mrs Swanson of Billy's sad demise. You'll find her at 27 Sheep Walk Road, a repulsive loudmouth of a woman. But don't let that prejudice you against her. You can tell her we suspect that Billy's friends did him in to shut his mouth. And if she can find it in her black heart to talk to the filth, she could help us put her husband's killers behind bars, as is the righteous duty of every grieving widow.'

'I know Kitty Swanson,' said WPC Bampton. 'I ran her in once, she was caught red-handed shoplifting in Woolworth's. Gave me an argument when I took her in charge. She gave the magistrates a sorry song and dance about bringing up three children with her husband out of work with a bad back. All the usual lies, so she got off with a caution.'

'They're a bad lot, the Swansons,' Bowker agreed with a grin. 'Including Jason. Now listen, this is important—if Jason's at home and stoned out of his mind on illegal substances, pretend you haven't noticed. I don't want him run in, understand? He's small fry in a bigger operation to collar a drug dealer.'

'Right, sir,' said WPC Bampton, admiration in her voice.

'What you must try to get out of Ma Swanson is what Billy has been doing today since he got out of bed. Anything he and Kitty did before they got up is too repugnant for us to bother with. Did anyone call? Did he go to his local pub? It's a nasty place like a public urinal called The Three Jolly Monks. Did he meet anybody there? And anything else you can find out.'

At the railway station he handed his tired-looking Honda over to her so she could drive herself to the Abbotsbury Estate. He stood in the forecourt for a moment, watching anxiously how she reversed the car out and drove off, not too much gear-crashing. *What a woman* he thought *she's built like a Russian shot-putter, on steroids. With ten like her I could stamp out crime in this miserable little town.*

The stationmaster was ready for him, a tall, very thin man in a dark jacket and a railway tie. Evidently Austin had talked to him on his mobile. But he informed Bowker he wasn't happy that the train had been taken out of service and was standing in a siding waiting for examination by railway engineers. And that meant the schedule was shot to hell, a train short, passengers off-loaded and grumbling, alternative transport to be arranged. And so on and so on. Bowker ignored his complaints and told him the train wasn't to be touched until Forensic had been there.'

Driver Flock was waiting in a cheerless little office full of filing cabinets and blue smoke. He had a thick white tea mug in one hand and a cigarette in the other.

Bowker didn't like the look of the man at all. He was only in his middle thirties but he was grossly overweight. The mystery was how he got into the driver's cab. Perhaps they had somebody stand behind him on a high box and give him a boost through the cab door—like the way Japanese railways had special employees on mainline platforms to pack commuters tight into carriages by brute force.

And Driver Flock had a furtive look about him—the shiftiness of someone who slides round the rules every chance he gets. Not for any particular advantage, but just to prove to himself that he's crafty enough to beat the system.

'I've been advised I don't have to talk to you,' Flock said.

The unprovoked attack threw Bowker into his Mad Mangler mode: fighting crouch, arms extended to grapple with his opponent and fling him headfirst out of the ring. Obviously Driver Flock was a fan of TV wrestling—his mouth dropped open as he thought he recognised a star.

'It's you!' he gasped, 'I didn't know you had a day job as a copper. Don't hit me, I'm your biggest fan!'

Bowker took a shuffling step nearer the sitting driver, hands reaching out to grip an arm and twist it off.

'All right, all right, what do you want to know!' Flock was in mortal terror for life and limb.

Bowker loomed over him, his face dark with rage.

'When you came under that bridge, what did you see, Flock?'

'The track was clear for half a mile ahead, all the way up to the right-hand bend before Bedlow station. Suddenly there was a flash of blue boilersuit and an almighty thump as somebody hit the train. I knew he was dead right away—nobody survives after a knock like that.'

'You're right about that,' Bowker growled. 'Where did he come from? From the left, the right, from above, from down between the rails, which direction?'

'I'm buggered if I know. Nobody was there, and suddenly there he was. It was like magic—he appeared out of thin air.'

'Did you see him on the grass bank either side before you hit him? That dirty boilersuit stands out against green.'

'He wasn't there,' Flock insisted and cowered back as Bowker clenched his hands into fists like sledgehammers. 'I saw clear to the bend, half a mile away. There wasn't anybody.'

'Right,' said Bowker, certain now that Billy had been dropped down from the bridge. 'Did you see his face in the split second before the train hit him? Were his eyes open or shut, as if he was unconscious?'

Driver Flock gave it some anxious thought, his gaze fixed on Bowker, watching his every movement and ready to duck.

'Not to say I saw it,' he said finally. 'A flash of white. It all happened so fast, I couldn't tell you if his eyes were open or not. There was only a blur, a hell of a thump, and something blue flying through the air up the bank.'

'Did you see anybody up on the bridge as you approached it?'

'I wasn't looking up there, I was watching the track.'

Not you, my lad, Bowker thought. *You were more likely sitting with your feet up on the windscreen, reading a comic and eating a ham sandwich. I know your sort.*

Naturally, Flock wasn't going to admit any such dereliction of duty. There was no more to be got out of him. Bowker snorted in contempt and moved back a couple of steps.

'We'll leave it there,' he said angrily. 'Come to the police station later on, we'll get your statement on paper, and you can sign it, for what it's worth.'

'OK,' said Flock, happier now he knew Bowker wasn't going to break him in half. 'I'll be there. Can I have your autograph?'

'Police officers are not allowed to give autographs.' Bowker didn't know whether to laugh at him or feel insulted.

'You give them at the ringside—I've seen you do it on TV. You ought to be a bit more obliging to a fan like me. You'd be nowhere without your fans,' Driver Flock whined.

9. $\cdots\cdots\cdots\cdots$ *kyte & pewsey cold store*

Dc Shirley Cote was in the Incident Room when Bowker got there after his useless questioning of the train driver. Her hair had been bleached and then dyed a fantasy shade of apricot, teasled and tousled, finger-waved, sculpted, layered, highlighted with silvery speckles. She had taken Bowker at his word and gone for broke. It could be a long, long time and maybe never, before she got another chance to treat herself to the full Monty at police expense.

Bowker stared at her in wonder and perched on a corner of her desk. He'd seen upmarket tarts touting for Arab millionaires in posh London hotels with hairdos like that. But he wasn't going to discourage DC Cote by telling her so.

'I hope it was worth it,' he said.

'Well worth every penny of the eighty quid it cost,' she said and she sounded pleased with herself. 'You'll love it when you hear what I found out. Moira Druce has started a new meaningful relationship, just as you thought she might. You must know more about women than I gave you credit for, sir.'

'Hah!' Bowker snorted.

'We had a lovely girlie chat while she supervised the stylist doing my hair. I told her I'd got a new boyfriend and wanted to look my best—that was to get her confidence. She opened up and told me about her new boyfriend.'

Bowker's thick black eyebrows came down in a X until they met above his nose.

'Don't keep me in suspense!' he growled. 'This is not Twenty bloody Questions—is it anyone we know?'

'Donald Vereker,' Cote said with an air of triumph.

Bowker was speechless.

'Two souls in grief and pain, sensitive, and suffering an unexpected loss. Or so Moira told me. She lost Ronnie Matthews in a tragedy, and Vereker's wife vanished at the same time. They were both shattered, she says, and somehow this brought them together. Very romantic, the way she tells it.'

Bowker grunted. 'Did she and Vereker know each other before Ronnie got flame-grilled? Did you think to ask that?'

'Of course I did—it was only natural to ask how they'd met. Part of the romance. One enchanted evening and all that. Their eyes meeting across a crowded room. Women love a good old chat about how they met the man in their life.'

'And?' Bowker was restraining himself.

'A shortage of romance. She'd known Vereker since she started her hairdressing business. He takes care of her fire-and-theft and third-party insurance.'

'All these connections,' Bowker grumbled. 'Bedlow is like one big happy family, except that they do each other in.'

'You should have been here last year when we were after a man who killed his four children because his wife had run away with his best friend. He was something in the Jehovah's Witnesses, a deacon or an elder or whatever they're called.

Four young kids smothered in their sleep. Dead a week before we found them—it turned my stomach over, I can tell you.'

'I hope the bastard got four life sentences,' said Bowker, an expression on his face that boded ill for whoever murdered the Matthews children.

'Not a chance. His lawyer put him up to pleading diminished responsibility because of temporary mental insanity. They sent him to a psychiatric place for treatment and I expect he'll be out again in six months. They're the worst of the lot, religious nutters; they're capable of anything.'

'God must be very embarrassed at times.' Bowker shook his head in doubt. 'But what about Vereker and Moira—did they have jolly get-togethers when Ronnie Matthews was alive?'

'From what I gather, sir, they'd always been friends. Vereker gives a cocktail party just before Christmas every year for his commercial clients. Booze galore, nibbles on sticks and a jolly chat, a kiss or two under the mistletoe for wives in their best party frocks. Winks and nods and bottom-pinching.'

'Are you saying Vereker's a bit of a lad with the women?'

'That's the impression I got from Moira Druce,' DC Cote said. 'She's very pleased about catching him herself, as if he's some sort of prize package.'

'Because you wouldn't want him for free with a jar of instant coffee, that doesn't necessarily make him a social leper.' Bowker thought furiously. 'He's not hard up and he's a flashy dresser. Maybe Moira thinks he's a fairy prince. And that gives us another possibility to worry about.'

'Vereker could have had the fire started to get rid of Ronnie Matthews so he could take over Moira?' Cote asked doubtfully.

'Never in a million years,' Bowker said impatiently. 'Not his style to be interested in any woman enough to risk his liberty. His main interest is himself. I meant, did he do his wife in?'

'Why would he do that?'

'Being married might have become a bit boring and restricting if he's a woman chaser. And Mrs Vereker's life might be insured for a ton of money. Nobody's better placed to arrange that than a broker. Three or four separate policies with different outfits so none of them know the real total. He'd get a discount on the premiums, being in the trade.'

'I see where you're going—he keeps coming here to nag us to agree she's been murdered and find the body so he can claim the money. No body, no death, no payout.'

'If you can see where I'm going, you're a lot bloody brighter than I am,' Bowker snarled, 'because I haven't got the faintest idea myself. If you find out where I'm going, let me know. This entire case is a bloody washout from start to finish.'

His irritation was deflected from DC Cote to Jack Knight, who came into the Incident Room with a angry red mark over his left eye and a smile on his face in spite of it. He had the look of a man who has achieved something, as he marched across to where Bowker half-sat on the corner of Cote's desk.

'Got the message to come straight back,' he said, 'I can pick up the search for Mrs Vereker anytime. They told me downstairs about Swanson diving under the Oxford flyer. Was he the one who started the blaze at Matthews' shop?'

'No,' Bowker said with conviction. 'Billy's exit was supposed to be suicide. The only one who believes that is Superintendent Billings—and *he* won't when the postmortem results come in.'

'A suicide under a train from guilt and remorse,' Knight said thoughtfully. 'I saw a movie about that years ago in Walsall. I had a teacher girlfriend then who belonged to an arty film club where you had to watch terrible old black-and-white movies they said were classics.'

Shirley Cote stared at him open-mouthed. In her experience, detective sergeants were not allowed to chat to detective inspectors about girlfriends and old movies during working hours.

'There was a rich married woman having it off with a Russian, an army officer,' Knight went on. 'Wore a uniform like a fancy-dress ball. It was in the days when the Russians had a czar and horse carriages and top hats and ladies in silk ball gowns that showed their chest nearly bare. Before they invented communism. Anyway, when she ran off with Fancy Dan, she left her little boy behind with her old man. It went wrong when boyfriend gave her the big elbow, I've forgotten why. She jumped under a train in a shunting yard at St Petersburg. Or Moscow. Or Vladivostok—some horrible bloody place with snow on the ground.'

'Have you finished?' Bowker demanded.

'Greta Garbo, I think it was,' Knight added blithely. 'Bloody terrible old movie, really. You don't think Swanson did himself in, then?'

According to scientists, 50-ton killer dinosaurs with fangs a foot long and claws like crane hooks had pea brains that worked so slowly and poorly that the entire species died out. And left the world safe for apes and their descendants. There were those who regarded Denis Bowker in the same unfavourable way. It was easy to assume that he had no brain worth mentioning inside all that muscle and brawn.

But his record showed a formidable intelligence that was concealed behind his kick-'em-up-the-crotch method of detection. His views were clear on why Billy Swanson was dead.

'He was suicided because he knew who set the shop fire. Or he guessed who did. Maybe he was asking for hush money—I wouldn't put it past him. When we went around the town shouting the odds at the suspects, they got into a muck-sweat over Billy, so they did him in to keep his mouth shut.'

'One down, six to go,' Knight shrugged. 'If the suspects keep on killing each other, we only have to wait for the last one on his feet and run him in. Simple, really.'

'If that's true,' said Shirley Cote very boldly, 'then Billy's death is your responsibility, sir.'

Bowker turned a cold eye on her. 'I didn't push him under the train, Constable. He mixed with the wrong people.'

'All the same. . . ,' she persisted and was silenced by a look of granite.

'How did you get that bad eye?' Bowker asked Knight.

'I'm glad you asked me that. I was punched in the face by Mrs Vereker's brother. Sholto Morley, Ph.D. He lives at Reading and teaches at the university there.

'Teaches what, karate? I know the politicians have destroyed education but what sort of tinpot university makes you a doctor of philosophy for kicking people in the proverbials?'

'He teaches some sort of computer mumbo-jumbo. I went to his home, which is a third-floor flat, and rang the bell politely. A voice asked through a squawk-box on the wall what I wanted. I said I was looking for Joanne Vereker, at which the door flew open, out came a bearded freak in a T-shirt and punched me in the face.'

'I hope you punched him back,' said Bowker, 'after cautioning him properly, of course.'

'He took me by surprise and knocked me over backwards. It was humiliating, being knocked down by a university teacher. And he tried to slam the door on me. As luck would have it, I fell with my foot over the sill and the bloody door slammed on my ankle—you wouldn't believe the bruise I've got. It hurt like hell and I was sure the evil swine had broken my leg.'

'God, what a saga!' Bowker said. 'It's a bloody awful way to run an investigation, letting yourself be knocked about. Surely they taught you that when you were still a uniform. Did you run him in?'

'I got up and punched him in the belly. And in the nose. Then it was his turn to fall down. I dragged him inside the flat and cautioned him I'd take down anything he said and use it against him and arrested him for assaulting an officer in the execution of his duty.'

'About bloody time! Why did he punch you?'

'He said he didn't know I was a copper. He took me for a goon from Vereker looking for his sister to drag her back to him. He doesn't like Vereker at all. He apologised for hitting me, and I told him he'd get six months in clink for what he'd done.'

'Is there a point to all this?' Bowker sighed.

'His nose finally stopped bleeding and he washed his face and put on a clean shirt. He poured us both a glass of refreshment to help his bellyache and my bruises, then he got co-operative in return for the charges against him being dropped.'

'Does he know where Mrs Vereker is?'

'The impression I got is that most of her friends here in the town know where she is,' Knight said. 'The only one in the dark is Vereker himself. Nobody likes him and all his wife's friends hate the sight of him, just like her brother.'

'Funny you should say that,' Bowker said with a malign smile. 'DC Cote has found somebody who actually likes Vereker—enough to let him get his leg over.'

'Who's that?'

'Moira Druce. Did you get Mrs Vereker's address?'

Suddenly Knight looked crestfallen.

'Morley wouldn't say, though I tried hard enough. He says she phones him for a chat once a week but they both think it better if he doesn't know her address. In case the goons get to him.'

'Goons indeed!' Bowker snarled. 'Is he right in the head, or is he living in a fairy tale? Why should Vereker hire thugs if he thinks his wife's been murdered? It doesn't make sense. I'm beginning to think they're a pack of loonies, the Verekers and the Morleys.'

'Vereker's a creep,' Cote suggested. 'Nobody knows what goes on in weird little minds like that.'

Knight was not pleased by her interruption. This was his report to Inspector Bowker, not an all-comers discussion.

'When I pushed Morley for the address, he said even if he knew it, he'd never tell. He said he'd rather rot in prison than have his sister hauled back to Vereker, after all she'd put up with. I told him there was no way on God's earth she could be made to go back to him if she didn't want to, it's not the Dark Ages. I gave him a solemn promise we'd never pass the address on, but we want to make sure she's all right so we can eliminate her from our enquiries—all that sort of Mary Ellen.'

'Did he tell you where we can find her?'

'He wouldn't budge. You know what these bloody intellectuals are like when they're standing up for a principle. They want to be ill-treated so they can tell the tale to the pinko papers.'

'He's right, in a way,' Bowker said. 'There's no law that says Vereker has to know where his wife is. We can well do without a self-elected martyr screaming police fascism and savagery.'

'You said her friends here in Bedlow know where she is,' Shirley Cote said indignantly. 'I talked to five or six of her women friends, and they swore blind they didn't know where she was.'

'That's because you haven't got my charm,' Knight said with a happy smile.

Bowker said, 'If she's alive and well and getting on with her life just as we always suspected, the theory that Vereker did her in for the insurance money goes down the drain. Not that I ever thought much of it as a theory. Vereker's in the business and knows what suspicious grasping bastards insurance companies are when it comes to writing out a cheque on a claim.'

'Vereker and Mrs Druce, eh?' Knight winked at Shirley Cote. 'Grieving and inconsolable for his missing wife he may be, but his natural urges are functioning well.'

'He's a toad,' she said.

'We don't know if we can believe Morley,' Bowker said with a marked lack of enthusiasm. 'We still have to trace Mrs Vereker, if only to prove her own brother didn't do her in. And to bring a smile to Superintendent Billings' face. But that will have to wait. Right now we've got urgent things to do, such as finding out who's responsible for the sudden murder of Billy Swanson on the railway line.'

'Do we know his movements today?' Knight asked.

'We shall know more than we do now when WPC Bampton gets back—I sent her to interview the weeping widow. I've asked for her to be assigned to the murder squad. She's a woman of talent.'

'What sort of talent?' Jack Knight was very interested.

'Remember that bouncer we met at Ronson's stately home? With the muscles all the way up to his scalp?'

'I remember him well. Ellis—the man with hairy arms.'

'WPC Bampton could pick him up and break him in half over her knee. That's real talent. Now, we're nearly home and dry on our murder case, all we have to do is nab whoever it was did Billy in, and we've got the Matthews killer. So we shall ask our suspects to tell us where they were when the train went under the bridge. The one who lies, that's Chummy.'

'Sounds easy enough,' Knight said, 'but it bloody won't be.'

'Inspector,' PC Purley interrupted, 'Hagen's on the phone for you, and he sounds urgent.'

'Put him through.' Bowker picked up DC Cote's phone.

'Sir, it's Hagen here,' an excited voice said in his ear.

'Where are you?'

'I'm in a public phone box in Reading, I had to leave the car and follow on foot the last part. So they wouldn't spot me.'

'Who wouldn't spot you, Ronson?'

'That's right, sir. I followed him here to Reading, He's gone into a cold store, with that thug of his. He parked his Porsche around the back, out of sight. Made me suspicious right away.'

'Maybe he's having friends in for Sunday dinner and he's gone to buy a side of beef on the cheap,' Bowker said sarcastically. 'Get to the bloody point, Hagen.'

'Yes, sir. While I was keeping observation on the premises, one of those giant trucks drove into the yard. They're unloading it now. It's a transcontinental job, got Swedish plates. That made me even more suspicious.'

'What are they unloading, frozen reindeer steaks?'

'Whatever it is, sir, it's not meat. It's in cardboard boxes—big ones—and there's a lot of them. Ronson's muscleman is on the loading dock giving them a hand.'

Reading, Bowker thought. That sounds about right. Middle-size town halfway up the Thames valley, a useful distribution centre, maybe. Oxford is about 20 miles upstream from there, and Windsor about 15 miles downstream. In that radius there's half a dozen towns besides Bedlow—there's Abingdon and Henley, Marlow and Newbury, Maidenhead. God alone knows how many villages as well, and even yokels have video players nowadays.

'Well, well, well,' he chortled, 'I think you've scored a bull's-eye this time, Hagen. You've found the hard-porn depot. Give me the name and address of the cold store, and I'll do an almighty dash to get a search warrant while you tell Sergeant Knight how we get to you.'

He scribbled it down on a blank lost-property form when Hagen spelled it for him, *Kyte and Pewsey, Rendelsham Road.*

'Need more than a search warrant, sir,' Shirley Cote reminded him. 'It's out of our area—it has to be cleared with Reading.'

'We haven't got a lot of time for buggering about—the birds will fly the coop if we don't get there quick,' Bowker snarled. 'Knight, take this phone and find out where Hagen's hiding. I'm going to see Superintendent Billings, God help me.'

'Are we all going, sir?' Cote asked, very keen.

'Yes, and we'll need a carload of uniforms. We'll pick more up in Reading when we get there. And if Bampton's back in time, we'll take her—she'll be handy if there's a brawl.'

'What about Sergeant Trimmer, sir?'

'If you can find him in time. Knight—get things organised.'

Hot pursuit is a matter of opinion. Explaining the situation first to the Superintendent and then to a magistrate took time. Then there was the matter of clearance with Reading police. And by then Ginny Bampton was back from her mission to Mrs Swanson, DS Trimmer was recalled from the charity shop facing Hinksey's off-licence—he had been filling in for Cote while she had her hair done at Moira Druce's salon.

A two-car convoy set off at last, Knight driving Bowker's old Honda, with DS Trimmer and Shirley Cote in the back-seat. After them came Ginny Bampton and three uniforms packed into a police car. No danger of sexual harassment there, Bowker thought with a mental grin. She'd flatten any silly copper who tried it on.

From Bedlow-on-Thames to Reading is only about fifteen miles as the rook flies it over the Chiltern Hills. But starting from Bedlow police station by the bridge across the Thames, there is a slow ride through the town to the main road—which is little more than an unimproved country road with slow-moving traffic.

Bowker was fuming none too silently at the delay. And when at last they reached the dual carriageway, he gave a loud snort of relief and told Knight to put his foot down flat. But there was no reason for the early-evening traffic to move over to let his unimpressive car through, in spite of the hooting and headlight flashing by Knight.

Bowker wound the window down and leaned right out to wave the police car past to take the lead. *'Use your siren!'* he bawled as it drew level. *'And drive like the clappers—I want to get there today, not next bloody Christmas!'*

The driver nodded and raised a thumb in acknowledgement as he floored his accelerator, flicked on his siren, and flashing blue light and took off down the road like a demented banshee.

After that the ride was short but exhilarating. Knight heard Bowker's bass rumble and in disbelief realised he was singing—God alone knew what. His gypsy-dark face was flushed darker yet, and his chest had expanded to barrel dimensions. No question of it, Bowker was happy!

Knight remembered some words he'd heard from a Salvation Army uniform preaching in the street—most likely it was a bit from the Bible: *He says among the trumpets Hah! and he smells the battle afar off, the thunder of the captains and the noise of shouting.* It looked very much as if Denis Bowker was hoping for a punch-up with the ungodly. Personally Knight hoped otherwise, he had a bruised shin and a black eye already—and that from a teacher, not a professional thug.

Where they turned off the dual carriageway in the suburbs of Reading, there were two police cars parked and waiting for them, packed with uniforms. Bowker got out and conferred briefly with the uniformed Inspector, a thickset man with a black moustache. Then the locals drove off to lead the way to the address Bowker had given them.

If Reading had any scenic areas, Rendlesham Road was not one of them. It had a dismal look, industrial buildings on both sides, run-down and dilapidated, looking as if they were hanging on to solvency only by their fingernails. A scrap yard, a wastepaper-collecting dump, a tyre-retread factory that had a vile smell, a zinc-plating plant. Down toward the end of the road was the Kyte and Pewsey cold store.

It was an old one-storey brick building, decrepit, neglected, and good for nothing much but demolition. It hadn't been a cold store for many a long year—Ronson had rented it for a song. A double gate stood open and askew on its hinges; beyond that was a yard for trucks, its concrete broken and oil-stained.

Across the front of the grimy old building ran a chest-high loading dock. The yard was empty, the loading dock was empty—the truck was gone. Whatever it had brought was now inside.

There was no time to look for DC Hagen in his phone-box. He'd make his way to the scene when he saw the action. As planned by Bowker and the uniformed Inspector, the convoy swept in through the gates and across the yard, the Reading cars racing down the side of the building for the rear, Bowker's two screeching to a stop below the loading dock.

'Come on!' Bowker shouted, dark eyes glowing. 'Straight in and arrest everybody in sight!'

They were up on the dock at once. One of the uniforms brought a sledgehammer from his car boot in case the door wasn't going to open when they knocked and flashed the search warrant.

'Cote, Bampton—there'll be an office somewhere inside, with a computer and floppy discs and stuff,' Bowker instructed them. 'You two ignore everything else and go and find that office and guard it. We haven't got this far to have some evil sod destroy the records.'

The front of the building was a series of roll-up metal doors—all rolled down and locked from inside. But at one end was an ordinary wooden door, brown paint peeling off it.

'Break it in!' Bowker ordered, not bothering himself with the niceties of knocking. The young copper with the hammer swung it and smashed the lock in two blows. It led into a passage barred by another door, and this one was made of steel. And locked and probably bolted inside.

The hammer man stepped up and gave it his best, ten or

twelve thumps that would have knocked down a brick wall. But the steel door held fast.

'Ronson's not keen on having visitors,' Bowker growled. 'He's installed a special door as a hint to us. Give me that hammer—I'll let him know we've come calling.'

He gripped the sledge down near the end of the handle, waited for the others to stand back out of harm's way, and thrashed at the door in a deafening attack. BAM BAM BAM went hammer head on thick steel plate. At the third hit, the lock burst, and only the bolts were holding the door shut. Bowker switched his onslaught to the other edge, and three more titanic hits broke the hinges. One last mighty clout, and the door fell inward with a ringing crash on the stained concrete floor.

The ill-lit passage went on toward the back of the building, but an open door to the right led into the main storage area, a big empty space between the rolled-down shutters and a line of six-inch-thick insulated doors to cold-storage lockers. All the doors stood wide open; there was no cold to keep in anymore. In the white-tiled lockers were stacked cardboard boxes and wooden crates.

Ellis the bouncer and four other men in work clothes stood in a bunched group in the open space. They had been alerted by the crash of broken-in doors front and back and were ready to repel boarders. Ellis had a long iron crowbar in his hand, useful for opening crates of videos or bashing in coppers' heads.

'Police!' Bowker bellowed. The sheer ferocity left no doubt in anyone's mind. 'You're all under arrest. Stand still!'

The workmen gauged Bowker's size and the sledgehammer he was carrying. They looked at the posse behind him, and then at each other with misgiving. Six coppers to five of them, and the one in front a maniac with a long hammer. Without a word, they came to a unanimous decision against giving Bowker any aggravation.

Not Ellis. His sleeves were rolled up his hairy arms. On his face was a look of intense loathing for all aspects of law and order. He hefted the crowbar high over his shoulder and sidled toward Bowker, shouting *'I'll get you, copper!'*

But before the clash began, in stormed the Reading squad—it had taken them longer to break in through the rear entrance and steel door. Now they were inside and at the scene of the action, their blood was up. They'd all drawn truncheons, the Inspector included, and were looking for skulls to rap.

Ellis still had it in mind to take on Bowker, crowbar against sledge, when two of the reinforcements rushed him from behind. A hard crack on his elbow paralysed his arm, and he dropped the crowbar on his toes. One of the uniforms twisted his good arm up behind his back to his shoulder blades; the other kicked his feet from under him. He hit the floor with a bruising thud, two beefy coppers kneeling on him while they got the handcuffs on.

'Cuff the lot of them!' Bowker glared around furiously. 'Their boss isn't here! Where's that wicked bastard Ronson? If he's got away, I'll go stark staring mad!'

He dashed back into the passageway, guessing the office might be at the far end. He was right. There was a door with a glass panel, and beyond it a square room, the brick walls distempered dark green. Shirley Cote was on her knees beside a battered old desk, on which stood a computer. She was picking up discs that had been scattered across the floor and putting them in a box.

Dougie Ronson, very smart in a peach-coloured suede jacket, a black silk shirt, and sky-blue slacks, lay face-down on the hard floor. Ginny Bampton was reciting the caution to him as she sat heavily on his back: *'You don't have to say anything but anything you do say will be taken down and used in evidence. Understand?'*

'Good work!' Bowker grinned like a hyena after a feast of wandering bushman's leg. 'You've arrested the top porn baron of the Thames valley. I'm proud of you both. What's he doing on the floor? Have the two of you been knocking him about?'

'He was trying to take off through the window with a box full of discs,' Cote explained happily. 'We grabbed his weedy ankles and dragged him back in. He dropped the box when he hit the floor.'

'This is police brutality!' Ronson protested from his awkward position. 'I'll bring charges against every one of you!'

'His solid gold medallion got hooked on the window catch when we hauled him in and nearly choked him to death,' said Cote. 'I was afraid we'd have to give him artificial respiration, though neither Bampton nor I wanted to do the mouth-to-mouth with him. His face got scraped when he hit the floor; we didn't do that. And I think his lovely jacket's ruined.'

Bowker sat down on the cheap swivel chair by the desk and got the warrant out of his inside pocket.

'I have here in my hand,' he said very pleasantly, 'a warrant which authorises me to enter and search these premises. Also to confiscate for further examination any goods or articles found therein which I have reason to suspect are in breach of various laws. And to take into custody at my own discretion all and any persons found on the premises.'

'That won't do you any good when I get you into court,' said Ronson. 'I'll have you kicked out of the police and into jail.'

Bowker laughed loudly enough to rattle the unwashed window.

'You're the one going to jail, Dougie. You've been laughing your head off at stupid coppers and playing at cock of the walk. Well, we're not all stupid, and you're wearing cuffs to prove it.'

'You're going to be sorry for this.' Ronson tried to bluff it out.

'After we've had time to sort through your stock, I'll have a guess how long you're going inside for: seven years or ten. You can let him up now, Constable Bampton.'

'Right, sir,' she said, staring at Bowker devotedly.

'I doubt if he's going to try anything silly,' Bowker went on blithely. 'If he does, you are fully authorised to disable him. Please bear in mind you are allowed to use the minimum force necessary to bring the prisoner under control. Which means you shouldn't break any of his bones—unless you have to.'

'Pig bastards!' said Ronson from down on the floor.

It was after ten that evening before Bowker went leisurely down to the cells in Bedlow police station basement. There were only four, it being thought unlikely a crime wave would ever hit the town hard enough to require mass jugging. The officer in charge of prisoners led Bowker to a solid door numbered 2 and opened a small viewing panel for him to take a look at Dougie Ronson.

The porn baron was sitting on an immovable wooden bunk like a shelf fixed to the wall. His arms were wrapped around his knees, his black silk shirt was bedraggled, his linen slacks creased. He had taken his white Gucci shoes off. His soiled suede jacket lay beside him on a rumpled and scratchy blanket.

His scraped face had been attended to by a doctor; a dressing was taped over one cheekbone. Although his bandaged profile was toward the door, there was no mistaking the look of dejection on his face. Which is how it should be, Bowker thought; crooks are crooks. But what struck him most was the stomach-curdling smell coming at him. He asked the uniform about it.

'Sorry about that, sir,' said PC Biddle. 'We did our best, but all our cells were taken when you brought him in. We kicked old Jango out to make room for this one, but there wasn't much time to clean up the cell between. We scraped the sick off the floor and sprinkled disinfectant about a bit. And we gave him a clean blanket, but that's all we could do for him. Old Jango's stink hangs about for a long time and is very hard to get rid of.'

'Who's old Jango?'

'Nobody, really. He's a hairy old tramp who drinks meths and dosses in doorways. We don't usually bother with him, but he was falling-about drunk in High Street this afternoon. The beat man brought him in for his own good. Sergeant Doubleday was furious at having the station stunk up and gave the beat officer a real telling off.'

'Isn't there a shelter for down-and-outs in the town?'

'Yes, sir, the Primitive and Particular Methodists run a place on Sedan Street. We've taken Jango there many a time, only they refuse to have in him now because he fights when he's drunk and he's filthy with lice. We black-bagged the blanket to send for fumigation in the morning, but there's enough livestock left in the cell to keep Ronson itching and scratching all night.'

'What have you done with the tramp?'

'He'd about slept it off by the time you brought this one in. We poured a pint of coffee down his throat and chucked him out. I think Sergeant Doubleday slipped a couple of quid in his hand and told him to go to the fish-and-chip shop for a meal. But he more likely spent it on liquor at the first pub that would let him in.'

'Has Ronson said anything since he's been locked up?'

'Nothing worth repeating, sir. He called me some nasty names. You were mentioned, too, but not in a friendly way. The first hour he was in the cell, he was shouting for a lawyer and going on about habeas corpus, but he's been quiet since then. He may be pondering his wicked ways, but I wouldn't bet money on it.'

'I'll have a few words with him before I go off to bed,' said Bowker. 'Just to wish him good night. Bring him upstairs in five minutes. I'll be in the Interview Room.'

As an afterthought, he asked if the cells were always so full.

'No,' said Biddle, 'it's the first time this year we've been this busy. New Year's Eve we packed them in three and four to a cell, but normally we've got space.'

'Today must be special, then,' said Bowker.

'You can say that—we've got a ragbag of guests staying with us overnight. There's a mental case in number 1 who ran his car off the road and ploughed into a bus queue. One dead so far and three seriously injured. Since he sobered up, he's been down on his knees begging Jesus to forgive him. In cell 3 we've a loony who stuck up a sub post office with a replica revolver. A woman waiting for stamps hit him with her shopping bag and kicked him in the identicals. He was doubled up when they brought him in.'

'At least he wasn't using a cosh,' Bowker commented wryly. 'A toy revolver can't do any damage. It's only a month or so since a post office clerk in Cowley had his head smashed in just like an egg and died of it because he wouldn't hand over the cash.'

'I read about that, sir. Nasty business it was. Now, in cell 4 we've got a loon who says he doesn't remember his own name, one of the total amnesia cases you hear about. But his real problem is being caught red-handed outside Bishop Peabody School. Maybe "red-handed" is not the right word for it; he was exposing himself to the young girls.'

'What a bunch!' Bowker said in disgust. 'A dangerous driver, an amateur stick-up artist, a flasher—and a smelly old dosser you kicked out! At least you've got a real villain now in your dungeon, Ronson the dirty video millionaire.'

'He doesn't smell as bad as old Jango, sir—not outwardly, at least.'

After the raid on the Reading cold store, Bowker and the black-moustached Inspector in uniform came to an arrangement. Reading got Ellis and the four workmen, charged with assault and affray and any other relevant crimes the Reading squad could think of, including conspiracy. And if Reading brought up a truck as well as a black maria for the prisoners, Bowker offered, they could have the contents of Kyte and Pewsey's cold store—except for a sample of each that he had his own men load into his car boot.

Ronson was Bowker's prisoner, no argument about that; he went back to Bedlow handcuffed. And since then he had been in a cell in the basement, a dismal and malodorous cell. Upstairs in the Incident Room, the murder squad became frantically and unusually busy, under the direction of Jack Knight. Bowker congratulated his team warmly and left them to get on with it.

He decided he'd earned a treat. His cold roast beef and salad lunch in The Black Dog pub was the faintest of distant memories now. He strode across the Thames bridge to the White Hart Hotel and into the dining room. The headwaiter tried to look pleased to see him again and seated him under the painting of huntsmen and hounds.

This time he knew better than to offer the elaborately bound menu. Bowker moderated his glare in acknowledgement of the man's gleam of common sense and ordered six lamb chops, well-done, new potatoes, and broccoli. Followed by a wedge of Stilton cheese—and accompanied by a pint of best ale.

'Draught ale from the barrel,' he said, wagging a finger the size of a frankfurter at the headwaiter.

Back in the police station an hour later, ready for anything, Bowker sat in the smallest Interview Room he could find, dominating it by sheer bulk. Knight sat beside him and they stared bleakly at Ronson over a cigarette-scarred table. He'd left his jacket in the cell, the gold medallion had been taken with his wristwatch, keys and money. In his bedraggled black shirt, he looked like an old-time Fascist on the run.

The porn baron was not in a helpful mood.

'I want my lawyer,' he said grimly. 'You've no right to stop me talking to him.'

'And you shall have him, Dougie,' Bowker said amiably. 'There were a few things we had to check before having a chat with you about your awkward predicament. Is it Mr Lloyd Davies you want to come and hold your hand?'

'I'm saying nothing before he gets here.'

'There's nothing I want you to say. We've got everything that we could ask for. You'll get ten years for what you had in your warehouse. I thought you should know that, Dougie, to put your mind at rest, in case the suspense was preying on your thoughts and keeping you from your sleep.'

'I'm not answering any questions without my lawyer here.'

'I've no questions to ask you, Dougie. We've printed out your list of distributors up and down the Thames Valley. They're due for an unwelcome call, all thirty-eight of them, as soon as we can muster enough bobbies to do the job. About four tomorrow morning, just as it's getting light and your chums are tucked up in bed.'

Ronson said nothing.

'Meanwhile,' Bowker said with a heavy sigh, 'teams of battle-hardened coppers are viewing your obscene video nasties to make notes for the prosecution. It's a dirty job, but somebody's got to do it. We'll have to send them for psychiatric counselling afterwards.'

Knight made tut-tutting noises, his face severe. For all Bowker's joviality, his brain was at work laying a trap for Ronson.

'I can guarantee you'll do ten years,' Bowker continued, 'but if we show one or two of your choicest items to a judge and jury, you might even get twelve years. We're going to do our best.'

'You're wasting your time.' Ronson tried to understand Bowker's tactics. 'I'm not saying anything. I want my lawyer.'

'You don't have to say anything, Dougie. WPC Bampton told you that when she arrested you. You can't have forgotten Bampton so soon, she's the big lass in uniform. If you take my advice, you certainly won't say anything. In fact, you'd be stupid to do so. You're standing in the clag right up to your chin. Keeping your mouth shut is the most sensible thing you can do.'

'I don't get it,' Ronson said in disbelief. 'You are advising me to say nothing to you? What are you playing at?'

'We're not playing, Dougie, we're dead serious about crime in the police force. It's our job. Read out a few of those titles, Sergeant.'

Knight opened the folder he was holding and read from a sheet of paper in a suitably awestruck voice.

'We've got samples of twenty-eight different videos from the cold store at Reading where we arrested Mr Ronson. And computer discs, fourteen different ones.'

'Pornographic computer discs for school kids!' Bowker snorted. 'That's real technological progress for you!'

'And sixty-five different magazines with very obscene pictures within the meaning of the Act,' Knight continued. 'The total haul from the cold store is estimated at two tons of material. All of the items in our possession are being closely examined, with a view to prosecution.'

'Very definitely a prosecution,' Bowker said sourly, 'but get to the video titles.'

'Our preliminary survey has produced the following titles:
Miss Whiplash 7
Nazi Torture Chamber 3
Death in Chains
Boy Scouts Camping
Schoolgirls without Knickers
Babes in Arms
Lolita's Little Sister
Benny's Twelfth Birthday Party
Little Girl Lost.'

'That's enough to be going on with,' said Bowker, thick black eyebrows drawn down in a terrifying scowl. 'You're not married, are you, Dougie? Got no children of your own?'

'I've nothing to say.'

'I'm glad to hear that. I can't imagine what a man could say, living in a stately home bought with money he'd made out of the sexual exploitation of children.'

'I only sell the videos, I don't make them.'

'We can't be sure of that.' Bowker's menace was enough to make Ronson very nervous. 'We're hoping to find someone looking like you in one of those twenty-eight videos. A ginger-haired chap in his forties, that's all we need.'

'Look all you like, I had nothing to do with making them, and you can't prove I did. They're all foreign, made abroad.'

'So you say. But maybe we can find somebody of your build in a black leather mask in the Nazi torture chamber with his parts hanging out. We won't need to see a face if we can get a public prosecutor to agree you're the star. You'll be bloody amazed at the charges you'll be facing.'

'You're trying to frame me!' At last Ronson was alarmed. 'You can't do that, it's not right!'

Bowker's grin was terrifying beyond words. 'You know all about right and wrong, do you?'

'I'm saying nothing until Lloyd Davies gets here.'

'It's after eleven at night. He won't be in his office, and we can't disturb him at home this late. He might be entertaining—think how annoyed he'd be if we dragged him here on the say-so of a doomed maggot like you. Even if we knew his phone number, which we don't.'

'I can tell you his home number,' Ronson said quickly.

'This isn't the bloody Ritz Hotel,' Bowker said. 'There's no all-night service. We'll phone him in the morning, when he gets to his office, and advise him you'd like him to trot round here for a consultation.'

'You bastard! I don't want to stay here all night in a dirty stinking cell!'

'We haven't got the home comforts of Cocker Park,' Bowker said with a malicious smile. 'No satin sheets. And no playmates. But whether Davies comes to talk to you now or in the morning makes no difference. You're staying in that cell for some days.'

'You can't do that to me.' Ronson was getting more alarmed.

'Dougie, you haven't understood the nastiness of the position you're in. One of the names on your list of distributors we got off the computer disc is Ronnie Matthews, deceased, of Minching Lane. The man you'd never met, the man you said you didn't know from Adam. Sergeant Knight wrote that down in his notebook.'

'Be reasonable,' Ronson said. 'You know I have to protect my associates.'

'I don't know any such thing. And I don't care if you protect them or not—they'll all have a copper on their doorstep a few hours from now. With a search warrant in his hand.'

Ronson shrugged. It was out of his hands to do anything about that now. But he was sweating. He knew many of them would agree to testify against him in return for leniency.

'What I don't understand,' Bowker said with a frown, 'is

your reason for having Ronnie Matthews killed. Your motive must have been a strong one, Dougie—what was it?'

Ronson realised he'd been guided to the edge of a sheer cliff. Another step would pitch him over into the abyss. He'd been out-thought by the thuggish Inspector sitting opposite him.

'You're off your bloody head!' He was seriously worried by the course of the interview. 'I had nothing to do with that!'

'You can kick and shout all you want. Dougie, Matthews was an important man in your network until you and he fell out and you thought it best to get rid of him. You sent a couple of minions to his shop by night to set fire to it. Your scheme worked very well; poor Ronnie was burnt to a crisp. After which he wasn't a threat to anybody, you included.'

'You've got it all wrong!'

'Mrs Matthews and two little girls died in that fire,' Bowker said with a cold menace that made Ronson stop fidgeting on his hard chair. 'One was seven years old and the other was nine.'

'I had nothing to do with it, I swear it!'

'This is not a formal interview, Dougie. We're not taping the chat, and Sergeant Knight isn't writing anything down. I haven't asked you any questions, and I don't want any answers. You don't have to deny anything.'

'So what the bloody hell are we all doing here?'

'I'm here out of a sense of fair play, to explain to you just where you stand.' Bowker sounded sincere but implausible. 'Then tomorrow you can beg your lawyer to save you.'

'If he takes the case,' Knight put in. 'This one might be too nasty even for Lloyd Davies. Bedlow's a small town, and he's got his own future to think of. You won't be a paying customer for ten or more years to come, which makes you very expendable.'

Bowker took up the thread. 'You can explain the porn charges to him better than I can. And you can tell him we're going to charge you with the murder of Ronnie Matthews.'

'You can't—I had nothing to do with it!' Dark patches were showing through the black silk shirt under Ronson's armpits.

'And the murder of Doreen Matthews, his wife. And the murders of Janice and Diana Matthews, their children,' Bowker added.

'Don't forget Billy Swanson, sir,' Jack Knight said.

'I'm not forgetting about poor Billy, dropped off a bridge to be mashed by a train. When I began to beat about in the bushes, you got worried about Billy because he knew it was you that had the Matthews family killed. He was a danger—the next time we ran him in for thieving, he'd shop you to get himself off. So it was safer to shut his mouth.'

'You're bloody mental!' Ronson exclaimed in great anxiety.

'Have a good long talk to your lawyer tomorrow morning—you need the benefit of his high-class and expensive legal advice—because the way I see things, you'll never be out of a cell for the rest of your natural life.'

'I'll be free on bail in twenty-four hours.' But Ronson didn't sound convinced about it.

'Not a cat's chance in hell,' Bowker said with a malign grin. 'You'll be in the cell down below, while we're wrapping up our enquiries. We'll take you to a magistrate's court and tell him the wicked crimes you've done. That's the habeas corpus bit you were so interested in. Davies will ask for you to be let loose on bail of a few thousand quid, but it won't wash. Not with the charges you're on. You'll be remanded in custody to await trial—which means you'll be kept in a cell in Reading jail for nine or ten months while the public prosecutor sorts his case out.'

'You bastard!'

Ronson was seriously disturbed, and Bowker piled on the agony.

'It won't be as nice as the cell you've got here, Dougie. We catch so many villains, there's a bad shortage of accommodation for prisoners on remand. You might even have heard about it on TV—the do-gooders are always going on about what a scandal it is, the way we lock criminals up in nasty little holes.'

'You don't scare me!' Ronson pulled himself together.

'I'm glad to hear it. You'll have to share a cell with other villains, not clean well-dressed crooks like yourself, riffraff from broken homes caught raping or drug dealing. You won't like them at all, not a man with your taste for high life.'

'You can't do that to me,' Ronson tried to sound confident.

'It's very historical, Reading jail. You must have noticed it every time you drove past in your Porsche, going to the cold store. A big, ugly old Victorian building. Oscar Wilde did time there for committing sodomy on lads. Back in those days, a judge could sentence you to hard labour, which meant six hours a day on a treadmill. Pity they've stopped doing that, Dougie. It kept the inmates very fit.'

'Who's Oscar Wilde?' Ronson asked.

'A fat queen who wrote stage plays. But forget about him, he did only two years. You'll draw life and they'll mean it— five murders is a bit bloody thick, Dougie. They'll lock you up in a long-stay jail. In the north, maybe, not around here. Very hard places they are, northern jails, full of unpleasant and violent people. Before you see the light of day again, you'll be a very old man with no interest in playmates with big chests. Assuming you survive that long.'

At midnight Bowker told his weary team to go home and be back in the morning by eight.

'You know it's Saturday tomorrow, sir?' DC Hagen asked, made bold by his success in locating Ronson's porn warehouse.

'I don't care if it's Mother's Day and your dear old crippled mum is moping in her sickbed and wondering why her wayward boy hasn't turned up with a bunch of roses,' Bowker said in a voice that would discourage Genghis Khan himself. 'Now that we've got one bastard in irons, we're not letting up.'

'No, sir,' Hagen gulped.

Bowker had thought about the most efficient route to locating Swanson's killer. He'd decided simplicity was the key.

'Sergeant Trimmer, we have to trace Billy Swanson's movements from the minute he left home to the time he was dropped down in front of the train. His widow is no bloody use; WPC Bampton has already established that.'

'Went out about ten,' Bampton confirmed. 'Didn't say where he was going. So she says, although she's a terrible liar. Nobody remembers seeing him in his usual pub all morning.'

'That terrible bloody boilersuit he wore and that wreck of a van stick in the memory,' Bowker rumbled. 'Use all the team and trace his movements, Sergeant. He drove somewhere for a meeting and got blind drunk before he was hauled to Windmill Lane to be murdered. According to Driver Flock, a mental defective if ever I saw one, his train put paid to Billy at 1.22 P.M. We've three hours to account for from the time Billy left home.'

'Right sir,' said Trimmer. 'We'll ask at every house on both sides of the street from Billy's house to wherever.'

'Except DC Cote,' Bowker said. 'I want her watching Hinksey's off-licence shop.'

'Where will you and Sergeant Knight be if I need to report to you?' Trimmer enquired.

'We'll be asking villains to account for their movements when Billy fell under a train and ruined British Rail's timetable.'

'No need to ask Moira Druce,' Cote said. 'She was telling her assistants what to do to my hair when Billy went off the bridge—she's in the clear.'

'I never imagined she lugged Billy about personally. She's by no means in the clear, Constable.'

The team drifted away in the direction of their homes. Bowker decided to leave his car in the police carpark and walk to The White Hart, to make sure of a space the next day. It was a warm summer night, and Knight was glad to stretch his legs after sitting down for hours viewing obscenely off-putting videos.

'So that's it, then?' he said as Bowker paused on the bridge over the river to look at the dark water swirling past beneath. 'We charge Ronson with all the five murders and collect as much evidence as we can find to get him put away forever. Why aren't you happy? You look positively moody.'

'It wasn't Ronson who had the Matthews family killed,' Bowker said morosely. 'We're no nearer than when we started.'

'Not Ronson?' Knight was almost shrill in his amazement. 'So what the hell was that romance about Oscar Wilde and treadmills you came out with?'

'That was just to give him sleepless nights. With luck on our side, he'll be so worried about taking the blame for the murders that he'll confess to the porn charges and save us trouble.'

'How can you be sure it wasn't Ronson did the dirty deed?'

'Ronnie Matthews was worth a lot of money to Ronson. And vice versa. I don't see Ronnie as an ambitious man, not living above the shop, the way he did. He was from a deprived background, and he wanted to squirrel cash away to make himself feel secure. He wouldn't go up against Ronson, not as I read him. The pickings were too good—four hundred thousand quid in less than ten years.'

'So if Ronson didn't have him burnt, who the hell did?'

'How do I know? But we've got a chance now—because whoever cremated the Matthewses suicided Billy. We've got a murder of our own to work on, we're not just stumbling along in Mason's footsteps like bloody King Wenceslas.'

'It wasn't him, it was the pageboy who trod in them. The boy loaded down with a side of beef and jugs of wine and bundles of firewood for the peasants.'

Bowker wasn't listening. He turned from his contemplation of the Thames and walked on toward the hotel. Not his usual great stride that had Knight almost trotting to stay level with him—this was a measured pace like a bobby walking a beat.

'Mrs Swanson could be lying—you realise that?' Knight said.

'Quite possible, the horrible slag. If Billy told her what he knew she might try to put the black on Chummy. She could end up dead because he doesn't mess about, whoever he may be. He just wipes them out in nasty ways. I'm wondering how to keep an eye on Kitty Swanson. No use sending Bampton to watch her—she's a bit too obvious.'

'Obvious?' Knight asked, 'What makes you think that a female weight lifter stands out in a crowd?'

'When I saw Billy lying dead by the railway, it put me in mind of Dombey,' Bowker said thoughtfully.

'Who's he—not another suspect?'

'*Dombey and Son*—it's one of Dickens' novels. Don't you ever read books, Jack?'

He rarely used Knight's first name. It was an indication they were off duty when he did.

'Not if I can help it,' Knight said. 'I like the flicks.'

'Dombey is a miserable sod who owns a shipping line, and a man named James Carker holds the top management job. This Carker wants to get his leg over Dombey's young wife, she being off her husband because he treats her like dirt.'

'Sounds more like a tabloid front page than a school book, if you ask me,' Knight said. '*Shipping magnate in love triangle.*'

'Right. Young Mrs Dombey and Carker run off together— France was the fashionable place then for guilty lovers, as they used to be called. Today they go to Majorca or Ibiza and don't feel at all guilty when they commit adultery.'

'They get embarrassed if they're politicians and the tabloids track them down,' Knight offered.

'You're not taking me seriously, Jack, and I'm trying to make a serious point. Mrs Dombey goes off Carker in France. He takes it hard, having chucked up a good job for her.'

'I don't see what this has got to do with anything—were you thinking of Mrs Vereker running off with a man?'

'No, it was Carker's death at the railway station that seemed to me to have some bearing on our case.'

'Railway station?' Knight sounded puzzled, 'I thought trains weren't invented in Dickens' time and people travelled in stagecoaches. A lot of Christmas cards have Mr Pickwick on top of a stagecoach wearing a funny hat. Snow on the ground, robins and holly, Yuletide greetings, all that—my sister sends me a card like that every year.'

'Didn't they teach you anything at school? The railways were built in Charlie Dickens' lifetime. He was mad keen on them and travelled all over England by train. He was in a crash once.'

They were in Bedlow High Street, deserted at this time of the night, a place of dark shop fronts between the street lamps. Up ahead was The White Hart.

'So what about Dombey and the man who ran off with his wife—what happened?' Knight asked.

'Carker was so fed up at being given the elbow that he jumped under the next train and was minced to shreds.'

Knight was thoughtful for a moment. 'I never had the pleasure of meeting Billy. That's if it was a pleasure. I don't believe Mrs Vereker ran off with him; he doesn't sound her type.'

'No woman in her right mind would run off with Billy,' Bowker agreed. 'He was a repulsive little crook, and he smelled sweaty. It's nothing to do with Mrs Vereker, there's another connection if I could think of it. It'll come to me eventually.'

'What about Dombey—did his wife go back to him, or what?'

'No, he went on being a miserable bugger on his own until his business folded up and he went bankrupt.'

'Make a rotten movie,' Knight pronounced his verdict. 'Bad as the one I told you about, where Greta Garbo jumps in front of a Russian train.'

They turned into The White Hart and made for the lounge for a relaxing glass of whisky before bed. Bowker saw two men sitting talking in a corner and his face turned black with fury. Donald Vereker, the bereft husband, with Frederick Morten, the enquiry agent. Morten had swapped his brown suit for a dark grey one. A half-empty brandy glass stood on the table in front of him. His little run-in with the traffic police hadn't changed his ways.

'I thought we'd got shot of that troublemaker,' Knight said. 'The other one's got to be Vereker, I've seen his photo. Do you think this means what I think it means?'

'We'll soon find out,' Bowker snarled as he strode across the room like a rhinoceros lumbering toward an unlucky tourist in the African bush.

'Evening.' He lowered himself uninvited into a chair. 'Glad I caught you, Mr Vereker. Saves calling at your office in business hours. We're still looking for your wife, and I want to ask if you know a man named Dougie Ronson. He owns Cocker Park, the big house out on the Wallingford road.'

Vereker paused before he answered the question. 'I know him slightly. Only because I arrange the insurance on his house, not socially.'

'What about a commercial property in Reading—a rundown old cold store? Do you fix the insurance on that? And the contents too, maybe?'

'Offhand, I couldn't say.' Vereker was cautious. 'I'll have to check my records, if you really want to know.'

'I'd like to know,' Bowker said with genial ferocity. 'Phone the police station when you've checked your records and leave a message for me. What was the name of the place, Sergeant?'

It was a game they played between them, Bowker pretending not to remember, Knight producing his notebook and flipping through it. Some suspects went paranoid when it was done to them.

'Kyte and Pewsey, Rendlesham Road,' Knight said solemnly.

'Better write it down, Mr Vereker,' Bowker suggested cruelly. 'It might slip your mind by tomorrow, and you won't know what to look for in your files.'

Vereker was becoming visibly agitated. 'I don't know anything about this man Ronson,' he said with a quaver in his voice. 'What his business is or anything. My only contact with him is to insure his premises.'

Morten butted in to save Vereker making any unwise admissions or divulge any useful information. He put his hand on Vereker's sleeve to warn him and grinned very evilly at Bowker.

'I bet you thought you'd seen the back of me, Inspector, after that little prank of yours with the traffic patrol. I'm not working for the newspaper anymore. I'm working for Mr Vereker. He's retained me to find the truth about what happened to his wife. I'm like a bad penny; I keep turning up.'

'For all I care,' Bowker said with a black scowl, 'you can be like Rin-Tin-Tin the wonder dog sniffing a cold trail across an acre of concrete carpark. Stay out of my way.'

After a massive breakfast of scrambled eggs, bacon, baked beans, and fried tomatoes, with toast and several pints of strong tea, for Bowker, that is—Knight ate much less—they arrived at Bedlow police station at ten minutes to eight. Bowker had told the murder team to be there by eight, and he meant to be in first.

The constable on the front desk was waiting for him.

'Morning, sir, there's a message for you. Some joker or other has been daubing the war memorial in the night.'

'Why do I want to know that?' Bowker asked, puzzled.

'It's your name that's been daubed on it, sir. Among the dead—that makes it a bit personal, I reckon.'

'Hah!' Bowker's thick black eyebrows crawled up his forehead. 'I've upset somebody. Who reported it?'

'The man on the beat last night, PC Tudge.'

'Has he signed off and gone home yet? I want to talk to him if he's still here.'

'His shift's over, but he stayed on to talk to you. He's up in the canteen.'

'And I want to see this miserable bit of vandalism, that's if it hasn't been cleaned off already.'

'Not much chance of that, sir. It's Saturday—the department responsible for street cleaning and bin emptying is off for the weekend. The whole town hall's more-or-less closed. There's an emergency man somewhere, but he'll take a lot of finding.'

'Not often the idleness of public servants is any advantage,' Bowker grunted.

In the canteen, PC Tudge was enjoying mahogany-brown tea and a fried bacon sandwich with three other bobbies. He was a stocky man in his forties, not overbright, but rock-solid and totally reliable. Bowker sat down at the table facing him, Knight stood and tried to look as if he was doing something important as the three unwanted uniforms moved to another table.

'Sir,' said Tudge, 'I waited on for you.'

'Good man. When did you spot the desecration?'

'Just after five o'clock this morning. If it was there when I went past before, I missed it.'

'What time was it daylight this morning?'

'Getting on for four, although it was nearer half-past before it was bright enough for the street lamps to switch off.'

'Did you see anyone near the war memorial any time during the night? Lurkers in shadows, skulkers in doorways, furtive prats or teenage terrorists, raiders of the lost ark, anyone?'

Tudge gave the question slow and careful consideration before committing himself.

'Not after midnight, not a soul. Except for Dr Brenthurst—he drove past in a tearing hurry soon after two o'clock. Called to an emergency, I should think, and well over the speed limit.'

'You're certain who it was?'

'I know his car, sir. Big brown Swedish Volvo. Reminds me of a biscuit tin on wheels. With a doctor sign on the windscreen.'

'I think we can rule him out,' Bowker said. 'He has no reason to hate me, mainly because he's never heard of me. We'll go and take at look at your discovery, Constable.'

Bedlow War Memorial stood on Spinster's Reach, a broad street along the river, with houses on one side and open grass on the other. The memorial was on the riverbank side, and it was like every war memorial Bowker had seen. On a white stone base four feet high stood a tall stone cross that went up another nine or ten feet. Around the base was a square paved area enclosed by a low black chain that looped down from posts.

The few usual lines of verse were inscribed on the front side of the stone base:

> *They shall not grow old, as we that are left grow old;*
> *Age shall not weary them, nor the years condemn.*
> *At the going down of the sun and in the morning*
> *We will remember them.*

On all four sides of the base were carved the names of Bedlow men killed in the Great War of 1914 and in Hitler's war of 1939—in alphabetical order, from Abrahams to Winters. And the name of his regiment, a sort of military guide to the Thames valley; Gloucestershire Regiment, Oxfordshire Regiment, the Berkshire Yeomanry, the Middlesex Regiment.

And not only the infantry. Bowker read Royal Artillery, Royal Armoured Corps, Royal Navy, and Royal Air Force. Bedlow men had mixed it with the best of them, and three hundred names and more proved it. A terse message had been spray-painted slanting over the B section. *BOWKER* it said *RIP*. Done in bright red.

'Your idea of lobbing a stone into the hornet's nest seems to be producing results, though maybe not what you expected,' Knight said with a shrug. 'First Billy Swanson has an accident under a train. Now you're being told you're a goner.'

'We've got Chummy worried,' Bowker agreed. 'I like that. Take a photo or two and let's get back—we've got work to do.'

Knight had pulled rank to borrow the camera Shirley Cote used for her surveillance of Hinksey's suspicious customers. He shot a few pictures for evidence.

'We know Ronson didn't do the artwork,' he said chattily, 'or send his hairy bodyguard to do it, both being well and truly in jug. And Billy's being cut up this morning to see if his mangy innards tell us anything. So that's crossed a few off the list. If I were a betting man, I'd put a fiver on the horrible Burton brothers.'

'It's a bad and spiteful thing to do.' PC Tudge gave his view unasked. 'There's a lot of people who'll see it as an insult to the dead. It ought to be cleaned off before too many people are out and about this morning to see it.'

'You're right,' Bowker agreed mildly. He walked right around the base looking for any other defacements, but there were none—the anonymous messenger had said all that he wanted to say on the front: *BOWKER RIP*.

'There's a Tudge listed here,' he said, 'Any relation?'

'My grandfather, sir. Killed in action in Crete.'

'I'll see what can be done to get a cleaning team here. You'd better be off home and get some sleep.'

Bowker and Knight walked back to the police station.

'You're right about the Burtons being the favourites,' Bowker said, 'but there's more than one horse in the race. The daubing could have been done by a woman. All it needs is a can of spray from Woolworth's and a very early stroll through empty streets—thirty seconds to spatter the war memorial, and straight back to bed for another couple of hours' sleep.'

'That may be,' Knight argued, 'but you have to admit that a woman couldn't heave Billy over a railway bridge. Not unless she was WPC Bampton. She could do it with one hand.'

'With her views on Billy and his loudmouth missus, she'd have given him the long drop on to the track with pleasure,' Bowker agreed gloomily. 'But this is not an inside job.'

'That means we're left with the Burtons, hot-pants Moira, the idiot Shane, and Cousin Arnie. If I had to set the odds, I'd give five-to-one the Burton brothers and twenty-five-to-one the others. And I've had a thought you'll like: maybe Lloyd Davies dunnit.'

'If only!' Bowker said, a sharklike smile on his dark face. 'The day we run that slimy little lawyer in I'll stand you the best dinner to be had in Bedlow—with champagne and brandy and a singing stripper, if I can find one!'

'That won't be too hard. The local newspaper's got columns of personal ads by women offering to deliver birthday greetings in black silk underwear and nothing else.'

'Since when have you started reading the local rag?'

'Since you snatched that copy out of the editor's hand in The White Hart and gave it to me. You read only the front page, but I went right through it. You learn some very interesting things from small-town newspapers.'

'Such as?' Bowker was disbelieving.

'Well, in the Thames Valley Sunday Cricket League, Bedlow beat Maidenhead B team by an inning and thirty-five runs. The Reverend Cricklade-Wender who is the vicar at St Bardolph's Church is eighty-three this year and thinking of retiring. There's talk of a woman priest taking his place and the usual batch of letters from good churchgoers saying if God meant women to be priests, it would say so in the Bible. And another half-page of letters saying it's high bloody time the wimps moved out of the pulpit and let the women have a go.'

'You waste your time reading rubbish like that when you could be improving your mind with a book. I'm disappointed, Jack.'

'I can see you buying a Dickens novel for my birthday,' said Knight with a grin. 'There's a feud between the people who live in Heathley Road, wherever that is, and a factory at the bottom end. They're enraged and disgusted because trucks drive in and out from early morning until late at night.'

'I don't bloody care if they have cargo jets landing hourly,' said Bowker. 'What sort of factory?'

'I didn't believe it myself—they make tin tacks. Ten-to-one Vereker arranges the insurance on it.'

The Inspector snarled to hear the deserted husband's name but made no coherent comment.

At Bedlow police station, Bowker stopped for a serious talk to the officer on the front desk. He told him he wanted the paint cleaned off in the next hour. The town hall stand-by man was to be winkled out of whatever dingy hidey-hole he was skulking in and sent forth with paint remover, scraper, and bucket.

On the way up to the Incident Room he reverted to the subject of Moira Druce as possible murderer.

'She's worth shorter odds than the twenty-five-to-one you're giving her. For all we know, Ronnie Matthews might have given her the sharp elbow—and a woman scorned can do very nasty things. She might have persuaded the Burtons to start the fire for her. And drive Billy to Windmill Lane to catch the fast train to Gloucester.'

'This is DS Trimmer's theory,' said Knight. 'I told you that—jealous passion and spurned love turning into bitter hate, just like the movies. But I can't see how she could get the Burtons to risk their necks for her. She's got a hairdressing shop. And if they're the drug dealers around here, as everybody tells us, it stands to reason they've got a lot more money than she has.'

'That woman we arrested in Long Slaughter—she found somebody to kill for her with no money changing hands.'

'That was different!' Knight objected.

'Every murder is different. People are different, that's why. Not all of life is about money. Some emotions are stronger than greed—everybody knows that.'

'Bloody hell!' Knight said in dismay. 'Yesterday we make the best pinch this month so far, and now you're looking for dumped girlfriends getting their own back! I can see Moira sticking a steak knife into Matthews in a sudden flush of hate if he tried to give her the soldier's farewell. But I can't see her having him killed by fire when it meant his children being killed with him. Not many women murder kids—you know that.'

'Not many,' Bowker agreed, 'but some do. And those who do can be crueller than any man. You know that as well as I do. Need I remind you about the hospital nurse who poisoned sick kids—ten of them in a few years?'

'Should have been sent to a mental asylum, not jail,' Knight commented. 'She couldn't have been right in the head.'

'Jack, *your* head's been tampered with by do-gooders!' Bowker said in alarm. 'Stop making excuses for evil. Young as you are, you must have heard of the Moors Murders of thirty years back—children abducted and tortured to death from sheer badness.'

In the Incident Room, Knight returned the camera to Cote. She checked it suspiciously, as if certain he'd ruined it, then off she went to her observation job.

'She hasn't fallen for your charm,' Bowker said with a wicked grin. 'You must be slipping.'

'She's crazy about me. She's treating me casually to hide it because she can't cope with her own feelings.'

'We have our final two suspects: horrible Arnie and his

loony cousin Shane,' Bowker went on with total disregard for Knight's assertion. 'For a start, there's two of them. That's convenient because it took two to get that fire going so fast. And we know Arnie's a wrong'un.'

Bowker didn't like having a desk; it pinned him down to paperwork and routine. He kept away from the one assigned to him and perched on a corner of Knight's desk.

'How do we know Arnie Hinksey is a wrong'un?' Knight asked, knowing it was expected of him to argue.

'He's pushing drugs. How much wronger can you get?'

'We've no proof he's pushing,' Knight observed. 'Shirley Cote is trying to find enough suspicious circumstances for us to ask for a search warrant. Then we storm his off-licence and hope to hell we find little cellophane bags of illegal white powder and dollops of crack.'

'You're being negative,' Bowker growled. 'We've met Arnie and we've talked to him. He's crooked all the way through.'

'Suppose for the sake of argument that he's pushing. We can't assume from that he murdered Matthews—they were best friends. They went fishing together.'

'Fishing!' Bowker said in huge disgust. 'Sitting like idiots on the riverbank for hours on end! If I hear about Arnie and Matthews going fishing one more time, I'll go mental. I tell you what we're going to do to Arnie, we'll get a search warrant. If not today, then tomorrow or the next day—it's only a matter of time. We'll raid him and run him in.'

'Sounds promising so far.'

'Somewhere on his premises there'll be a suitcase of unlawful substances. We'll slam him in a cell downstairs. Open-and-shut case, no defence possible, quick trial and seven years inside.'

'Nice,' said Knight. 'I like it.'

'We'll take his shop and his flat apart, we'll scrutinise his lousy little life all the way back to the first time he shaved. There's bound to be incriminating paper of some sort, bankbook or whatever. Something to tie him to the Burtons. And something that tells us why he killed Ronnie Matthews and his family.'

'Maybe,' Jack Knight said very doubtfully.

'When he's at his lowest ebb, we'll accuse him of the murders; Ronnie and family and Billy Swanson. We'll pull Shane in as his accomplice and grill him till he can't remember his own name. A few hours of Shane helping us with our enquiries—that's all we need—and we'll have enough to convict them both.'

'I like it,' Knight said again. 'There's only one problem.'

'What problem?' Bowker snarled.

'They didn't do it.'

Bowker's chest swelled. His hands were balled into fists.

'Look at this.' Knight found a piece of paper on his desk and smothered the explosion in the nick of time. 'The dabs' reports arrived on that newspaper Trimmer found in Billy's van. The one he thought was a suicide message.'

'What does it say?'

'So many fingerprints on it, they hardly know where to start—half the population of Bedlow read that particular paper. Maybe it was used to wrap fish and chips in!'

'Are Billy's prints on it?' Bowker demanded.

'Yes they are, five sets and two full palm prints. That's got to be a setup—nobody holds a paper like that to read it. Some villain pressed Billy's hands on it when he was drunk. But it's a bit bloody amateur.'

'Just as I expected,' Bowker said. 'What time this morning is Billy being cut up?'

'Ten sharp, pathology department of the Prince Albert General Infirmary. I suppose you want me to go and see the fun?'

Bowker never went to postmortems. He wasn't squeamish—he'd seen enough of them when he was a detective-sergeant and before that when he was a detective-constable.

But it made him furious to watch a human being sliced open and gutted like a rabbit. He saw it as a denial of the value of life. Useful as it often was to have an inside look at what caused the victim's death, Bowker didn't want to be there.

'I had it in mind to send you,' he said glumly, 'but a change of plan seems called for. It may be Saturday, but Superintendent Billings will be in before long, or I'm a Dutchman. He'll want to have a gloat about collaring Ronson. Which is only right and proper, and every senior officer deserves a gloat when things go right on his patch for once.'

'He might recommend you for promotion,' Knight said hopefully and to himself he added 'and me.'

'Not when he hears Morten is back in business looking for Mrs Vereker. He'll go demented.'

Jack Knight grinned to see Bowker in a quandary. It was not a thing that happened often, and was worth enjoying when it did.

'You want me to get out there and find her before the private eye does?' he asked.

'He's not a private eye,' Bowker snarled immediately. 'This isn't bloody Hollywood. The black eye her brother Sholto gave you has developed well—if you find her looking like that, she'll be so bloody scared she'll run away again. Get an eye patch for it.'

'You want me to go out looking like a bloody pirate?' Knight was outraged.

'And in answer to your question, I don't want you to look for her—not just now. There's too much happening in Bedlow. I need you here; otherwise, I have to rely on the murder team I've been given.'

'Good coppers, all of them,' Knight said with a gleam of pure malice in his eye. 'The Superintendent said so himself.'

Bowker glared at him hatefully.

'I want to run Arnie in over the weekend, if we can swing it. If I'm here when Superintendent Billings arrives, he'll ask what my plans are. And the less he knows, the better. Senior officers have dizzy spells if they hear the rules might get twisted just a bit in the pursuit of justice. So I'll go with you to Billy's postmortem.'

Having committed himself to attending the dissection of Billy Swanson, Bowker so arranged it that he and Knight arrived late, just as the pathologist was finishing. Billy was laid out on a stainless steel table, and the assistant was sewing him up where he'd been sliced open from rib cage to below the navel.

Billy dead was even less prepossessing than Billy alive, if it was possible. Divested of his scruffy blue boilersuit, he was revealed as potbellied and slightly knock-kneed. He'd lost two toes from his left foot, but that was years ago. On both of his forearms there were poorly executed tattoos of daggers, crowns, and roses—most likely souvenirs of his various stays in jail.

Bowker introduced himself and Knight. The pathologist stared coldly at them through overlarge spectacles, as if they were a pair of second-rate specimens for his knife. Something he could do without. He was kitted out from head to foot in operating-theatre style, from head cover to rubber boots, as if about to perform some vital surgery on Billy, such as a brain transplant.

'I'm perfectly certain you were informed the postmortem would begin at ten sharp,' he said. 'You're too late, Inspector—it's been done.'

'Pressure of work,' Bowker said. 'These things happen. Murder enquiries always need more time than is available.'

Dr Denzil Thornton didn't quite say *Rubbish!* but the look on his face made his feelings clear. He was a tall, thin man with a long face that had a naturally sour expression.

'A particularly interesting specimen,' he said after a pause. 'You've missed a once-in-a-lifetime opportunity by being late—a cadaver with massive internal injuries. Almost every bone was broken and most organs ruptured, but hardly an external mark at all apart from bruising. Quite fascinating—I understand that he was struck by a train?'

'What a shame to miss medical history in the making,' Bowker said in a tone colder than the mortuary refrigerator that Billy had spent the night in.

'Killed instantly, of course.' Thornton blinked at the unexpected reply. 'Multiple fractures of the spinal column, the spleen ruptured, both thighs broken, hips smashed, liver ripped and intestines torn, ribs fractured and heart pierced—'

'I've got the picture,' Bowker interrupted. 'The grisly parts can wait until I read your report. How drunk was he?'

'Astoundingly drunk. I've never seen so high a blood-alcohol content before. He was in a deep coma when the train killed him. He never knew what hit him.'

'A small mercy, at least,' Bowker said.

'He'd never have recovered.' Thornton blinked again at Bowker's expression of sympathy with the deceased. 'Without any intervention by the train, he would have died of acute alcoholic poisoning, I'm certain of it—the amount he consumed must have been stupendous.'

'Probably poured down his throat after he passed out. Did you find any sign of that?'

'No. But I wouldn't expect to—if he was already unconscious, his muscles would be relaxed. It would not be difficult to hold his mouth open and pour more liquor down his throat.'

'Was he hit front or back?'

'The impact was to his chest, pelvis, and thighs. Not the head, or his nose would have been broken, and it isn't. As you can see for yourself.'

'Our theory is that he was rolled over the parapet of a small bridge as the train came under it. But obviously not headfirst from what you say. They must have laid him along the parapet in readiness and given him a shove at the right moment.

Down went Billy sideways, head clear of the train when it hit him.'

'At least he's in one piece,' Thornton said sniffily. 'Train victims I've seen in the past have always been cut into several parts by the wheels.'

'Billy was lucky.' Bowker was sardonic. 'The impact threw him about twenty feet up an embankment and he landed soft on grass.'

The pathologist thought it over for a moment and decided that he was not being addressed with the respect due to him.

'I believe you know the time of death precisely, Inspector.'

'According to the man who drove the train that hit him, it was at 1.22 P.M. yesterday,' Bowker agreed, 'but we know British Rail timekeeping is not the same as normal timekeeping. We put the time of the shunt somewhere between 1.15 and 1.35. Ten minutes each way means nothing to British Rail. And exactness of time's not all that vital to us, for once.'

'I don't think you and I have met before,' Thornton said in a way that implied he was not sorry. 'Have you been transferred to Bedlow recently?'

'I'm here temporarily to clear up the deaths of the Matthews family last April.'

'And that has something to do with this?' Thornton gestured at the remains of Billy Swanson, neatly stitched up and covered with a white sheet by the assistant, before being taken back to the deep freeze.

'I'm certain of it,' Bowker said. 'Did you do the postmortem on the Matthews family—two adults and two small girls burnt to death in their beds?'

'I remember it now,' Thornton conceded. 'It was a formality; the cause of death was all too obvious. But Inspector Mason was in charge of that investigation—I remember he was here at the time. A very sound and sensible officer, always punctual.'

The unstated opinion was that Bowker was neither sensible nor sound. And certainly not punctual.

'Those who decide these things had a change of heart,' Bowker said carefully. 'DI Mason is on another case. The four Matthewses are mine now.'

'Then I wish you good luck.' But Thornton didn't sound as if he meant it wholeheartedly. 'There's nothing more I am able to tell you, beyond the details you'll find in my report. "*Grisly*," I think you called them, Inspector.'

There was a sneer in his voice on '*grisly*.' Bowker bridled and Knight wondered why the Inspector always seemed to fall foul of medical men. It was because Bowker saw a pathologist gutting a body as the final insult, but Knight didn't know that. He spoke quickly to forestall any Bowker outburst.

'Did Billy eat breakfast before his last booze-up, doctor?'

Thornton turned his attention to Knight, blinking through his big shiny spectacles.

'That's a nasty-looking black eye you have, Sergeant. How did you get it—interviewing a suspect?'

'I walked into a fist,' Knight said curtly.

'To answer your question—the deceased ate a meal some hours before he died. I take it to be breakfast because it consisted of cornflakes of some kind and fried black pudding.'

'Bloody hell!' Knight said. 'Not together, I hope.'

'And fried bread,' Dr Thornton added.

Bedlow High Street was busy. This was Saturday, and shoppers were out in force. Back from the hospital, Bowker told Knight to put the Honda in the White Hart carpark.

'Not going back to the police station?' Knight asked. 'Still dodging the Superintendent?'

'Yes, we bloody are!' Bowker snapped. 'I saw a coffee shop in the shopping mall. We'll go there for a progress discussion.'

'We'd do better in The White Hart,' Knight suggested.

'He knows we're staying there, he might have left a message. Besides, if Morten's there, I don't want to see him.'

'You're getting paranoid about that private eye, sir,' Knight said in disapproval. 'I can't see what he does matters much.'

'Don't argue with me, just park the car at The White Hart.'

As Knight feared, the coffee shop was crowded with women and children, fed-up looking husbands, and plastic bags bulging with the results of hours of determined shopping. They found a table near the wall, and Bowker handed Knight a ten-pound note.

'Get me a large black coffee and three doughnuts—those with the jam in the middle. Postmortems make me hungry. And whatever you want yourself.'

Knight joined the queue at the counter, baffled by how seeing a dead body sliced up could give anyone an appetite. But Bowker seemed to be outside the ordinary rules.

He carried a tray back to the table with coffee and doughnuts for them both, nearly tripping over a four-year-old down on the floor playing with a plastic Action-Man toy.

'The Benedict they named this place after,' he said. 'Why did they make him a saint? Was he from round here?'

'He was an Italian.' Bowker was amazed by the question. 'He founded monasteries all over. Hundreds of years ago, that was.'

'Why?'

'How the hell do I know why?' Bowker was devouring his third doughnut. 'Maybe he wanted to get away from the Ronsons and the Burtons of his time.'

'All very well,' Knight said with a frown. 'It's not natural, though, depriving yourself of women.'

'It wouldn't suit you or me, Jack. But each to his own. There was a lot of holiness about in those days. Or so they say.'

'Not much of it left today, even in a small town like this. I never saw a body hit by a train before. He looked peaceful, all things considered. What sticks in my mind is we're dealing with a prize bunch of amateurs; that suicide wouldn't fool anyone.'

'Amateurs at killing people, but bloody good at it,' Bowker said. 'No knife or gun to find and trace, no blunt instrument—nothing we can use to identify Chummy. A fire and a fast train—he's ruthless and deadly.'

'Nasty,' Knight agreed, 'very nasty. We're not looking for a scoutmaster on this one. The little trick with the war memorial seems in character. What do you make of it?'

'It means he's getting irritated. We must be doing the right thing, whatever it is we're doing.'

'What *are* we doing? Tell me so I know in case Superintendent Billings asks me.'

Bowker gave him the cold eye. 'We still haven't checked alibis for the time of Billy's dive under the Oxford express, so that's what we're going to do next. I'll take the Burtons, you take Arnie and his idiot cousin Shane. We'll meet in the bar of The White Hart and have a pint of ale and compare notes before lunch. Then we'll arrest our murderer.'

'You'd better let me take the Burtons,' Knight said quickly. 'They're the type who provoke you to rage, and we don't want any brawling on the forecourt. You check Shane and Arnie.'

Bowker stared at him as if assessing his mental stability. 'That's the feeblest bloody excuse I've ever heard. You want to interrogate that niece of theirs!'

The look of incredulity on Knight's face was awesome.

'You think I fancy Cilla? Never in a million years, not even stranded with her on a desert island!'

'Why should I stand in your way? If you're that keen on her, you take the Burton filling station, and I'll do the off-licence and the boatyard.'

Knight let the discussion drop; he couldn't win it now.

'There are public phones outside,' Bowker said. 'If you've

had enough of that slush-favoured coffee, give the Incident Room a buzz and check if anything of interest has happened while we've been out.'

'You think the Superintendent is still there?'

'Why take chances? Go and phone, Jack.'

He was gone for the best part of ten minutes. He came back to the table to find Bowker finishing yet another doughnut.

'Interim report from DS Trimmer,' said Knight. 'Some progress, but not much. His team has managed to trace Billy as far as the Burton filling station. He was there about ten-thirty yesterday morning.'

'The Burton brothers!' Bowker's dark eyes gleamed.

'Just what I thought. But he didn't stay or talk to either of the brothers. He bought a gallon of petrol and drove off.'

'A gallon? *One?*'

'So Cilla told Trimmer. Remember the yellow swimsuit?'

'I could tell you fancied her by the way you were leering at her. She's got a sort of blank nobody-at-home look in her eyes. There's a lot wrong with the Burton family. What do you deduce from one solitary gallon?'

'That Billy was broke. And maybe that was the bait to get him to meet Chummy—the promise of cash in hand. Billy climbs into his scruffy old wreck and gets to the Burton filling station on the vapour in the fuel pipe. Spends his last quid on Four-Star and drives off to meet his doom.'

'Sounds about right,' Bowker conceded. 'Not too hard to track him that far, because the Burton place stands on the corner of the Abbotsbury estate. After that he's on Gallow-gate and could have turned into the town or away from it. If he went away from Bedlow, Trimmer has his work cut out to follow him.'

'So you reckon we can cross the Burtons off the list?'

'What are you talking about? If they were going to get Billy blind drunk and do him in, they wouldn't be seen with him at the filling station. They'd have arranged to meet him some-where out of sight; that stands to reason.'

'Seems to me the only way we ever cross any names off is when we find them dead or they're locked in a cell when the deed was done,' Knight complained. 'There's more news. DC Cote called in from her observation of Arnie's off-licence. She saw something interesting and took a few snaps for you. But she wanted you to know right away.'

'Know what? Don't keep me dangling!'

'Your favourite lawyer stopped at Arnie's this morning, about eleven o'clock. He came out again with a crate of cham-pagne and six bottles each of vodka, Scotch whisky, and brandy. And French brandy at that, not that cheap Greek muck. She's got a good eye for detail, the DC with the flashy hairdo who adores me.'

'Lloyd Davies, the crook's friend,' Bowker said in a malig-nant whisper. 'He's giving a party.'

'Arnie was out on the pavement in person to help him load all that booze into the back of his BMW.'

'He parked outside the shop on the double yellow line? Where was that bloody traffic warden who gave me a ticket?'

'Shirley Cote didn't mention her, so obviously she was away on her coffee break, or whatever traffic wardens take. What do you think—could your wily lawyer pal have bought anything besides expensive booze from Arnie for his party?'

Bowker had the unbelieving look of a man who's just heard his lottery ticket has won the ten million-pound prize.

Lloyd Davies owned a house in the new executive part of Bedlow, a suburb created for those citizens doing well enough to afford the monthly payments on a loan of £250,000. There were only nine houses in Summerfield Close—they were set well back from the road and had green space and trees between them.

This highly desirable residential area was on the far side of the Thames to the realities of Abbotsbury Estate. The Close ran off a pleasant tree-lined avenue of almost as expensive houses, at one end of which was a parade of half a dozen shops to serve them. Knight had been shown where Lloyd Davies lived by Trimmer on his guided tour of Bedlow villains' homes—he drove Bowker there for a stealthy look.

'See that?' Bowker said in grim satisfaction as they passed the shops. 'There's an upmarket off-licence on Davies' doorstep—or as near as makes no difference. Why does he drive into the town to buy from Arnie and risk a thirty-quid parking ticket if that Nazi woman is out on the prowl? Because Arnie can supply something he can't get elsewhere.'

'Maybe Arnie gives him long credit,' Knight suggested, feeling uneasy about the operation in hand. 'Or maybe he's in love with Arnie's sexy missus and dropped in to beg her to dump Arnie and move in with him. I would, if I earned as much as him.'

'And maybe Arnie retails prohibited substances, such as a man giving a party for his criminal friends might wish to buy.' Bowker wore an executioner's smile on his face.

'You don't know his friends are criminals,' Knight protested.

'They're not members of the League of Purity,' was all Bowker would say.

Lloyd Davies' home was a large brick-built house, with a red-tiled roof and a white neo-Georgian porch. It had a garage for two cars to the right and parking space on the gravel drive for five or six more.

'Don't get too close—we don't want to be seen,' Bowker said. He was scrunched down in the back of his tired-looking Honda in an impossible attempt to make himself inconspicuous.

There was half an acre of neatly trimmed lawn in front of the house and two oval flower beds with clumps of yellow roses. The BMW stood in the drive, gleaming in the sunshine. Presumably Davies had unloaded it.

'Nice,' Bowker said critically. 'Must be four bedrooms there, five maybe, several bathrooms. Sitting room and dining room and the rest of it downstairs. Big garden at the back. I'd guess we have four doors to cover. He's not married, someone told me; no kids for us to worry about upsetting.'

'He's divorced. How so four doors?'

'Fancy front door where we charge in. French doors opening on a patio at the back. A side door for the milkman and tradesmen to make deliveries to the kitchen.'

'That's only three.'

'And a door from the house into the garage so that our lawyer pal doesn't have to get wet if he goes out when it's raining.'

'Right, four exits to cover if they make a run for it. But if they get stuck into all that booze Shirley Cote saw, they'll be legless when we turn up.'

Bowker's grunt might indicate satisfaction or the opposite.

'Are we really going to waltz in on a lawyer's party and tell him he's breaking the law by handing around drugs with vodka and tonic and the onion-flavoured crisps?'

Knight was becoming ever so slightly desperate. 'I'd like to know because it could be a sticky end to two careers dedicated to law and order.'

'Everybody has to take chances, Jack. Otherwise the criminals would always come out on top. What sort of world would it be if that happened—it's bloody bad enough already. And anyway, you are acting under my orders, so nobody will hold you responsible if it's a total botch-up.'

'Then why have I got this sick feeling in my belly?'

'That's because you didn't eat a proper breakfast. I've told you scores of times how important good, regular solid meals are. Now drive us out of this nice little suburban hideaway, easy as my old granny enjoying a Sunday-afternoon spin in the country. No screaming tires—we don't want to attract attention.'

True to its name, Summerfield Close was a dead-end. Without going any nearer Lloyd Davies' house, Knight eased the car round and moved silently away. He was still very uneasy.

'It's not as if we suspected him of the Matthews murders,' he complained. 'Ronnie was worth good money to Davies. He paid him fees for buying houses. You can bet Davies bumped the fees well up because it was done in used ten-pound notes, which showed it was illegal money. If Davies buys a packet of reefers to liven up his party, it's nothing to do with our case.'

'We're coppers,' Bowker said in disapproval. 'Crime is always our business. I thought you knew that. Besides, reefers are for spotty teenagers and students, not grown-up crooks.'

'We're not in Bedlow to do a Wyatt Earp and clean up the town—they've got coppers of their own for that. We're here only to find the killer of Matthews and his family. The proper thing to do is pass on any suspicion we may have about pushers and dope fiends to Superintendent Billings and let him decide what to do about it. It's his town.'

'I never thought I'd see the day when a sergeant of mine said a thing like that!' Bowker was outraged. 'If you're as worried as that, you can take the rest of the weekend off. Starting now.'

'And miss the fun of running a lawyer in? I was only telling you what the proper thing was, in case you'd forgotten. I never suggested actually doing it. Sod the promotion—if you want to play gangbusters, I'm with you.'

'That's more like it, Jack. Stick with me—you'll be a real copper, not a desk detective.'

'I haven't felt so bad about a job since that Balls Pond Road fiasco,' Knight said.

'Where's that—up in that hellhole you came from?'

'Where else? I was one of a team trying to get a loony with a gun to come out and give himself up.'

'What sort of gun?' Bowker asked.

'It was a revolver. Old army issue, I think. He'd bought it in a pub. He was a born loser. His girlfriend gave him the elbow and went back to her mum's house, taking the baby with her. He went after her, and there was a screaming match for hours. The girl's mother tried to shove him out of the door when he waved the gun about and threatened to shoot himself. The next-door neighbours called us when they heard a shot.'

'Had he done himself in?'

'No such luck. He shot his girlfriend's mother in the back as she ran for help. When we got to Balls Pond Road, she was lying in the front garden bleeding, and he was at a downstairs window threatening to shoot anybody who came near the house.'

'Usual sort of hostage situation,' said Bowker. 'A loony half out of his mind waving a firearm about. You're supposed to play for time and talk him down, but it's tricky if there's somebody hurt. What happened, did you rush him front and back?'

'The Super in charge wanted to rescue the woman in the garden first and asked for volunteers. Me, silly young uniform needing my head testing, said I'd go. I crawled across the pavement and into the garden and there the bugger was at the open window. He couldn't miss me. There was this woman moaning and bleeding—I got her under the arms and dragged her away. Big woman she was, weighed a bloody ton.'

'It's like that *Crimewatch* programme on TV,' Bowker said with a distinct lack of patience. 'Tedious. Did he shoot you?'

'He shouted very nasty things at me while I was rescuing Mum. But he didn't fire at me, or I'd be bloody dead. Instead he went into the room and shot his girlfriend. She was stone dead when we broke in and nabbed him. Mum bled to death in the ambulance, leaving us with a nutter and a baby needing a change of nappy. It was a bloody fiasco.'

Bowker shook his head in sympathy. 'It's a rough old world. We do what we can. Why do you think tonight is going to be a fiasco?'

'There's a big problem in bagging the lawyer.'

'Only one? I can think of ten.'

'Crooks' friend he may be, but Lloyd Davies is a big number in Bedlow. He's sure to be on the committee of half the charities and do-good outfits in the town. The mayor will be his drinking pal. He'll get invited to garden parties by the

Lord Lieutenant of the county. I don't have to tell you how these legal buggers organise themselves into all the right places.'

'For all I know, he gets asked to dinner at Buckingham Palace by the Queen herself. Doesn't make any difference, a crook is a crook and he ought to be behind bars.' Bowker was very firm.

'But when you mention his name to Superintendent Billings and say you're applying for a warrant, he'll go psychotic.'

'I never doubted that for a moment. He'll go all sweaty about his promotion to Chief Superintendent. So we save him all that useless anxiety by not telling him what we're doing until after we've done it.'

'Bloody hell!' Knight moaned. 'You take chances!'

'In the ordinary way of things, I'd tell him what I'm doing,' Bowker said with a total lack of candour, 'as I did when we had the chance of nabbing Dougie Ronson and his porno stock. And he co-operated nicely by phoning Reading and getting their coppers to back us up. It's not the usual way of things this time, it's Saturday and it's after one o'clock.'

'We'll never get away with it!'

'The Superintendent will be home having lunch by now, and this afternoon he'll be playing tennis with his pals. He's very keen on the tennis, somebody told me. This evening he'll very likely be taking his wife out to dinner somewhere nice. It would be a shame to wreck his leisure time harassing him about details we can handle ourselves.'

Knight abandoned the argument. 'What do you want to do about Arnie?' he asked. 'Pull him in first? Or at the same time?'

'I want him left alone. He'll lead us to the Burton brothers eventually. I think I want Wayne and Gary Burton for the murder of the Matthews family. I'm not a hundred percent sure yet, but that's how it begins to look.'

'I've been telling you that pair did it ever since we arrived in

Bedlow. So we let Arnie run for a while and keep observation on his shop. Shirley Cote's going to hate you if she's stuck on that job much longer.'

'Hagen can take over from her as soon as Trimmer's got as far as he can with the search for where Billy went in his van.'

'Don't hold your breath waiting.' Knight was not impressed by the detecting abilities of the local coppers.

Bowker scowled. 'One thing might upset the applecart, and that's if Lloyd Davies has hysterics when we grab him and points the finger of guilt at Arnie as his supplier. I doubt if he will—not straightaway—he'll hang on to the information in hope of doing a deal with us later. Sell Arnie to us in return for letting him off.'

'I'm holding you to your promise,' Knight said. 'You stand me the best dinner to be had in Bedlow when we run the lawyer in—with champagne before and brandy after and a stripper. I'd like a young blonde with long legs and a big chest.'

'There's work to be done before you go berserk over undressed young women. How many times have I said we'll check alibis for the time of Billy's unfortunate death? Every bloody time I say it, something comes up to stop us. But not this time—we've got hours before we stroll in on the lawyer's party and ruin it. So drop me off by the bridge to have words with Shane while you go and talk to the horrible Burtons.'

Soon after ten that evening, Bowker's dusty grey car slid into Summerfield Close. Saturday evening and porch lights were on to deter burglars while the owners were out to dinner or at one of the nearby theatres. There were extra cars parked in the drives of three houses: guests for dinner. At Davies' house, seven cars stood in the drive.

Knight eased to a stop across the end of Lloyd Davies' drive, blocking in the visitors' cars parked on the gravel. Two police cars followed silently, roof lights switched off, then a large van—it parked at the end of the Close, blocking the road. Two uniforms stayed by it to intercept any escapees.

Bowker was in a bad mood. The cherished theory of solving the Matthews murders by deciding who dropped Billy Swanson over the Windmill Lane bridge had turned to smoke and ashes. The Burtons said they took the day off on Friday to go to Windsor races. As surly as ever, they gave Knight names of two trackside bookies they'd bet with.

Arnie Hinksey had also been out of Bedlow. He left for London by train at nine Friday morning and didn't get back until after five. And yes, he told Bowker with ill grace, the man he'd gone to see on business would confirm it. His name was Brown and his telephone number was et cetera. When Bowker asked him the nature of the transaction with Mr Brown, Arnie went silent.

'That kind of business,' Bowker said. 'I see.'

That left Shane at Batty's boatyard, with his gold earring and vacant expression. He had to think hard about his whereabouts the day before, but eventually a smile crossed his suntanned face.

'Mr Batty gave me the day off because I'm here on Saturdays and Sundays all through the summer. So Friday I had a lie-in till the middle of the morning, and then I took a boat up the river with Mr Batty's agreement, and I did some fishing. My mum made me a big packet of sandwiches. I had a nice day though I didn't catch much.'

'There's an evil scheme against us,' Knight said when Bowker related his frustration with Arnie and Cousin Shane. 'Every one of them with an alibi, and every one of them could be bogus. The first race at Windsor would be about 2.15. That gives the Burtons plenty of time to drop Billy under a train and get to the course to put a few bets on before the meeting ended. And Arnie could get off the train two stops down the line and be back in Bedlow to do Billy in and then go to London for his fake alibi with a crooked pal.'

'The smell of dead rat is overpowering,' Bowker said glumly.

'They all have somebody to vouch for them,' Knight agreed.

'Except Shane Hambleton,' Bowker pointed out. 'When I talked to Batty, he said Shane went off in the boat about half-past ten and wasn't seen again until after six. He could have moored out of sight and gone anywhere. I'm having the lock keepers checked to see if anybody remembers seeing him go through.'

'But he's mentally lacking,' Knight protested. 'You can't for a moment believe Shane is up to organising Billy's departure by train. What it comes to is we're back where we started—bloody nowhere.'

The white double garage door at Davies' house was up and over to show the BMW and a Japanese 4-wheel drive. And a door inside into the house. Bowker motioned one of the uniforms to watch it and walked silently across the trim lawn to the porch.

Knight was beside him. Ginny Bampton and three more uniforms followed—one with a sledgehammer in case more than a search warrant was needed to get them into the house. They waited for the rest of the force to fan out around the house, to cover the side door and garden door.

The curtains were drawn across all the downstairs windows and the thumping bass beat of rock music could be plainly heard. An excited high-pitched laugh, men's voices, two or three together—then a shout from the house across the road: *What's going over there?* Someone had spotted the police cars and had come out on his front lawn to stare.

'That's buggered it!' Bowker said. 'Ready or not, here we go. Stand by with the big hammer!'

He beat a thunderous rat-a-tat on the door with his clenched fist while Knight put his finger hard on the bell push and held it down. Nothing much happened inside the house; the rock music thumped on, the voices carried on. The nosy neighbor opposite advanced to the pavement on his side of the Close and repeated his question in a loud voice.

'What the hell's going on over there? Who's in charge?'

'If he opens his mouth again, I'll run him in!' said Bowker.

'For what?' Knight asked.

'Committing a public nuisance.'

Lloyd Davies' door opened. But it was not the lawyer himself, it was a pretty fair-haired woman in a blue party frock—short enough to show her thighs almost to where they joined. She had a big smile on her face and a half-full glass in her hand.

'Don, darling, we'd nearly given you up!' she burbled, before she got a good look at Denis Bowker under the porch light, huge and menacing in his crumpled dark suit, with a wolfish grin on his swarthy face.

'You're not Don.' She sounded amazed.

Bowker was reconciled to being mistaken for a chain-saw mass murderer by nervous women at night. It was part of the general unfairness of life. But this one didn't fly into a blind panic or try to slam the door. She threw herself at him and jumped up to wind her arms about his thick neck, her glass spilling vodka and melting ice cubes right down the back of his suit. Her warm body pressed very close to him.

'Come in!' she burbled. 'A real man at last—where have you been all evening?'

Bowker prised her loose and showed her his warrant card. But no sign of comprehension dawned on her face. He handed her over to WPC Bampton.

'Keep a grip on her, Constable. She's drunk. Or high. Come on, then, the door's been opened for us. No need to break it down.'

Inside was an entrance hall, a staircase on the right, open doors to the left and straight ahead. The rock music came from the room to the left. Bowker sent two uniforms upstairs to look around, the rest of them into the room with music. With Knight following him he charged straight ahead. He had caught sight of Davies through the open door and meant to run him in personally.

Ahead was a large sitting room, two extra-long settees facing each other, and low armchairs dotted about. Four people sprawled on the settees. One of them was the lawyer. He was in expensive casual wear: a collarless pink silk shirt, grey linen slacks, and cream moccasins with tassels.

His dark hair was untidy and he had an arm round the waist of a young woman Bowker and Knight recognised. She was in a black miniskirt and a semi-transparent white silk blouse with no bra. Even so, she was wearing more than the last time they saw her. She was one of Ronson's breakfast-time poolside playmates and she been naked then, except for tiny white bikini briefs.

It was Minky, the blonde who had fled into the house looking sick when Bowker mentioned little girls burnt to death.

'Hello, Minky,' Knight said with a smile. 'Why are you hiding your charms tonight?'

She was fuddled, but she knew she knew him and smiled back at him. A lot of women smiled at Handsome Jack—even when he had a black eye.

'What the hell's going on here?' Lloyd Davies shouted as he jumped up from the settee in a rage. 'What are you doing in my house?'

He was at least a foot shorter than Bowker and less than half his bulk. Under the circumstances, the confrontation was guaranteed not to be a success. The grin on Bowker's face became fiendish beyond description. He was staring at an expensive lead-crystal bowl on the coffee table between the facing settees. It held a fine white powder. There were traces of the powder on the green onyx tabletop itself.

Here's the sly little bugger who gets the local criminals off with a fourpenny fine, Bowker said to himself in glee. *Got him.*

'Evidence, Knight,' he said, 'take charge of that bowl—mind you don't smear any fingerprints on it.'

Davies made a grab at the bowl, although there was nothing he could do to make it or its contents disappear. Knight was there first. He snatched the bowl away, a handkerchief between it and his fingers.

'I'll take it out to the car for safety,' he said. 'That is if you can cope without me for a couple of minutes.'

'Now look here.' Lloyd Davies struggled to recover the situation. 'You can't invade my house—there'll be hell to pay over this when I talk to the Chief Constable.'

'Lloyd, what's going on?' the man on the facing settee said, his hand now away from his girl's thigh. He was in his fifties, silvery-haired, and in a fawn cashmere casual jacket. He looked important, or as if he believed he was important. The brunette beside him was thirty years younger and half-gone, her head lolling on his shoulder and her eyes closed.

'What are you going to do, Lloyd?' he went on uneasily. 'You know I can't afford to be arrested. There mustn't be a scandal, you understand.'

Bowker flashed another smile that would stop a runaway truck. 'I'm sorry to hear that because you are arrested. And when we've had a look at the rest of the house, we shall take you to the station to get your details and bring charges officially.'

'Lloyd!' the man complained. 'Do something!'

Bowker informed him, 'I have to tell you that if Mr Davies is your lawyer, you've got a problem. He's under arrest himself and won't be able to represent you.'

'There's no need to take this tone.' Davies abandoned bluster for a more conciliatory approach. 'Let's have a private talk, Inspector, you and I—I'm sure we can come to a sensible agreement. You may think you wish to charge me, and naturally I shall contest any charges vigorously at the proper time. But we may find all that unnecessary if we discuss it calmly first.'

'Caught in possession,' Bowker said. 'I'll be very interested to hear how you try to slither out of that.'

'If I am threatened with arrest, I shall make a phone call, and you will be compelled to apologise to me. But don't think that will be the end of it—I intend to pursue you relentlessly for your outrageous and unlawful behaviour.'

'You're not being threatened with arrest,' Bowker said with a malignant grin, 'you're being arrested. This is the real thing. You don't have to say anything, but anything you do say will be taken down and used in evidence. I bet nobody ever said that to you before.'

The lawyer's face flushed, but he controlled himself. He felt something was not right. This policeman was a bruiser, no brain to speak of; you only had to look at him to know that. Compared with a first-class legal mind, he was a non-starter. Davies made the same mistake other lawbreakers had made, to their cost.

'The thing is this, Inspector,' he said, 'there's no need for you to arrest any of my friends or subject them to the dreadful indignity of appearing in a police station. They're innocent of any wrongdoing; you can see that. As I am myself, though maybe I'm overgenerous in my hospitality.'

'That's an unusual way of looking at it,' Bowker said with undisguised relish. 'Offering your friends South American white snuff is taking hospitality a bit far, some might say. A judge, for instance. Sometimes judges get very shirty to find gents of the legal profession in front of them. They think it's letting the side down. A really irritated judge might think seven years in chokey about the right length of time for you to repent.'

Davies pushed his heavy glasses up his nose and ploughed on, trying to retrieve the irretrievable.

'My suggestion is that you let everyone leave except me. I have no objection to going with you. Any charge will be a formality.'

'I have a counter-suggestion.' Bowker beckoned to WPC Bampton to come in from the hall. 'This officer will escort you to a police car we have waiting outside. Your friends will join you at the police station shortly.'

He had chosen weight-lifter size Ginny Bampton to make Davies feel inadequate.

'You're making the worst mistake of your life.' Davies was in an intimidating mood again. Bowker grinned happily.

Now the house was secured, he called the rest of his team in.

'Trimmer, everyone in the house is under arrest. Caution them and put them in the black maria ready to leave when I give the word. Cote, take charge of the women. Go through their handbags while Sgt Trimmer is having the van brought up. Hagen, you look through this room and the other downstairs rooms for any little packets of banned substances hastily chucked under furniture to bamboozle us.'

Knight was back from stowing the crystal bowl and contents in an evidence bag in Bowker's car.

'The neighbours are out in strength,' he reported. 'They seem annoyed about police activity in their Close. It sort of lowers the tone. You'd think we were the Ku Klux Klan burning a wooden cross on the lawn, the way they're carrying on.'

'They'll very likely write a letter of protest to the *Times*,' said Bowker. 'I've a good mind to tell them that we're raiding a whorehouse—that'd do wonders for their property values. But duty before pleasure. We'll take a look upstairs; there must be people we haven't found. I counted seven cars outside, and we've seen only a few people so far—and one of them lives here.'

'Four couples were dancing in the dark in the room next door, all of them out of their skulls,' Knight said. 'I glanced in on my way back. One of them decided to get tough with the uniforms and is lying on the carpet with handcuffs on.'

Two of the bedrooms had been in use. Under the sardonic stare of uniformed coppers two glassy-eyed men were getting dressed—and two very much younger women were trying to do the same, but not very seriously, giggling and flaunting themselves.

'Go downstairs,' Bowker said to the nearest uniform. 'I want WPC Bampton here to take charge of these shameless young ladies whose bodies you're goggling at. Find her and send her up.'

One of the young ladies stuck her tongue out at Bowker.

'You're spoiling the party,' she said dreamily. 'Why don't you go away and leave us alone? Nobody invited you.'

'True,' Bowker agreed. 'I'm just a gate-crasher. Knight, look in the drawers of that bedside cabinet. See if there's any more prohibited on hand.'

'There's going to be trouble over this,' said the man sitting on the edge of a bed putting on his dark blue socks. 'A lot of trouble. This is a private house; you've no right to break in.'

Bowker grinned and waved his search warrant.

'This gives me the right. You're under arrest, if you haven't been told already. And so is the young lady putting her bra on. Anything either of you say may be taken down and used, et cetera. Feel free to say whatever's on your mind. And you're absolutely correct, there's going to be big trouble. But you're the one on the receiving end of it.'

'Aha, look what I've found!' Knight's hand was in the top drawer of a bedside cabinet, on which stood an empty champagne bottle. He came up with a handful of blue and red capsules.

'Give you the energy of a nineteen-year-old, do they?' Bowker said to the man sitting on the bed. 'You look about fifty to me, flabby round the middle, bit of a boozer. I can understand you need a pill or two to keep up with the young lady when she strips off. Sad to say, for men suffering from the droops, it's against the law to have those capsules, unless your doctor prescribed them, which he'd be a bloody fool to do. But we'll ask him.'

'They're not mine! I've never seen them before!'

Ginny Bampton loomed up in the bedroom doorway behind Bowker, broad, muscular, and hard-faced in her blue serge uniform.

'You want me, sir?'

'This young lady is having difficulty getting her clothes on. And there's another in the next room. Take charge of them, will you, and bring the men downstairs with them. I want to have all the prisoners out of the house in the next ten minutes so we can start processing them at the station. Otherwise we'll be at it all bloody night!'

Downstairs DS Trimmer had marshalled all the available partygoers into the police van now parked outside, under the eyes of the neighbours and their guests.

'Sergeant Trimmer, Bampton's bringing the last four down from the bedrooms. They're to go to the station with the others. All except Lloyd Davies, of course. He's on his own in a car and is to be kept separate. Send him off first and keep him away from the others at all times.'

'Bloody hell!' Trimmer muttered as Ginny Bampton brought her four prisoners down the stairs. 'Did you know you've got one of our local magistrates in that lot, sir?'

'Not surprised. Bedlow's an interesting town, very close-knit and matey. I've even come across someone I know: a pretty young woman with a nice chest who calls herself Minky. She might turn into a useful source of information about the Matthews fire, if she's ever ready to talk. She's on leg-over terms with a lot of your local villains. As for your magistrate, I think his letter of resignation will be in the post tomorrow. That's if he feels well enough to write it. Any others you recognise?'

'Bald-headed man who was dancing with a little redhead. She'd taken her clothes off. I know him by sight—he's area director of a bank in High Street. I'm not sure which until we question him.'

'There'll be more surprises in store,' Bowker said blithely, 'Mr Davies is sure to have a wide circle of important friends.'

'There's been nothing like this in Bedlow for years,' Trimmer said, 'not since the Evangelicals were caught running a teenage vice racket. Girls and boys, they had. The town was overrun by reporters from the Sunday newspapers when that happened.'

'Skip the unholy past and listen very carefully,' Bowker told him. 'Keep Davies away from all the others. Sling him in a cell to wait until I get there. Process his guests. Get their names, addresses, and the rest of it. Put the frighteners on them; tell them that serious charges will be brought against them. If they feel like giving a statement blaming Davies, encourage them.'

Trimmer got his notebook out and started to scribble in it as if afraid of forgetting his instructions.

'When that's done, send them off home with a warning they'll be notified when and where to appear,' Bowker added.

'I'll have the buggers shaking in their shoes,' Trimmer said happily. 'You want me to hang on to Davies, sir?'

'Fingerprint him. Then just lock him up and let him stew.'

'If I can ask, what are the fingerprints for?'

'Just for fun, to depress him.'

But privately Bowker was wondering if there was any chance of Davies' prints matching any of the many found on the newspaper in Billy Swanson's scruffy old van. It wasn't likely, but still worth checking—a copper could always hope.

'Where will you be while we do all this paperwork, sir?'

'I'm staying here for a while with Knight and we're going to look through everything in the house, from attic to dog kennel. And most especially any documentation we find. This is a never-to-be-repeated chance of thumbing through the lawyer's secrets. There's no telling what nasty little items we might find.'

'Just the two of you? It would be quicker with a team.'

Bowker hated teams, but he knew better than to say so.

'Right, Sergeant, many hands make light work. Leave me a couple of uniforms to poke around in the garage and the garden shed and the bins. If Davies cracks up and wants a lawyer after he's been in the cell for ten minutes, remind him it's Saturday night and he's drunk.'

'Drunk?'

'Drunk,' Bowker repeated straight-faced. 'When I arrested him, his speech was slurred, and he was swaying on his feet.'

'Nearly fell down,' Knight added. 'Very wobbly.'

'Advise him to sleep it off. Then you'll see what can be done for him in the morning, and all that old Mary Ellen.'

'Got it, sir. And if you don't mind me saying, this is a good night for us. I never expected to see Lloyd Davies run in.'

'I'm glad you're enjoying it too, Sergeant. I feel as if I've put my hand in the church bazaar lucky-dip tub and pulled out a solid gold bar. Nothing that feels this good can last.'

'Pity the Burton brothers weren't invited to the party,' said Knight. 'Especially as they provided the necessary via Hinksey. Bit like the ugly sisters at Cinderella's ball—too downmarket to mingle socially.'

'A pair of bloody roughnecks,' Bowker agreed. 'But we'll get them, never fear.'

Sunday was normally a day off for Superintendent Billings. He'd phone Bedlow police station about eight-thirty, after finishing breakfast, to check which drunks, vagrants, and housebreakers had been taken in charge on Saturday night. No action was necessary on his part—he could sag into an armchair and immerse himself in the Sunday newspapers.

His comfortable routine was dynamited by the news of Bowker's Saturday-night raid. Billings was astounded to hear of the haul of miscreants the Inspector had brought in. And perturbed.

By nine o'clock that morning, Billings was at his desk. And so put out that he wasn't wearing his smart uniform with the shiny silver buttons. An old tweed sports jacket with leather-patched elbows—he'd never been seen at the station before dressed so casually. It was taken by subordinates as a sure sign of mental distress.

'I don't know what to say to you.' He stared at Bowker across his desk. 'You've ignored me and deliberately flouted my authority. I don't begin to understand your motive. You must be aware that you've created a situation that can turn into total disaster.'

'I thought I'd arrested a handful of lawbreakers, sir.' Bowker was dangerously muted. The *sir* was a warning note to anyone not wholly deaf.

'Why didn't you tell me what you were planning?'

'I saw no reason to involve you in a routine arrest.'

Billings' eyes rolled upward dangerously. He was fast losing his grip on his temper.

'You're being deliberately obstructive,' he said sharply. 'It was not a routine arrest, and you knew that damn well. I want no prevarication from you, understand? You went ahead in the full knowledge that the outcome would be embarrassing to me.'

'Why is that?' Bowker tried to sound interested.

'This is a small town. I know most of the men you arrested. I get asked to their charity dinners and business lunches. One of them is a member of the tennis club where I play. My wife sits on charity committees with the wives of some of these men. How do you suppose she or I can face them again?'

'Pity about your social life,' Bowker said in a voice like an iceberg colliding with the *Titanic*. 'What's that got to do with running in lawbreakers?'

'Don't pretend to be dense!' Billings snarled.

'What would have been bloody embarrassing last night would be finding you with your friends at the party,' Bowker countered.

It wasn't a question of thinking the unthinkable—he'd said the unsayable. Billings' face turned black with rage. How could anyone bracket him with dope fiends?

'That remark was outright insolence,' he said. 'Slighting and injurious. Make no mistake about it, Inspector, I fully intend to bring disciplinary charges against you. There's no place for misfits like you in the modern police service. I don't know how you've lasted this long—God alone knows how you got promoted up to Inspector.'

It was in Bowker's mind to tell him, but he decided he'd let the moment go. A certain respect was due to senior officers— even the stupidest ones. Billings was not disposed to ease off. He had rank, but not Bowker's intelligence; he didn't even then fully comprehend what the Inspector had done.

'You'll be lucky if you're still in the service when I finish with you,' he declared savagely. 'The very least you can expect is to be reduced to constable in uniform.'

'Friendship I can understand,' Bowker said, 'although there's not much of it about anywhere. But sympathy for fat businessmen jolting themselves with drugs to get a leg over young girls—I find that hard to understand. Perhaps you can explain it to me. *Sir.*'

This second *sir* was very definitely an act of insolence.

The Superintendent took a sheet of paper from his blotter. On it was a list of names, neatly typed.

'If I had to compile a *Who's Who in Bedlow-on-Thames,* most of these names would be in it,' he said unhappily. 'You arrested a respected magistrate, a prominent town councillor in line to be mayor next year, six influential businessmen, including a local director of the West Country Bank.'

'I was impressed myself when I saw the list of names,' Bowker said very cheerfully. 'When we ran them in, they were anonymous punters snorting up cocaine and fumbling young women's private parts. Pathetic and sad and small-time. To think they turn out to be the upper strata of this pleasant riverside town!'

The mockery in his voice was unconcealed. Billings glared at him as if wishing him dead, as very probably he did.

'One of the women you subjected to the indignity of transport in a police van happens to be a daughter of Sir Osbert Nunally, the biggest landowner for miles around,' he went on, staring at the list with an appalled expression. 'I see she's charged with possession of controlled substances!'

'A loose woman.' Bowker shook his head. 'She ought to know better. Offering her body for drugs, that's all it amounts to. If her father were a bus driver, you'd know what name to call her. But as he's titled, I suppose she's just high-spirited.'

'Fortunately, I don't recognise any of the other women.' Billings ignored the jibe.

'I can help you with one name.' Bowker grinned. 'Minky, she calls herself in company. Real name Maureen Pilcher— she's eighteen years old, and her father's a carpenter. She left school with no qualifications beyond the ability to read fashion magazines. Slowly. Life ambition: to become an international fashion model. Career progress to date: bare-breasted modelling in photos for low and sleazy men's magazines.'

'I know nothing of her,' Billings said firmly.

'Of course not,' Bowker agreed. 'But she has breakfast in the nude with someone we take a close interest in—Douglas Ronson, the porn baron. She knows things about him we'd like to know. I have hopes she'll decide it is to her advantage to tell us what she knows.'

Billings put the list down carefully and tried to collect his thoughts. If he had been a smoker, he'd have been on his fifth or sixth cigarette of the interview by now.

'There may be something in what you say. But all the same, it won't do,' he said, 'heads are going to roll over this. Yours.'

Bowker ignored the dark warning. 'You've left out the best part.' He grinned ferociously at the Superintendent. 'Mr

Lloyd Davies, legal eagle and wrongdoer's best friend. Caught in the act and charged not just with possession but also the distribution of unlawful et ceteras.'

'How do you get to that?'

'We'll say he was taking cash for the coke he supplied. He'll deny it and ask his guests to say it was free. If they back him, it's an admission they were snorting it. And if they decline to back him, he's got no evidence he wasn't selling it to them.'

'Too damn devious,' Billings said. 'Isn't it enough to charge him with possession?'

'Don't like half-measures. I'd rather go for broke. Meanwhile, Davies is in custody till we put him up at a magistrate's court tomorrow morning. They'll have to find another magistrate, not the one I had the pleasure of meeting last night. He was in bed with a girl young enough to be his granddaughter. On speed.'

'There can be no doubt Davies is a man of doubtful character; I will concede that much,' Billings said through gritted teeth. 'And as I understand it, you have a serious case against him, if the substance recovered from his house proves to he cocaine. Or heroin. Those are questions of fact, though Davies will have an answer, believe me.'

'His fingerprints all over the bowl it was in. That makes a solid case.'

'You haven't got the results yet. But supposing you're right; that should prove the case against him. But the others—do you know the firepower you're facing?'

'Sod that!' Bowker said aggressively. 'What matters is to put Davies out of business permanently. Get him convicted; get him struck off by the lawyers' union. The effect of that will be to land most of the serious criminals in Bedlow behind bars.'

Billings sat up straight in his chair and gave Bowker an icy glare. 'Inspector, you were not sent here for that purpose.

You came here specifically to investigate the murder of Matthews and his family and to apprehend those responsible. And as far as I know, you have achieved nothing on the case, nothing at all. Even the confounded private detective brought in by the newspaper editor has done more than you. You have blundered about on non-related cases.'

Bowker's blood pressure was rising toward the high numbers at the implication of Billings' accusation.

'The Matthews case is well in hand,' he growled. 'These other crimes came to light during my investigation. So I ran them in, as any copper would. I'm damned if I can see you have anything to complain about.'

This time he didn't bother to say *'sir.'* He'd had enough of the Superintendent and wanted to get out of his office. He had work to do. He had been hoping to take Sunday off and go home to see his wife and children for the day; but after last night's catch, there were things to be done to extract the maximum advantage. The family outing would have to go ahead without him; he'd call his wife and explain.

'After what's happened, I'm having difficulty taking what you say seriously,' Billings said.

Bowker fixed him across the desk with a glare that would halt an Alpine avalanche.

'I've been in Bedlow four days,' he blared. 'Four bloody days—your lot got nowhere with the Matthews case in three months! So don't come the old soldier with me. You'll have the murderer in your cells in another four days—maybe less.'

There was a spiteful glint in Billings' eyes as he scribbled something on his blotter.

'Four days,' he sneered. 'I'll remind you that you said that. As far as I'm concerned, you are completely discredited.'

'I can see from the look on your face that the Superintendent was thrilled about us running that bunch in last night,' Knight said when Bowker reached the Incident Room. 'Instant promotion for all of us, is it? Recommended for the Queen's Medal?'

Bowker's scowl brought his thick black eyebrows right down to the bridge of his nose. He said nothing—any regret about the four-day promise he'd made under provocation was his own affair and was not for discussion.

Knight went on, 'To add to your festival mood, Lloyd Davies is now talking to a lawyer. Apparently he expected to be given the use of an interview room for the consultation, maybe even a blonde secretary. The uniform in charge of the cells today had other thoughts, and Mr Davies is talking to his legal adviser in the comfort and privacy of his cell.'

'Bloody good thing, too,' Bowker muttered fiercely. 'I'll buy that copper a pint when he's off duty. What else?'

'DS Trimmer wants to talk to you—he's hovering over there.'

Bowker crossed the room and stood by Trimmer, topping him by a head. 'Give me some good news, Sergeant. I'm losing that good feeling we had last night. I knew it couldn't last.'

'About Billy Swanson, sir. We placed him at Burtons' filling station about 10.30 on Friday morning, as you know. He seems to have turned toward the town centre on Gallowgate, and we found a traffic warden who remembered seeing that scruffy old van go by and hoped he'd park so she could write him a ticket.'

'Not that Nazi woman who attacked me!' Bowker's face darkened dangerously.

'No, from what I heard, that was just off High Street. Billy's van was spotted the other side of the railway bridge. If it was his. We can't be certain Billy had the only dirty old blue van, though I've never seen another like it.'

Bowker took Trimmer by the arm and led him to the town map on the wall.

'Just there'—Trimmer stabbed with his finger—'she was

doing a line of parked cars outside the shops along there. A bonanza for her, she told me. She'd ticketed eight in a row and the van would make it nine, her lucky number. But though he dithered as if he meant to stop, he drove on when he saw her.'

'And she lost interest and didn't see where he went?'

'No reason to, except that he was heading for the railway arch, which means he was going to the town centre.'

'He was on his way to meet someone,' Bowker said. 'But who?'

Trimmer studied the map. 'If he turned right after he'd gone under the bridge, he'd be in Penny Lane. Where Mrs Druce lives.'

'The thought had occurred to me. But it's a bit public around those blocks of flats to lug a dead-drunk about in day-light and load him into a van. Have you got somebody out there asking?'

'Hagen's there right now, ringing doorbells—if anyone saw a blue van, he'll find them.'

'If Billy went past Penny Lane and along the High Street, he'd come to Old Church Yard, where Hinksey's off-licence is. But he couldn't park there because of that demented woman in uniform.'

'No, sir.' Trimmer had been warned by Knight not to get involved with Bowker in any chat about meter maids.

'If Cote had been on observation over that Help the Hope-less charity shop we'd know if Billy turned up to put the squeeze on Arnie. Then we'd know Arnie was the right one to run in for the Matthews job. Why did he have to choose that day to get himself done in—the one day I told Cote to get her hair done at Moira Druce's salon and pick up the gossip?'

'Bit of bad luck,' Trimmer said carefully, not wanting to get caught up in any nasty recrimination Bowker had in mind.

'If that's where Billy was going, where could he park his van without getting a ticket?' Bowker asked.

'Maybe in the streets back of St Bardolph's Church. Parking's allowed there, if you can find a vacant space.'

'Maybe even in Minching Lane, the kerb outside the burnt-out shop!' Bowker said in disbelief.

'In my experience, the parking meters in those streets are all taken by the residents, from early morning to six at night. Far more likely, he'd go to the public carpark, behind the shopping mall. I've sent WPC Bampton there to question the attendant who takes the money when you leave. It's a long shot, as he must see hundreds of cars every day, but you said yourself: Billy's van is distinctively horrible.'

Bowker stared hard at the map. 'Wherever he parked, if he did, he didn't necessarily go to call on Arnie Hinksey. He could just as easily have strolled down to the river bridge and Batty's boatyard. Except Shane Hambleton had the day off Friday—but he was there to pick up a boat and go fishing.'

There was so much outright loathing in his voice when he said 'fishing' that Trimmer thought it best to keep silent.

'Batty gave me the impression that Shane went off on his own, but he could have put in to the bank somewhere along Spinster's Reach to pick up Billy, if they'd arranged it on the phone.'

'True enough,' Trimmer agreed. 'I'll send someone to ring the doorbells all along there to ask if anyone saw a boat pick up a man in a dirty blue boilersuit. Useful, Billy wearing that. It makes him easy to remember.'

'Except so far nobody remembers seeing him.'

'Early days yet, sir. We'd have done all this house-to-house yesterday, except we were busy raiding Ronson's cold store full of pornography. Come to think of it, we've had a busy time ever since you arrived in Bedlow, what with last night's raid on the lawyer's party. Is it always this busy where you are?'

'Busy?' said Bowker, straight-faced, 'It's been a rest cure, coming to Bedlow. I like these quiet little towns where nothing much ever happens.'

Trimmer stared at him sideways, wondering whether to take him seriously.

'Keep at it, Sergeant,' Bowker encouraged him, 'and give your informants a good kicking—some nasty little Bedlow crook must know what Billy Swanson was up to. I'm taking Knight with me to make Vereker's life a misery.'

'Why, what's he done?' Trimmer asked.

'It's what he *hasn't* done that's irritating me. The last time I saw him, I asked if he brokered the insurance on the warehouse in Reading for Dougie Ronson. He pretended he couldn't remember and promised to check and let me know. And he hasn't.'

Vereker's house in Cherry Tree Way was large and modern. And empty. There was no answer when Knight rang the bell, though he kept his finger on the button for half a minute. No answer even when Bowker used his fist on the door like a hammer.

'Ten o'clock on a Sunday morning, and he's not at home.' Knight grinned. 'It's a bit early for the pub. Do you think he's gone to church?'

'He struck me as a churchgoing man the minute I laid eyes on him,' Bowker agreed gravely. 'A lot on his conscience, I imagine. If he's got a conscience.'

'Pity he wasn't invited to Lloyd Davies' snorting party. Then we'd have him all nicely bundled up.'

'I think he was invited,' Bowker said. 'When I knocked on the door, it was opened by a woman wearing the shortest skirt that I ever remember seeing outside an ice-skating rink. I took her to be a tart when she flung her arms round my neck and rubbed her chest against me.'

'I noticed that,' Knight said. 'I fully expected her to wrap her legs round your waist and rub the rest of her against you—I was kicking myself for not having DC Cote's camera with me.'

Bowker gave him a killer look and went back to his old Honda.

'At the police station, she was identified as Deborah Nunally,' he went on, 'Superintendent Billings chewed my ear off because she was pulled in and charged.'

'Well he might,' Knight said with a broad smile, 'daughter of Sir Country Squire who owns half the land round here. I'd like to have a girlfriend like that, from the upper crust. Champagne for breakfast, horseback riding to get the circulation going, a sly leg-over in the back of Daddy's Rolls-Royce on the way up to London for the opera.'

'She's a junkie.'

'I know,' Knight said. 'We can't all be perfect.'

Bowker realised his leg was being pulled. 'The point is, when she opened the door and before she saw me properly, she called me "Don." Someone by the name of Don was expected. And we happen to know a Donald. An irritating insurance broker.'

'She must have been a long way gone on the illegal substances if she mistook you for Vereker. But he can't be the only Donald in Bedlow.'

'I'll give you that. But in small towns there are connections—we've seen plenty of it here already. Connections in business and other shared interests. Vereker is a client of Davies. I know that because I asked Davies when I was in his office.'

'Even so, it's a bit bloody thin.'

'Moreover and notwithstanding, there are only two names in Lloyd Davies' address book with a first initial D. I went through it carefully to check on his pals. The woman you lust after, Deborah Nunally. And Donald Vereker.'

'I'm glad you found something useful for all those hours

that we spent going through Davies' house. What a waste of time that was—not a scrap of evidence about anything. That lawyer's got some sort of compulsion—it's a mental disease, being neat and tidy as that.'

'Disappointing,' Bowker conceded, 'but not a total write-off. We know his shoe size and who's on his Christmas-card list.'

'For the sake of argument, say Vereker was asked to the party. He wasn't there when we gate-crashed, so we've nothing on him,' Knight said. 'Maybe he meant to drop in later and it was closed down by the time he arrived. A touch of the flashing blue light outside the house, and he wouldn't even turn into the Close.'

'Maybe he decided not to go at all. You can bet it wasn't the first sniffing party Lloyd Davies gave. Vereker would know what to expect. It could explain why his wife left him.'

'What's that got to do with the price of tea in China? It's not our job to find runaway wives; you said so yourself.' Knight was mystified. 'Even if you overlook that and send me off to be punched in the eye every so often.'

Bowker was patient with him. 'What I'm saying is that on a Saturday night Vereker wouldn't stay home alone with a can of beer to watch a third-rate comedy show and a terrible old movie on TV. Turning down the lawyer's party and a romp with Minky or the squire's daughter or both of them—he must have had something else planned. Like taking his girl-friend out.'

'Come to think of it,' said Jack Knight, 'I might even prefer Moira Druce myself—she's got the look of a stayer. Debbie and Minky look like hit-and-run girls to me. Like eating a Chinese meal—an hour later, you're wondering why you bothered with it.'

'All this back-street fantasising!' Bowker said. 'We've work to do and a murderer to catch. Vereker didn't bring Moira home for the night, or they'd still be here eating bacon and eggs and drinking coffee. So they probably went to her flat. Start this car and take us to Penny Lane.'

'That's what they call deduction, is it? I've often wondered how it was done. What if they've gone to Brighton for the weekend and are shacked up nice and cosy in the Grand Hotel down on the seafront? Your detecting will look sick and sorry then.'

Bowker bared his big square teeth and said *'Drive!'*

The Benedict shopping mall was closed Sundays, and Bedlow High Street was deserted but for a few people outside St Bardolph's Church—mostly elderly couples looking mildly uncomfortable in their go-to-church clothes. It would take a lot more than women priests to make anyone take religion seriously, Bowker thought. Not counting the loony varieties, of course, where the members wave their arms about and spout gibberish and think they've got a personal message from up above. There was always a market for loopiness.

A police car was parked in Penny Lane. No sign of DC Hagen or the uniform who drove the car—they were in the building named Isabella, pursuing sightings of the dirtiest old van in Britain and a little crook in a greasy blue boilersuit.

Moira Druce opened her door fairly promptly this time. Bowker had his warrant card in his hand, even though he was sure she'd remember him. Once seen, never forgotten. But he didn't want to go through the rape routine so early in the day.

Moira was looking inviting this morning. She was dressed in a flimsy silk negligee that looked very new, her hair was fluffed out, and there was a happy look on her face. It faded the minute she saw Denis Bowker—she recognised him, all right.

'You've come at an inconvenient time,' she said, getting over her initial surprise, 'Why don't you call back this afternoon?'

'It's all right, Mrs Druce,' Bowker assured her with a smile he tried to make appealing. 'It's Donald Vereker we want a word with.'

'In that case, you'd better come in,' she said and led him and Knight to her sitting room. Vereker was sitting in an armchair, legs crossed and very much at his ease. He held a cup of coffee in one hand and a Sunday newspaper in the other. He was wearing just shirt and trousers, no tie or socks, relaxing after a late breakfast. His fair hair was arranged casually.

He looked up from the paper in surprise and then scowled when the two policemen marched into the room.

'Sit down,' Moira said to them. 'Would you like coffee?'

Bowker lowered himself on to the striped sofa and said they'd only be a minute.

'What do you want?' Vereker demanded, suddenly aware that he was the subject of their interest, not Moira.

'Just a couple of questions.' Bowker made it sound so menacing that Vereker's hand shook and coffee slopped into his saucer. Knight made a great performance of producing a notebook and ballpoint pen, as if to write down every word Vereker said.

'Look here, Inspector, it's a damned liberty bursting in here on a Sunday. It's an invasion of privacy, and I intend to make a formal complaint about it.'

'By all means,' Bowker said with ferocious affability. 'Write that down, Knight—Mr Vereker is lodging an official complaint about being interviewed on Sunday.'

'*Official complaint,*' Knight murmured, writing the words down very slowly to make Vereker feel a fool.

'Our problem is this,' said Bowker. 'Crime does not stop on a Sunday. It may surprise you, a man used to having his weekends free for leisure pursuits, but we have to work a seven-day week to keep up with all the wrongdoing that goes on.'

Although Vereker was only half-dressed, the heavy gold watch was on his wrist. He was the type to keep it on in bed.

He gave an impatient sigh and twisted his arm to glance at the dial.

'Make it as brief as you can,' he said unhelpfully.

'The last time we met,' Bowker said, 'you were talking to Fred Morten, the private enquiry agent in The White Hart hotel. He volunteered the information that you'd retained him to look for your wife.'

'I wouldn't need to spend money if you did your job and found her,' Vereker said spitefully. 'Have you any idea what that man charges an hour?'

Bowker ignored the question as beneath contempt. 'I asked you on that occasion if you handled the insurance of a man named Ronson. In particular the insurance on a commercial building in Reading. You promised to let me know.'

'It slipped my mind,' Vereker said quickly. 'I've been busy.'

'When do you think you'll have time to check it?' Bowker was still being affable.

'I'll do it sometime tomorrow. Why do you want to know?'

'Perhaps you haven't heard—Ronson has been in custody since Friday. He's not enjoying it at all, locked up in a cell on his own twenty-four hours a day. Meals from the police canteen—it almost counts as cruelty, feeding him that garbage.'

'I didn't know.' Suddenly Vereker was very cautious.

'The reason he's locked up is because we went over to Reading to see this dilapidated cold store, which I'm sure you'll tell me you never heard of. You wouldn't believe what we found there—tons and tons and tons of pornography Ronson imports for sale up and down the Thames valley. Knight, remind me of some of the video titles.'

Knight turned through the pages of his notebook with a solemn expression on his face.

'*Nazi Torture Chamber 3,*' he read aloud. '*Boy Scouts Camping. Lolita's Little Sister. Benny's Twelfth Birthday Party.*'

'And a lot more like that,' Bowker cut in, seeing the look of disgust on Moira's face as the implications dawned on her. 'Not just videos but magazines with photos of leisure activities you wouldn't think humanly possible.'

'No!' Moira's hand flew to her mouth.

'Worth a lot of money when sold to armchair perverts,' Bowker went on. 'I've been wondering how Ronson could cover his stock against fire, flood, and theft—the usual risks. No respectable insurance company would touch it. He'd need bogus documentation to prove it was knitting patterns and keep-fit videos. And help from a friendly bent broker would be very valuable to him.'

Vereker went red in the face. 'Are you suggesting I'd be involved in something like that!'

'You don't know if you brokered the insurance till you take a look at your files,' Bowker said with genial ferocity, 'in your best interests, the question ought to be cleared up fast. That's why I'd like you to consult your records in the office tomorrow. I'll drop in at midday for a look at any papers you find.'

'I will not be blackguarded in front of a personal friend and take it lying down!' Vereker said loudly. 'Do what you like at midday. Long before that I shall be in Superintendent Billings' office, reporting your crass and bullying attitude. You're going to regret bursting in here this morning.'

Bowker grinned at him, the hangman's grin he kept for people with a high opinion of their own importance, the grin they saw just before the trapdoor opened under their feet. 'If you won't tell me what I want to know, it will take me no time at all to get a warrant to inspect your records and remove anything with a bearing on Ronson's illegal business operations. He's facing serious charges, and he'll get a prison sentence.'

'That's nothing to do with me!'

'Furthermore,' Bowker went on, his tone hardening to granite, 'there's a link between Ronson and Matthews, the newspaper shopkeeper who was burned to death with his family some months ago. Matthews was one of Ronson's outlets for videos. So you see why we're interested in everything to do with Ronson and his porn.'

Vereker had the sense to keep his mouth shut. Moira blushed a fiery red at the mention of Ronnie Matthews and videos, and she stared at Bowker in shame and dire dismay. A romp on a TV video before a romp on the bed was one thing; burning people to death was altogether another.

Bowker ignored her and glared hard at Vereker. 'Were you invited to a party that Lloyd Davies, the well-known lawyer, gave at his house last night?'

'No!' Vereker shook his head vigorously in denial.

'But you have been to parties at his house in the past?'

'I don't think so.' Vereker was very cautious. 'But perhaps I have—I know a lot of people, and I'm asked to a lot of parties and functions. I'd have to check with my diary to be certain.'

'Write that down, Knight—he can't remember for sure whether he's been to parties at Davies' house or not.'

'I don't understand the point of this,' Vereker complained in a nasty tone.

'We dropped in on last night's party.' Bowker's smile was horrific to see. 'As a result of what we found, Lloyd Davies is in custody. Not the next cell to Ronson, we can't have them doing a Monte Cristo and tapping on the wall to confer. But his cell is just as dismal as Ronson's.'

'Good God!' Vereker muttered. 'Lloyd in a cell!'

'The reason I mention this'—Bowker rose up from the sofa to his full height, much like Godzilla striding out of the sea to stamp Tokyo flat—'is because you stand in need of legal advice and Davies is no longer available, being in stir.'

'Why should I need legal advice? I've done nothing.'

'When I raised the question of Ronson's insurance two minutes ago and you handed me all that Mary Ellen about looking up your records, the fact is that I knew the answer. When we ran Ronson in, we impounded his records at the warehouse, and that led us to another building where he rented office space, and so on and so on. You get the general picture? To our astonishment, the dirty old porn store at Kyte and Pewsey was insured through your good services.'

'I've no idea what he used the building for! He told me that he imported American computer magazines.'

'Not knitting patterns? Never mind. Put your shoes and socks on, Mr Vereker. You're accompanying me to the police station to make a statement. You are not under arrest. Not yet. But I must caution you that anything you say may be used in evidence.'

'But what's he done?' Moira demanded. 'This is harassment!'

'Don't be too upset,' Jack Knight soothed her. 'We won't keep him overnight, not unless he wants to confess to something very nasty. He'll miss lunch with you, but he might be back in time for dinner.'

'What happened to your eye?' She was suddenly solicitous as the Knight charm impressed itself on her.

'Punched in the face in a hand-to-hand with four bank robbers with iron bars and sawn-off shotguns.' He gave her his Handsome Jack smile.

'On the way to the station, we'll stop to collect your diary,' Bowker said to Vereker, his teeth showing like a shark about to bite a swimmer in half. 'I'm interested in how many of Davies' parties you've been to. I take it you're also a close friend of Deborah Nunally, tearaway junkie daughter of Sir Osbert?'

'I don't know what you're talking about,' Vereker muttered, a sheepish look on his face. But Moira understood what Bowker was suggesting and gave Vereker a hard look. He wasn't going to eat dinner in Penny Lane that evening—that was clear enough.

To the surprise of all, Donald Vereker returned of his own free will to Bedlow police station on Monday morning, a little after nine. He asked to see Inspector Bowker, claiming it was of the utmost importance.

'You know why he can't stay away from us,' Knight said. 'It's that cup of brown sludge they call tea we gave him while he was here yesterday. The canteen ought to be sued for misleading and fanciful descriptions. I don't know what they brew it from, but it's habit-forming.'

Vereker had spent over two hours the day before explaining to Bowker and Knight that he knew nothing about Ronson's business. And nothing about Lloyd Davies' parties. And having said it two or three times, with mounting insistence, he watched them write it down as a statement for him to sign.

Bowker glanced in disbelief and derision at the signature

and warned him that he'd be advised of proceedings against him. The insurance company concerned would certainly want to take action for fraud or deception or whatever they thought appropriate.

As for the parties and the drug taking and frolics that went on at them, the Inspector stated he had reason to believe Lloyd Davies was going to co-operate fully in the hope of getting off lightly. If Vereker's name was mentioned, he'd be advised.

If the strict truth were told, Lloyd Davies had given not the least hint he would offer any information, but Bowker saw it as only a matter of when. Meantime, his edited version seemed more likely to achieve results with Vereker.

'The local paper will have its spiciest front page ever,' he said with a grin. *'Drug Orgies in Lawyer's Home.* You can be sure the national press will pick up the story. And with the list of names Davies will give us, I'd guess your business here is done for. What do you think, Knight?'

'Not much call for insurance brokers with criminal records,' Jack Knight said solemnly, shaking his head. 'And he'll do time for the phoney insurance job, no doubt about that.'

'One way and another it looks to me that you'll have to make a fresh start in another town when you're back on the streets,' Bowker said in a tone suitable for announcing the ending of the world when a comet hits it next Tuesday. 'With another name and doing a different job—van driving, maybe—if any employer will take you on. You don't look strong enough for bin emptying.'

Vereker was staring at him like a rabbit crossing a busy road and caught in the headlights of an oncoming thirty-ton truck.

'I'll say very little at this stage about the connection with the murder of the entire Matthews family,' Bowker continued. He sounded like a medieval torturer deciding to have a change from pushing long pins under the suspect's fingernails to a red-hot branding iron in the armpits.

'Enquiries are being made into the drug business around here, and arrests will be made shortly. Everyone with even a remote link to drugs can expect a hard time. We take a very serious view of people being murdered. Especially children. Trouble and woe and aggravation are on the way for every accomplice or concealer of information. Get yourself a lawyer, Mr Vereker. You need one.'

After that they let him go, a worried man. Here he was again, of his own accord, asking to see the Inspector.

'Might be the so-called tea,' Bowker said while he and Knight made their way down the stairs to the Interview Room, 'or maybe our gold Rolex pal has come to do a deal. Do you think I scared him yesterday?'

'I don't know about him, but you scared *me*. The most he'd get for faking Ronson's insurance form is twelve months suspended and a telling-off from the geriatric old bugger judging the case. You made out he was up for trial in an Arab hellhole where he'd get a hundred lashes, his right hand chopped off, twenty or thirty years in solitary, and the confiscation of everything he owns.'

'I said nothing of the sort! I told him he'd be charged with serious offences—that's all.'

'It's the way you tell 'em,' said Knight. 'You terrified the bugger. And all he wanted was for us to find his wife for him.'

Vereker was alone in the interview room. He looked unwell. Dark smudges under his eyes from not sleeping. He'd changed his shirt and put on a grey-striped business suit, but it was bluff. Very obviously, he was being eaten away inside by anxiety.

Jack Knight slipped a new cassette into the tape recorder and sat down beside Bowker, facing their twitching visitor over the cigarette-scarred tabletop.

'Don't switch that on,' Vereker said. 'I want to talk off the record for a minute or two.'

'Strictly against the rules,' Bowker rumbled. 'Everything has to be open and above board. I'm a copper and you're a criminal. There have to be proper rules. Well, strictly speaking, you're a suspect until a jury says you're a criminal—but you know and I know it's only a formality. Still, I'm a fair man. Switch the recording machine off, Knight.'

'I haven't switched it on yet.'

'What do you want to say off the record, Don?'

'I don't know anything about the Matthews murders; you've got to believe me! I'm just a businessman trying to make a living—maybe I was a bit careless over Dougie Ronson's warehouse, but I had no real idea what he was using it for.'

Bowker made a *tcha* noise that indicated profound disbelief.

Vereker went on quickly, 'I guessed it wasn't on the level, and I was fool enough to shut my eyes to it.'

Bowker interrupted, 'I can't be doing with all this rubbish. You said all this in your comedy statement yesterday. I didn't believe a word of it then, and I don't bloody believe it now. So stop wasting time. If you want a shoulder to cry on, don't come to me, try the Salvation Army.'

'No, wait—there is something I can tell you to prove that I'm not involved.'

'Such as?'

Vereker took a grip on himself and went into his negotiating mode, for all the world as if he was selling insurance.

'I've heard rumours about drug selling in Bedlow. Some people say the Burtons who own the filling station on Gallowgate have a lot to do with it. I'm not suggesting they do because I don't know anything about that sort of thing.'

'Except how to snort it up at Davies' parties,' Bowker said.

'I deny I've ever in my life done any such thing!'

'What is it you want to tell me?' Bowker let his boredom and impatience show very clearly.

'The Burtons' insurance goes through me. Their home and their filling station. And one other property. I don't know what it's used for, but I've often wondered.'

Bowker and Knight looked at each other and grinned.

'You're a regular encyclopaedia of useful information,' said Bowker. 'What sort of property are we talking about, Don?'

'A dilapidated old house insured for a few thousand pounds. I used to think they'd bought it as an insurance swindle to burn down and claim on. But they've had it too long for that.'

'How about the contents?'

'There's no contents insurance. Maybe it stands empty, but I don't think so.'

'So what's the address of this interesting property.'

'What's in it for me?'

Bowker shook his head mournfully at this new example of human greed and self-seeking. 'I can't do much for you,' he said, shaking his head, 'not if you're an accomplice after the fact to murder. The simple truth is you're in deep clag—any minute now it will close over your head and suffocate you.'

'I've had nothing to do with murder—I swear I didn't!'

'I'll pretend to believe you for the time being. What *are* you an accomplice to, Don?'

'Fiddling the insurance proposal for Dougie Ronson—nothing else at all.'

'Fraud and intent to deceive,' Bowker said bleakly. 'How much did he pay you?'

'Not enough, considering the trouble he's landed me in!'

'You landed yourself in it. And don't think that's the end of your troubles. There's the crime of concealing information from the police.'

'What do you mean?' Vereker was sounding harassed.

'If you have information about a crime and don't report it to the police, you are committing an offence yourself. You've just admitted to knowing where the Burton brothers store their dope. The judges are very hard on everything to do with drugs because there's a sort of crisis going on, silly young buggers drugging themselves to death left, right, and centre. What do you suppose Don will get on that charge, Knight?'

'Two years at least, depending on the judge.' Knight pursed his lips solemnly. 'Might be three years. And no chance of it being suspended—he'll do it inside.'

'I came here in good faith,' Vereker protested. 'What's wrong with reaching an agreement?'

'What did you have in mind?' Bowker's face had same look The Mad Mangler displayed in the wrestling ring before he threw his opponent ten feet in the air and let him crash on his head.

'Drop your charges against me, and I'll tell you the address,' Donald Vereker offered.

'I can't believe what I'm hearing!' Bowker said in outraged astonishment. 'You expect me to conceal knowledge of a crime? You must be demented!'

'Come on,' said Vereker, bolder now he was on his own ground, or thought he was, negotiating terms. 'It's not much of a crime—who tells an insurance company the entire truth? And there's been no claim on the policy, so there's no swindle.'

'You were a part of Ronson's pornography racket, whatever you may say to get off the hook. Why should I offer you any sort of deal now you've admitted knowledge of yet another criminal act, drug trafficking? All I have to do is arrest you here and now. I can get a search warrant within the hour and go through your office files till I find the address I want.'

Vereker began to sweat visibly.

'You said you were a fair man,' he reminded Bowker.

'Did I say that? It must have been a joke. This is as far as I'll go—tell me the address, and we'll take a look. If there's dope on the premises, I won't charge you with being part of the drug ring. If the information is a dud, I'll lock you in a cell in the basement between your friends Ronson and Davies.'

'No charge at all?' Vereker was pushing his luck.

'Are you raving? You expect me to enter into a conspiracy to pervert the course of justice? I have to inform the insurance company that Ronson's application was false. What they do about it is their business. They may decide to prosecute you.'

'I can handle that. The address you want is 8 Kitchener Row—it's an old terrace of workmen's cottages that should have been pulled down years ago.'

Bowker went to inform Superintendent Billings that he was getting a search warrant and had some expectation of finding the Burton dope cache. Nothing to be gained by antagonising him again, two days after the Davies party pinch. Let him think his lecture on insubordination had inspired total allegiance. Meantime Trimmer and Knight were organising a reliable squad of uniforms to take along in case of trouble.

Bowker sounded baffled when he returned to the Incident Room. 'I'm not sure I heard him right. He said he's coming with us, or that's what it sounded like. I told him it might turn into a brawl, and he said he'd waited years to see the Burtons put away and he's not going to miss being in at the kill.'

'Hope he doesn't get his nice uniform torn,' Knight said with a smile of great charm. 'Be a pity to see those silver buttons ripped off by thugs and crooks. This arrived for you while you were chatting to His Nibs. It doesn't look like fan mail to me. Are you expecting any more death threats this week?'

He pointed to a plain brown envelope on Bowker's desk.

'Pushed under the street door,' he said. 'Nobody's touched it since the desk officer saw it and guessed what it could be. If we're lucky, there might be a fingerprint or two.'

The envelope was addressed in capital letters, just BOWKER.

'Not much inside,' said the Inspector, flipping it over with a pencil. 'Not a bomb, that's for sure. I'm disappointed.'

Knight, Trimmer, and Hagen were crowding around Bowker's desk, agog. Shirley Cote would have been there too, but she was up in the empty flat above the charity shop keeping watch on Hinksey.

'Open it!' Knight pleaded. 'This suspense is too much— cold sweat's dripping off us.'

Bowker held the envelope flat on the desk with his pencil and slid a plastic letter opener under the flap. Three more seconds, and he'd emptied out the contents. One Polaroid photo—that was all there was.

The three standing detectives craned their necks to see what it was a photo of. Two young children, a boy and a girl, riding on a one-humped camel. A red X had been drawn over their faces. Bowker's fortissimo roar of rage caused the surrounding coppers to leap away from his desk.

'My kids!' he bellowed, 'the bastard followed them yesterday to the wildlife park!'

'It's a second warning,' Trimmer said not very helpfully. 'A reminder. First it was your name on the war memorial. Now this is to let you know he can hurt your family.'

Bowker was black-faced with fury. He raised his arms over his head and smashed both fists down on the desk. The wood split. A crack opened right across from one side to the other.

'Photos take fingerprints well,' Knight became practical, to give Bowker time to regain control. 'Hagen—take the photo and envelope to the dabs department and tell them it's bloody urgent—we want any prints matched inside the next twenty minutes.'

'I was going to be there,' Bowker said between gritted teeth. 'They enjoy seeing the animals. We take a picnic with us. But I called off because we'd just run Davies in and there was a lot to do here. So my wife took the kids on her own, and some wicked bastard was watching my house yesterday—he followed them.'

'It's the Burtons,' said DS Trimmer. 'Stands to reason. They heard about the Saturday-night raid, and they moved very fast to put the squeeze on you. They thought Davies might drop them in the acky to get himself off. They're frightened men.'

'If that's the way of it, it's bloody ironic,' Bowker said in a grating voice. 'We got nothing out of Davies, not a word. And then Vereker strolls in off the street and tells us where they store the drugs.'

'You have to take this straight to the Superintendent,' Knight said, a rough sympathy in his tone.

'And he'll take me straight off the case!' Bowker was sour.

'It's the right thing to do, take you out of the picture till the evil sods threatening your family are behind bars.'

Bowker reached for the phone without comment. Inside a minute, he was talking to his wife, explaining that there was a risk and she must collect the children from school fast.

'There'll be a police car outside the door in five minutes.' He nodded at Knight to get on another phone and make the arrangements. 'Take yourself and the kids to my mother's for an unexpected stay. Phone her and say you're coming. It'll only be for a day or two, I promise.'

How Bowker's wife responded to the emergency only he heard. A most uncharacteristic look of concern drew his dark gypsy face down into a mask of anxiety. How does a woman react to a threat against her children? Knight wondered while he was hanging on, waiting to be put through. Fear and anger, very obviously—but any woman hardy enough to marry Denis Bowker was likely capable of fighting marauders off with her fingernails and feet.

He still hadn't met Bowker's wife. He wanted to find out what she was like, as did many of their colleagues, to see what sort of woman could cope daily with The Mad Mangler. But Bowker kept his job and his personal life very well separated.

Some facts were known about his children. The boy was ten and already a promising pianist. The little girl was eight and a model who appeared in shampoo ads on TV and magazines. Which was mind-boggling—given their father's rough-hewn looks and sandbagging personality.

'Have you fixed an escort?' Bowker asked when Knight put the phone down. 'Who did you speak to?'

'Chief Superintendent Horrocks,' Knight said grandly.

'Bloody hell—I don't believe it!'

'He wasn't keen to talk to a mere detective-sergeant and kept on muttering I'd been put through by mistake. But after he grasped that it was about your kids, he switched into overdrive. A car is hurtling toward your house right now, with siren wailing and roof light flashing. Might be two cars. Or three if the DCS got very busy. With firearms and attack dogs. There's no chance the Burtons can get anywhere near your family without being grabbed and beaten senseless. If not actually shot to death.'

'That's all right, then.' Bowker gave a great sigh of relief.

'Orders from the Chief,' Knight went on. 'He says in case you may have forgotten, you're only on loan to Billings—your real boss is still Horrocks himself back at the ranch. He told me to tell you to tell Billings—get yourself taken off the case and Returned to Sender.'

'That's what DCS Horrocks said, is it?' Bowker growled, grey eyes slitted as he glared suspiciously at Knight.

'More or less his exact words. You know you've got to do it.'

'What I have to do this very minute is get a search warrant,' Bowker said stonily. 'We're near the end of the bloody case, and I'm going to see it through.'

'You can't just ignore Horrocks' orders. He'll go through the roof. The least you'll get is a severe reprimand.'

'When have I ever ignored a senior officer's orders?'

Bowker asked innocently. 'Never once, not since the first day I put on my new blue uniform and was sent out on foot patrol to keep the Queen's peace.'

'Then you'll tell Superintendent Billings?'

'It's turned out convenient that he wants to come with us on the raid because I can tell him about the photo just before we kick the door in. Even he wouldn't be heartless enough to send me off the field just before we score a touchdown.'

'You surely do take chances,' Jack Knight said, 'but why not? Who wants to be a desk detective like Billings! Promise me one thing: if either of the Burtons is there when we storm in, you won't kill him with your bare hands. Not in front of Billings.'

'*Superintendent* Billings,' Bowker corrected him. 'Respect for senior officers—how often do I have to tell you?'

Kitchener Row was a lost and forgotten part of Bedlow, out of sight and out of mind for generations. A short terrace of small red-brick houses put up when Queen Victoria was on the throne—and Lord Kitchener was a national hero for killing off a lot of Sudanese fuzzy-wuzzies to avenge the death of General Gordon at Khartoum up the Nile.

Not that the general would have taken any pride in the street named after him, even new it had not been much. The railway ran past the backyards. Every train that passed rattled the house windows.

'They'll see us coming all the way along the street.' Bowker briefed his team of detectives and uniforms. 'There's no element of surprise possible, not unless they're all drugged to the eyeballs. Which I doubt. So it's straight in hard from both ends of the street and both sides of number 8.'

Superintendent Billings attended the briefing, but he had the grace to keep silent. The point about delegating responsibility was that somebody else got his backside kicked if things should go wrong.

Bowker went on, 'Teams of four. In those poky little houses, we can expect two rooms downstairs and two up-stairs. DS Trimmer goes in by the back door with his two teams, and DS Knight takes the front door with his two. I want a team of four men in each room of the house, up and down, five seconds after we kick the doors down. Anybody offering resistance, lay them out and do it fast, before they have time to jump out of a window or pull out a shooter. Got me?'

The taking of 8 Kitchener Row was the sort of action that the coppers of Bedlow-on-Thames dreamed of—they'd seen it done only in TV movies and crime documentaries. It was Christmas come early, an adventure to brag about in the pubs forever. The cars were left at the ends of the Row while uniforms and plainclothes charged the house like Vikings gone berserk for pillage and rape.

Superintendent Billings stayed in his car until he heard the thud of sledgehammers on doors; then he strolled up the mid-dle of the street, resplendent in his uniform and peaked cap. To be frank with himself, he suspected there might just be incidents in the heat of the action, which it would be better for a senior officer not to witness.

Bowker was invited to make the short journey to Kitchener Row in Billings' car, a superior vehicle with a uniformed con-stable at the wheel. During the ride, Bowker mentioned the photo of his children and the steps he had taken to counter the threat.

'This is absolutely outrageous!' Billings said. 'I've never come across anything like it before, threats against the family of an officer! How do you explain it?'

'Could be the Burton brothers.' Bowker wondered why he had to explain it at all. 'If so, they'll be in custody shortly and no longer a threat to anyone.'

'Look here,' said Billings, 'I have to take you off the case; that's the procedure. You shouldn't even be here.'

'Take me off the case in an hour's time,' Bowker suggested in as reasonable a tone as he could manage. 'Let's get the Burtons under lock and key first. Or do you want to take over the raid yourself?'

'Why didn't you tell me about the threat before?'

'I was so busy planning this jaunt, it slipped my mind.'

'We're here, sir,' the driver said to Billings, pulling to a halt behind two other police cars at the north end of Kitchener Row. 'There they go!'

It was a stirring sight, uniforms and suits in full cry along the pavement from both ends toward number 8 in the middle.

'Am I in charge or not?' Bowker demanded in anguish of mind, seeing the action start without him.

'Carry on, then—we'll talk later.' Billings was reluctant to make himself responsible for the operation at this stage, which was what Bowker had been relying on. At once he was out of the car and haring toward the house, choosing the rear entrance.

He knew that cornered crooks would more likely try to get out by the back rather than the front door. His long legs covered the ground in seconds—he was with Trimmer's group as the back door finally gave way under the pounding of a sledgehammer. It was reinforced inside with steel bars, as he'd warned his squad to expect.

Over the heads of the coppers in front of him, Bowker saw into a small kitchen. A youngish man with a dirty beard and long hair was standing just inside the door. He was dressed in the usual ragged denim, a typical squatter in a derelict house—if he hadn't been holding an axe in his hand, ready for use on the first head to come within reach.

To no avail. The rush of coppers into the kitchen knocked him down and he was trampled under big heavy feet as orders to rush the stairs and secure the upstairs rooms were obeyed zealously. When the stampede had passed over him, he struggled up on hands and knees, groaning and looking the worse for wear.

The lethal-looking axe was still in his hand so Bowker kicked his elbow with his size 15 brogue and he dropped it with a loud screech.

'You're under arrest,' Bowker said. 'Get down on your face on the floor and stay there!'

'You've broken my arm!'

'There's worse to come,' Bowker told him furiously.

Shouts and stamping resounded through the house, upstairs and down. Bowker snarled in frustration, he was missing the action. If he joined in now, the bearded axe-man would surely make a run for it. Trimmer should have left a man to cover runaways—but you couldn't expect too much. It was bloody aggravating, being left standing about like a plain girl at a dance.

The tumult and the shouting were soon over. Bowker ordered his prisoner to get up, grabbed his good arm, and shoved him forward into the next room. On the bare wooden floor stood a table with four chairs around it and leftovers of a meal. Fish and chips, paper plates, empty beer cans. Four of Trimmer's uniforms were talking enthusiastically about the raid, and they had one man in custody. He was sitting on a chair, handcuffed and glum.

'You can have this one, too.' Bowker pushed his captive toward them. 'Caution him properly and make a note he's charged with assaulting a police officer with intent to commit grievous bodily harm with a deadly weapon. It's the axe on the floor out in the kitchen—pick it up and bag it as evidence.'

In the front room were more coppers, but no prisoners. Just an old sofa with the springs showing through threadbare upholstery and two armchairs facing a TV set. It was covering horse racing from Kempton Park.

There was no sign of drugs. Must be upstairs safe and out

of sight, Bowker told himself anxiously; they wouldn't want nosey neighbours watching their business through the windows. If that creepy little sod Vereker was having a laugh by sending them to the wrong address . . . no, it didn't bear thinking about.

He stamped up the dusty wooden stairs. The two small bedrooms were crowded with big coppers and he saw they were in the right place. His face positively beamed as he stared round at stacked bales of cannabis, big wooden boxes packed with plastic bags of white powder, cardboard containers of coloured capsules.

There were two more prisoners, hairy and dirty as a brace of Hell's Angels. Evidently the cover for drug running was to look like squatters. They both lay face-down on the dirty floor with their wrists cuffed behind them.

'Well done!' Bowker's mood was angelic. 'Any trouble?'

'That silly bugger reached for a sawn-off,' DS Trimmer said. 'Ginny Bampton clobbered him with her baton and he's out cold.'

'We'll put her in for a commendation.' Bowker radiated so much good humour that Trimmer stared at him as if he was off his hinges. 'Going for an armed criminal, she ought to get a medal. When this evil thug wakes up, we'll do him for attempted murder, besides everything else.'

The windows were covered with cheap net curtains, filthy with the dust and grime of years. In the front bedroom Bowker used a pencil to move the net aside and stared out through the cracked and dirty glass. There stood Superintendent Billings, right in the middle of the roadway, staring at the house, with a hand on one hip. He'd brought a leather-covered swagger stick with him and was tapping it against his thigh.

What a sight, Bowker thought. It was years since he'd seen a swagger stick; he'd assumed they'd gone out of style except for when a Chief Constable was presented to the Queen to be given a knighthood. Somebody should take a bloody photo of him, Bowker thought, but he didn't say it in DS Trimmer's hearing.

'What next, sir?'

'Take the prisoners to the station and charge them. Send for a truck and have all this stuff taken to Forensic, to make sure it's what we think it is. Have a dabs team go through every rat-infested inch of this nasty slum—we want to prove the Burtons were here. Meanwhile I'll take two of your men and award myself the pleasure of running in the brothers. Got all that?'

'Yes, sir. What about Hinksey at the off-licence, do you want him picked up now?

'Later—he's small-fry, and we've got enough on our hands for the moment. He'll keep.'

Bowker went down the creaking old stairs and out through the little front room, collecting Jack Knight on the way. In Kitchener Row there were people standing outside their doors, watching the drama in openmouthed wonder. A particular object of their attention was Superintendent Billings, whose stance consciously embodied the might and majesty of the law.

Knight saw him and sniggered. 'Bloody hell—do you think we should salute him?' he asked in an undertone as he and Bowker approached.

'Shut up, you bloody clown,' Bowker muttered.

'Satisfactory, Inspector?' Billings asked grandly.

'Enough drugs for a New Age rock concert. And four ugly thugs under arrest, two a bit damaged. I've left Trimmer in charge to tidy up while I collect the brothers Burton.'

'Good work!' Billings sounded nearly friendly. 'How many men are you taking with you?'

'DS Knight and two constables.'

'Then I'm coming,' Billings said. 'It's been years and years since I arrested a crook. I might never get another chance.'

'Sure you want to?' Bowker asked, aghast. 'We're going after a pair of bruisers with everything to lose. I really can't see them giving up quietly and saying they're sorry.'

Billings was not a complete fool. He saw the glow in Bowker's eyes and heard the eagerness in his voice.

'You're hoping there'll be a roughhouse, Inspector. I'm well aware of that. But before you start punching heads in, remember that you've no proof the threat against your children came from these two criminals.'

'I'll bear that in mind. Shall I get on with the briefing now, or will you take over?'

Billings nodded curtly to indicate he should proceed. Bowker waved his men close into a circle. He'd chosen the two biggest uniforms—their names were Salter and Thorpe—they were high on the excitement of raiding Kitchener Row. With Jack Knight, they formed a small circle to hear Bowker's orders.

The Superintendent was included. Although he took a half-step backward as if to say that he was part of the action, but not quite part of it.

'We're going to grab the two Burton brothers at their filling station. It has to be another up-and-at-'em job because there is no cover at all as we drive in. I'll go with the Superintendent in his car and take Constable Thorpe along. DS Knight will ride in a police car with Constable Salter. We'll go fast but silent till we're a hundred yards away from the filling station—then it's foot down hard and on to their forecourt like bats out of hell.'

'Right!' Jack Knight said enthusiastically.

Bowker continued, 'The Super's car will lead, and take the first entrance and block it. The second car will take the other entrance and block that. I expect car doors open and everybody out and running before the wheels stop turning.'

Knight grinned. Evidently he was wondering if that *everybody* included Superintendent Billings.

'You've all seen the filling station and know the layout. Up at one end there are second-hand cars for sale—if we're lucky, one of the Burtons will be buggering about with them, fiddling the mileage, maybe. If so, DS Knight's team goes straight at him and grabs him. The other Burton will probably be in the office at the back, and I'll go for him with PC Thorpe.'

'And if we're not lucky?' Knight asked.

'If they're both in the office or out among the wrecks, we go at them bald-headed. The Burtons are in a violent and dangerous trade, drug dealing, they're not Sunday-school teachers. So be bloody careful if they cut up rough. Make sure they get all the grief, and not us.'

There was a pause, in which the Superintendent could be heard to clear his throat.

'Bearing in mind that we are officers of the law, not a lynch mob,' Bowker added virtuously.

'Well said, Inspector,' Billings commented.

The operation went well. Cilla was in her booth, reading a paperback. There was a punter at one pump, filling up an estate car with a huge yellow dog peering out of the window. Customer and Cilla stared in amazement as two cars screeched to a tyre-scorching stop on the forecourt and out poured burly men—some of them in uniform.

The used cars with their over-optimistic price stickers stood forlornly alone. Bowker shouted and pointed at the door to the office, leading the rush himself. He kicked the door wide open without halting for an instant and in he went, bellowing, *'Police—stay where you are, you're under arrest!'*

In the small office, Wayne and Gary Burton were on their feet, alerted by the noisy arrival of the cars outside. They ignored Bowker's shouted warning—the brother behind the desk snatched the phone and threw it at his face; the other came in from the side with swinging fists.

Bowker ducked fast. The phone broke up against the wall.

He blocked Gary's roundhouse swing and landed a hard jab into his middle. Then the office was full of policemen and there wasn't room to fight. Gary bent over, gasping for breath, while Thorpe put the cuffs on him. Wayne clambered up on his overturned desk and took a header through the window.

'After him!' Bowker shouted, struggling to break through the massed bodies. Gary was pushed over in the scrum and fell down on his face, cursing and swearing now his breathing had started to function again.

By the time Bowker reached the forecourt, Knight close behind him, no-neck Wayne was lying on the concrete moaning, a hand to the bridge of his nose. Superintendent Billings stood over him, a smile of pleasure on his face and his broken swagger stick in his hand.

'This one almost got away Inspector,' he said very primly. 'I thought I'd stop him for you. Pick him up and I'll caution him. It's been a long time since I had the pleasure.'

'Right, sir,' Bowker was polite. This time the *sir* didn't sound quite so disrespectful.

Wayne was built like a heavyweight boxer. Bowker picked him up with one hand and slammed his back against the office wall—a hand the size of a mechanical digger clenched tight about the place where the throat would be on a normal person.

Superintendent Billings tapped Wayne's shoulder to secure his attention. He ignored the gagging noises Wayne was making as he slowly strangled to death and recited the caution to him, word-perfect, a beatific smile on his face.

'I'll leave the prisoner in your custody, Inspector,' he said and drifted away toward his car.

'That was the official bit, sunshine,' Bowker growled through gritted teeth. 'Now it's my turn. Which of you was it took that photo of my kids: you or your stupid brother? Tell me before I throttle you to death.'

Wayne's eyeballs were bulging out as he threw a tortured look round the forecourt in search of relief. But the Superintendent was sitting in his car. The two constables were tactfully busy escorting Gary Burton to the other car. Knight had an elbow on Cilla's booth and was assuring her, through the glass panel, that she wasn't being run in with Uncle Wayne and Uncle Gary.

'Photo?' Wayne choked. 'What the hell you talking about?'

'You'll try to escape again,' Bowker said, 'and when I try to stop you, you'll trip on my foot and smash your head against the wall and give yourself brain damage. Then I'll lose my balance and accidentally step on you and crack most of your ribs. Tell me about the photo.'

'I don't know anything about photos!' Wayne insisted wildly.

And for once in his life it sounded as if he was telling the truth. Which was vexatious, to say the least.

15. ·············· *tommy raffles's betting shop*

In the hurly-burly of running in the Burton brothers and their scruffy henchmen—with evidence to put them all away for years and years—there hadn't been time to evaluate the door-to-door enquiries Trimmer set in motion on Sunday.

Hagen had done the round of the flats in the four oddly named apartment blocks in Penny Lane. No one admitted to seeing Billy Swanson or his shabby old van on the morning he was hurled into eternity by Driver Flock's train. But as Hagen pointed out when he reported in, if it was Mrs Druce Billy called on, she wasn't likely to admit it.

Ginny Bampton had more luck, although the carpark behind the shopping mall was free on Sundays and the attendant had the day off. She tracked him to his home, and he remembered a dirty old blue van on Friday—only because the man who drove it away and paid was not the same person who brought it in and it surprised him to think two different people would ride in such a wreck.

As to who took it away, that he didn't recall, except that it was a man. Young, old, tall, short, fair, brown, business suit, T-shirt, bearded, clean-shaven? He didn't recall. 'Might have been a one-eyed Mongolian midget in a wet suit!' Bowker snorted in derision when WPC Bampton reported to him.

'If he took a shortcut through the shopping mall he was well on his way to Hinksey's off-licence,' Knight suggested, 'but if the Burtons were going to do him in, why would he go to Arnie's place? They wouldn't tell him to meet them there because then Arnie would know they did it.'

'I've gone right off the idea that the Burtons did Billy in,' Bowker said with a black frown, 'Gary and Wayne know bugger all about stalking my kids and sending the photo—neither's a good-enough liar to lead me up the garden path. So if it wasn't them trying to warn me off, it wasn't them who got rid of Billy.'

'Hang on a minute!' Knight protested. 'Billings let you stay on the Matthews enquiry because you told him the Burtons were doing the threatening, and that's all finished now we've got the pair of them under lock and key. Now you say it wasn't them at all, which means the villains are still out there somewhere.'

'You didn't think I'd let myself be shoved off the case after we've got this far, did you?' Bowker snarled at him. 'My kids are in a safe place and being guarded by uniforms while we find the nasty bugger responsible for all the aggravation.'

'I'm starting not to like this,' Knight complained. 'Are you sure about the Burtons?'

'The search parties didn't find a Polaroid camera where they live. Nor at the filling station, nor at that dump in Kitchener Row. No camera at all. The young lady you were trying to grope, Cilla, said in her statement she'd never in her life seen Uncle Wayne or Uncle Gary with a camera. She doubts if either of them would know which end to point at the land-scape.'

Knight was baffled. 'Not that what you're saying makes any sense, but I'll take your word for it. And where does that leave us?'

'Right back where we started from. If the Burtons didn't kill Billy, then they didn't set fire to the shop and burn Matthews. So we're left with Arnie—though I'm blessed if I can think of a reason why he'd want to do his best friend in. After all that going fishing together.'

'This is a farce!' Knight was dismayed by Bowker's change of heart. 'It's like Twenty bloody Questions!'

'Billy was broke,' Bowker said. 'He couldn't afford more than one gallon of petrol at the filling station; we know that much. He was lured to his fatal mishap with the train by a promise of money. Let's go and walk the ground and see if we can see where Billy's bonanza was going to come from.'

'How about grilling Wayne and Gary for another few hours? It seems a wasted opportunity to leave them sleeping peacefully in the cells.'

'Plenty of time for that when they're remanded in custody for trial. They're not going to tell us anything; they're thugs who keep their mouths tight shut and pay a crooked lawyer to plot a route out of the clag for them. And we've taken their favourite legal adviser out of circulation. Mr Lloyd Davies regrets he's unable to lunch today.'

It was Tuesday morning. Bowker was restless after the success of the day before; he didn't want to sit at a desk with a split top and concoct a report. Knight recognised the signs. He stood up and put on his jacket, ready to go.

From Bedlow police station they walked in the summer sun down to the four-arch stone bridge over the Thames. They saw a dozen white swans gliding across the water, but no rowboats yet—not at ten in the morning. On Spinster's Reach, a little beyond the war memorial, a man in a striped pullover and a floppy-brimmed hat was sitting on a little folding stool with a fishing rod in his hand.

Bowker made a bloodcurdling noise in his throat at the sight, and Knight grinned from ear to ear. When they reached the High Street, they turned into the shopping mall.

'St Benjamin would be proud of it,' Knight said. 'Dress shops and TV shops and jewellery shops and book shops. I bet they had nothing like this where he came from.'

'Benedict, not Benjamin,' Bowker growled, marching toward the security guards. He halted in front of them and showed them his warrant card before they went into panic.

'Last Friday.' He spoke slowly and distinctly. 'Soon after ten in the morning. A man wearing a blue boilersuit.'

The two guards looked at each other doubtfully, the young one and the old one, their brains grappling with the information.

'Did either of you see him?' Bowker asked.

'Not me,' the young guard said with satisfaction, 'ten in the morning, I'm thinking about my break and a bacon sandwich. And a cup of tea. Twenty minutes, that's all we get off from clocking on till half-past twelve lunchtime.'

'Would he be a scruffy sort of chap, bald in front?' the old guard asked. 'About forty and dirty-looking?'

'Sounds right,' Bowker said encouragingly.

'I saw him. I remember thinking he must be a window washer in that boilersuit. Only they're on contract. They have to be out before the shops open.'

'I remember now you pointed him out,' said the young guard in awe of his colleague's feat of memory. 'I told you he might be a pickpocket.'

'And I told you he was too bloody clumsy for that—he walked like a duck. Breaking into gas meters was more his mark.'

'Which way was he going?' Bowker interrupted the discussion.

'Didn't notice,' the young guard said.

'He went out into the High Street,' said the other guard.

Bowker thanked him and headed back that way, fairly sure that the right man had been sighted. He and Knight walked along High Street, looking at the banks and building-society offices.

'Plenty of places to get cash along here,' Knight said. 'It's going to take days to go into every one to ask if a scruff in a blue boilersuit came in last Friday.'

Bowker agreed, 'It's a job for the whole team, but as we're here, let's nip into that shop. It's the right sort of place to interest the late Billy Swanson.'

He was making for the betting shop, tucked discreetly between a café and a health-food store displaying the usual lentils and dried apple slices.

Tommy Raffles said the sign over the door. *Turf Accountant.*

Inside was a long room with a counter across the end, guarded by a thief-proof metal grille. One entire long side was taken up by TV screens, row above row. As racing hadn't started anywhere in the country yet, the screens were running videos of football matches to give an impression of sporting activity. Early as it was, there were a few customers already, getting their bets on for the afternoon's horse racing.

Bowker glared through the steel lattice in as friendly a way as he could manage and showed his warrant card. He asked for Mr Raffles. The woman behind the counter eyed him suspiciously and told him to push his identification under the grille to her. It was given a thorough inspection before she eventually accepted it as genuine and notified the proprietor the law was here.

Tommy Raffles was a thin man in his fifties. He was in shirtsleeves and wore broad yellow braces with a horse-head pattern and glasses with thick black rims. He scrutinised the two policemen through the grille before nodding at an inconspicuous door at the side. They waited, hearing the rattle and snick of chains, bolts, and bars, before the door opened for them.

'What's it about?' Raffles asked when they were in his small private office. It had a metal desk, a heavy green-painted safe standing in a corner, and half a dozen TV screens side by side on a long shelf, all of them blank.

'Nothing to do with your business,' Bowker assured him. 'Just a routine enquiry you might be able to help us with.'

'Always glad to help the police.' The bookie sounded virtuous and very sincere. He plucked at his braces with his short thumbs. 'Somebody been passing fake twenty-quid notes again? I haven't taken any lately—not that I know of. It's the bloody Iranians who print them, you know, they're trying to destroy our economy because of that book writer with a scraggy beard who upset them over religion. I said as much to Inspector Mason, when he came chasing the last batch—just before Christmas it was.'

'I'll pass your theory on to the Foreign Office,' Bowker said with a straight face. 'It's something different we're here for. We're tracing the movements of a man in a blue boilersuit last Friday morning. He was seen in the shopping mall between about ten and ten-thirty, heading this way.'

'Oh, him!' Raffles said. 'Yes, he was in last Friday. Sue had a dentist appointment and wasn't here till nearly midday, so I was on the counter myself. He put a ten-pound bet on a runner at Doncaster. Twenty-to-one, never stood a chance. He was a mug to back it.'

'Why do you remember him in particular?' Knight asked. 'Must be hundreds of punters come in to put bets on sure losers.'

'Right!' Tommy Raffles agreed enthusiastically. 'I remember that one because he'd been in plenty of times before, always in that terrible dirty old boilersuit. Couldn't miss him.'

'We know he didn't have any money,' Bowker said, 'and

now all of a sudden he's making a ten-quid bet. Where did he get it?'

'How do I know? Maybe from the chap with him.'

'I think so,' Bowker agreed, a savage grin spreading over his face. 'Tell me about this chap with him.'

'I'll do better than that, I'll show you a picture of him.'

Bowker and Knight gazed at each other in delight.

'The security camera,' Bowker said as Raffles rummaged inside a metal cabinet. 'A bloody fine invention.'

'One camera up over the TV screens pointing at the door,' the bookie explained. 'Nobody comes in without getting his picture taken. Both of you are on today's tape. The other camera's over the grille. It sweeps side to side slowly to pick up any silly sod pulling a sawn-off from under his raincoat to threaten Sue. I usually keep the tapes a week.'

He found a videocassette labelled Friday 8 July and slotted it into the VTR beneath one of his TV sets.

'We open at ten,' he said, fiddling with the fast-forward. 'I can soon find the mug you're looking for.'

Bowker and Knight were sitting on stark uncomfortable chairs of chrome tubing with thin-padded seats. Knight opened his note book and leaned forward toward the screen. Bowker was enjoying the moment. He leaned back at ease and waited.

'There he is,' said Tommy Raffles, playing with the controls, 'in the horrible bloody boilersuit. And there's his pal.'

The view of the betting shop was black and white and unclear, but there—unmistakably—was Billy Swanson with a betting slip in his hand, talking to a bigger man with his back to the camera, a man wearing a short dark jacket.

It was the hairdo that gave him away instantly. His head was clipped to the skin at the sides and back leaving a thick mat on top.

'Hallelujah!' Bowker said happily.

The man with Billy turned as he talked and the camera had

him in profile. He had a cheerful smile on his face and an earring like a curtain ring dangling from his earlobe.

'You can tell a Shane a mile off,' said Bowker, 'even if you can't see his tattoos. There are questions he knows the answers to. You've been a great help, Mr Raffles. We'll take the video with us as evidence. Detective Sergeant Knight will write you a receipt. And I need to use your phone.'

While Knight scribbled a receipt on a sheet of paper provided by the bookie, Bowker phoned Trimmer at the police station—he told him to bring a car and two biggish bobbies and meet him at Batty's boatyard.

Shane Hambleton was stripped to the waist in the sunshine, busy filling the tank of a white cabin cruiser moored alongside the short pier where the pumps stood. Bowker waited until he'd finished and collected the money and the boat cast off. Then he approached Shane smartly, Knight and Trimmer a step behind him. The two uniforms waited a few yards back on the concrete apron, in case Shane broke through the first line and made a run.

'Come along, Shane,' Bowker said briskly. 'I'm arresting you. We want you at the station to answer a few questions.'

'You can't arrest me,' Shane said slowly. 'I've done nothing. What do you want me for?'

'For committing a public nuisance. Spraying paint on the town war memorial.'

'This some sort of joke?' Shane was puzzled.

'Do I look as if I'm joking?' Bowker's tone would have taken the paint off a steel battleship. 'You can be fined twenty quid for vandalism like that. And bound over to keep the peace.'

'I don't know what you're on about,' Shane muttered uneasily. It was dawning on him by stages that three detectives backed by two uniformed coppers was over the top for vandalising.

Bowker continued, 'While we're about it, I'm also arresting you as an accessory to murder. You helped your cousin Arnie do Billy Swanson in. And that's a life sentence. You don't have to say anything at all. If you do, we shall write it down to use as evidence, one way or the other.'

That's how he's going to play it, Knight thought—give Shane an opening to rat on Arnie. Not a bad way to tackle him. Nobody in his right mind would ever believe Shane had enough upstairs to plan dropping Billy in front of a train. Or burn down a shop in the middle of the night. Shane was just muscle; the thinking was done by Arnie Hinksey.

'You'll get into terrible trouble over this,' Shane said solemnly. 'I've read in the newspaper how chaps arrested by the police for things they never did got paid out thousands and thousands of pounds compensation. And the coppers got sacked.'

'I'm glad you can read, Shane,' Bowker said with a terrifying cheerfulness. 'You'll be able to understand the charge sheet.'

Knight was poised to jump at the first sign of resistance. He was balanced solidly, feet apart, hands clenched lightly. But Shane grinned and picked up his shirt and went quietly with them to the waiting police car.

'Lock him up,' Bowker said to Trimmer. 'I'll charge him when I get there with Hinksey.'

'We haven't got any cells left,' Trimmer told him. 'We've run so many crooks in since last week, we're clean out of space.'

'Not my problem,' Bowker said. 'I only catch 'em. Bung him in with the tracker dog in the kennel behind the station, for all I care.'

'Cruelty to dumb animals,' said Knight. 'Can't do that or the Animal Liberation freaks will burn the police station down.'

'You should have some backing if you're going after

Hinksey,' Trimmer advised. 'If you're right and he's done five people in, he might very well cut up rough. He was in the Paratroopers, and he could have a gun tucked away somewhere.'

Bowker sounded amazed. 'I've got backing. DS Knight is with me. But when you've taken Shane to the lockup, send the car to Arnie's off-licence with a couple of uniforms to collect him.'

'I see what's in your mind,' Trimmer said thoughtfully. 'You think he's the one who threatened your kids. You want a word in private with him.'

'I'm thinking he's the evil bugger who burnt Matthews' little girls to a crisp. Get about your business, Sergeant, we've both got work to do.'

From the boatyard by the bridge to Old Church Yard along High Street was five minutes' walk. Bowker didn't seem to be hurrying but Jack Knight was almost trotting to keep up with him. He had something to say to the Inspector.

'I didn't like the way Shane gave up so easily. All that Mary Ellen about compensation for wrongful arrest—maybe he's not as thick as we thought. What do you think he's playing at?'

'He's gone to ground like a badger. The hounds are on him, and he's vanished down a hole. He's defying us to dig him out. He's been told we can't prove anything if he keeps his mouth shut.'

'You can bet Cousin Arnie's briefed him well on that,' Knight said. 'Of course, he doesn't know about Tommy Raffles' video. If we get him to say he never knew Billy Swanson, and then run the tape for him, that should rattle him.'

'You're learning at last,' Bowker said in rough approval.

They turned off High Street into Old Church Yard. Bowker's face went black as thunder at the sight of the same meter maid, humming to herself as she wrote a parking ticket to stick on an estate car standing at the kerb. Some good soul was delivering cast-off clothes to the charity shop and was fair game for Miss Traffic Gestapo.

Bowker glanced up at the windows of the flat above the shop—he couldn't see DC Cote, but he knew she was there keeping watch on Hinksey's off-licence, long-lens camera at the ready to snap anyone of interest going in or coming out. He waved, making her understand that he wanted her to come down and join him.

'Need her to take charge of Mrs Hinksey after we arrest her,' he said in reply to Knight's unspoken question.

'We're arresting her as well? Marilyn Monroe's double?'

'Jayne Mansfield,' Bowker corrected him. 'Even bigger around the chest. Hinksey's missus is an accessory after the fact. She must know her husband killed Ronnie Matthews. And why. I should have seen it the day I told you about *Dombey and Son* and Carker jumping under a train. I had this feeling in my bones there was a connection somewhere.'

'Let me into the secret,' Knight begged, 'Charlie Dickens did the murders—he rose from the grave like Dracula and burnt the newspaper shop down, right?'

Shirley Cote dashed out of the charity shop and over the road to join them.

'You won't believe this,' she said, sounding sure of herself, 'but soon after Hinksey opened up this morning, in trotted Kitty Swanson.'

'You recognised her?'

'I was the arresting officer when Jason was picked up. I know Kitty very well because she tried to pull my hair out.'

'How long did she stay with Hinksey?'

'She's still there. It doesn't take two hours to buy drugs if that's what she came for. I was just going to call in with the news for you.'

'Billy must have told her what he guessed, and she's trying to put the squeeze on Hinksey for money,' Bowker said. 'Billy came off second best when he tried it. Bloody hell—I hope we're in time. Come on, quick!'

The bountifully figured Avril Hinksey stood behind the counter. Her long blonde hair was coiled into a ponytail; a white shirt did wonders for her bulwarks. She stared at Bowker through pale blue eyes and smiled fetchingly.

'You've come back, Inspector.'

'I want to speak to your husband,' Bowker said hurriedly. 'Is he upstairs?'

'Sorry, he's gone out. But if you come back later—he's sure to be back sometime this afternoon.'

Bowker glanced at DC Cote, inviting her to say her piece.

'I've been watching your premises ever since you opened,' she told Mrs Hinksey. 'He hasn't gone out, he's upstairs.'

'You can't go up there!' Mrs Hinksey said sharply, as Bowker raised the counter flap and made for the staircase.

'You're arrested!' he shouted to her over his shoulder. 'Grab her, Cote, don't let her get away!'

Knight ran up the stairs after Bowker. Before they got to the top, Arnie Hinksey loomed above them on the landing.

'You're not coming up here, copper!' he bawled and launched a fast kick at Bowker's head.

Bowker smothered the kick and absorbed the impact without any more damage than a bruised shoulder. He threw a punch at Arnie, and being a few stairs down, his fist landed below the belt. It made Arnie screech and totter back, with his hands clasped over his afflicted articles.

Bowker reached the landing and clubbed Arnie down with a fist like an iron mace.

By the time Knight got to the landing, Arnie was sprawling on his back senseless, blood smeared on his face. Through the open door into the kitchen, Knight could see Bowker down on one knee beside Kitty Swanson on the floor. She lay on her side, wrists tied behind her back with wire, a plastic bag over her head.

'She's dead, poor cow,' Bowker said mournfully. 'Been dead an hour or more. Cuff Hinksey—this brings his score up to six.'

Arnie Hinksey was tougher than either of them gave him credit for. He was conscious again. Knight bent down to turn him face-down and cuff him, Arnie drew both legs up very fast and lashed out with his feet—he caught Knight on the chest and threw him backward into the open doorway. He caught his head on the doorpost and went down like a sack of wet sand.

Bowker leapt to his feet, bellowing in fury. His suspect was escaping; Knight was blocking his way. Shirley Cote down in the shop wouldn't be able to stop Hinksey. Bowker took two running steps and hurled himself in a flying rugger tackle that cleared Knight, who was moaning and stirring. Hands big enough to crush coconuts reached out for a hold on Arnie.

But Arnie had stumbled to his feet, dazed but determined, and was heading for the stairs and the street. Bowker's tackle fell short. He meant to bring Arnie down hard, but his hands clamped on one retreating ankle. Arnie's impetus carried him on, though he screamed as his foot was twisted sideways in Bowker's grasp and his ankle broke. He pulled free, only to fall headlong down the steep stairs.

Bowker was up in a moment, unwinded, and trampling downstairs in pursuit of Arnie's head-over-heels crashing descent. When he caught him at the bottom, he meant to disable Arnie by twisting an arm up his back while he cautioned him. Then handcuff him to something solid to keep him safe while Bowker ran back upstairs to see if Knight was badly hurt.

There was no need. Arnie reached the bottom of the stairs and lay huddled and still. Bowker was wary after what had happened to Knight. He crouched behind Arnie and gripped the back of his neck hard to immobilise him while he got the cuffs on. The head rolled loosely in his grip, and Bowker realised the neck was broken. Arnie was already dead.

Outside was the caterwauling of a police car siren. Two large uniforms came into the shop where Shirley Cote stood guard over Avril Hinksey. Bowker stood up straight to glare at the rescue team DS Trimmer had sent him.

'You took your bloody time!' he said nastily. 'My sergeant's upstairs hurt, there's a murder victim up in the kitchen, and a mass murderer dead at the bottom of the stairs. And DC Cote has a prisoner to take in. Get on your radio—I want an ambulance, a scene-of-crime team, the police surgeon, DS Trimmer, the rest of my murder squad. And I want them here in the next ninety seconds or sooner. And pass a message to Superintendent Billings while you're about it—tell him we've got the bastard who killed the Matthews family.'

He went upstairs to the landing. Knight was sitting up, his back against the doorjamb. There was a streak of blood in his hair, and he was holding his chest and wincing.

'You all right, Jack?' Bowker asked anxiously, kneeling down beside him.

'No, I'm bloody not. That bastard broke my ribs. Did you catch him?'

'Well, of course I caught him. He fell all the way downstairs and broke his neck. He's as dead as the poor silly bitch on the kitchen floor with a bag over her head.'

Knight breathed in and gasped at the pain in his chest.

'There'll be an enquiry,' he said. 'Some stupid sod will want to prove you did him in because he threatened to hurt your kids—you didn't, did you?'

'Between you and me, it passed through my mind that the world would never miss a nasty sod like Arnie Hinksey. But he did the job himself. Now stop talking—there's an ambulance on the way. You'll soon be in the hospital having your ribs strapped up and your head sewn back together.'

'Tell me one thing,' Knight pleaded. 'Before we came into

the shop, you were giving me that farrago about Dombey jumping under a train. What the hell was it all about?'

Bowker was using his folded handkerchief to soak up the blood from Knight's split scalp. At the hospital they'd have to shave some of his hair off before they stitched the gash—Knight was going to be peeved about it. A black eye was bad enough, a bald patch would restrict his social life for a while. Unless he got a hat to wear while he was chatting up susceptible women.

'Not Dombey—it was James Carker jumped under the train,' Bowker explained. 'Carker wanted to get his leg over Dombey's wife. I remember you saying it was more like a tabloid front page than Charlie Dickens. It started a glimmer in my mind, but I couldn't get hold of it.'

'What's it got to do with Hinksey incinerating the Matthewses—that's all I'm asking—I'm in no fit state for a discussion on literature. I don't even like reading. Start with Billy on the railway line; that's what set you off talking about Dickens.'

Bowker pressed the handkerchief hard against Knight's head to staunch the bleeding.

'That bloody hurts,' Knight complained, 'I've got a headache you wouldn't believe.'

Bowker explained, 'It was like waking up trying to remember a dream you've just had, but it's slipped away and you can't pull it back into the light. Burning Ronnie Matthews and his family was so cruel and nasty, we took it for granted that local organised crime was responsible. But when we ran the local professionals in, we found it wasn't them. So after we'd eliminated everybody else, it had to be Arnie—only where was his reason for it?'

'I've got it now. The big blonde down in the shop. Arnie's wife. Matthews had his leg over, and Arnie found out. Instead of giving him a decent thumping, he wiped him out, and his wife and kids with him. That's wicked!'

'Matthews was Jack-the-lad with women,' Bowker said. 'We know about Moira Druce, and if we ferreted around, I'm sure we'd find plenty of others he had the privilege of. Not that we need look for them. It doesn't matter now Arnie's dead.'

'You're arresting that gorgeous sexy wife of his? You reckon she knew he set fire to Matthews' newspaper shop?'

'She must have guessed after the fire,' Bowker said. 'Why she kept silent about it, God knows. When we start questioning her, she'll tell every lie she can think of. She never suspected him for a moment. Or if she did, she was too terrified of him to say anything. All that sort of clag. The truth is that two little girls were burnt to a black crisp, and she stayed with the cruel swine who did it.'

'And Shane, he's as bad as her,' Knight said. 'Worse, because he was there helping light the fire. And he gave a hand to drop Billy Swanson off the railway bridge.'

'Where there's no sense, there's no feeling. Shane hasn't got much in the upper storey. Cousin Arnie was his hero. He did what he told him to do and slept easy at night.'

Jack Knight was looking very pale. Bowker could hear a second siren outside and hoped fervently that the clutter of emergency vehicles in Old Church Yard was giving the meter maid grief and woe. Two paramedics appeared and began fussing over Arnie's body.

'Leave that rubbish!' Bowker roared at them. 'Here's the one that matters, up here. Move yourselves!'

They came pounding upstairs with a folding stretcher.

'Handle him carefully,' Bowker said. 'He's got broken ribs—and he needs a compress to stop the bleeding on his head.'

'Who are you, a doctor?' one of them asked.

Bowker rose to his feet, chest inflating, shoulders spreading, and eyes glaring—more aggressive than The Mad Mangler himself in the ring smashing an opponent's head against a corner post.

'If this officer isn't in the casualty department of whatever miserable hospital you come from inside ten minutes, I shall run you both in for criminal negligence!' he roared.

16. ············· *oxford, by the river*

Superintendent Billings stared uneasily at Kitty Swanson's body trussed up on the kitchen floor, her eyes wide open and bulging in the plastic bag over her head. Her mouth was open, too, in her final agony of trying to draw breath. In death as in life, Kitty was a shapeless bundle.

The police photographer was snapping away from all sides. The doctor had been and gone, pronouncing her dead, his preliminary diagnosis being suffocation.

'We could bloody well see that for ourselves,' Bowker said to nobody in particular.

The Superintendent had already taken a brief look at the body of Arnie Hinksey lying crumpled at the bottom of the stairs. He had to step over Arnie, as everybody else did, to get up to the flat. It was inconvenient, but there was no point in saying so. There were routines to be followed before either body could be taken away.

The Superintendent was wearing his best uniform. It was newly cleaned and pressed, the silver buttons shone brightly, and his neat black shoes were polished to a gloss he could see his face in. Bowker thought sourly that he looked like a bloody Bolivian admiral. All he needed was a triple row of medal ribbons.

When his cursory inspection of the two sets of mortal remains was complete, he told Bowker to follow him into the sitting room of the Hinksey home. He did not invite him to sit down, nor did he sit down himself.

'I don't understand how your mind works, Inspector,' he said. 'All this comes at a very bad time—I've had to cancel a lunch with the Assistant Chief Constable. I was actually getting into my car when your message reached me. Your action has again put me in a bad light—I cannot afford to acquire a name for being unreliable.'

Bowker said nothing. Any comment he made would have been very insolent. He folded his arms and concentrated on looking blank. What this rigmarole was leading to, he couldn't imagine, but he assumed he was being reprimanded.

'Having cancelled an important official engagement to be here in response to your message, I find a man dead in circumstances that could prove awkward,' said Billings. 'Our job is to arrest criminals, not eliminate them. Fortunately for us, the body of a victim is here on the premises and there can be little room for doubt that this man Hinksey was responsible for her death.'

'It didn't look like suicide to me.' Bowker was bored. 'It's bloody hard to wire your wrists together behind your back while you're suffocating with a plastic bag on your head. I think she was done in, poor cow.'

Billings flushed with annoyance at Bowker's sarcasm and tried to stare him down. He did not succeed. He turned away and went to the window and looked down into the narrow little road where a red-faced meter maid was haranguing the drivers of the police vehicles parked on the double yellow lines.

'I'm sorry to hear your sergeant's been hurt. What's his name—White—how bad is he?'

'Knight,' Bowker said. 'He'll be on his feet in a day or two. He wasn't bleeding from the mouth, so the ribs probably haven't punctured a lung. I think he's slightly concussed from the bang on the head. I'll make him take a few days' sick leave after the hospital's finished with him.'

But Billings wasn't really listening. His interest in Jack Knight was minimal. What was giving him the shivers was whether Bowker had got his facts right about Hinksey.

'I'm glad he wasn't seriously injured,' he said. 'There's too much violence toward the police these days. I blame it upon the lack of parental responsibility. Discipline seems to be a thing of the past.'

He turned to look hard at Bowker when he mentioned discipline and its absence. Bowker made no comment.

Billings continued his complaint. 'I need to know all the facts before the press get on to what has happened here. There's already a man from the *Bedlow Herald* outside; I spotted him through the window just now. The officer on the door will keep him out for now—but when he sees bodies being carried out, he will expect to be told what happened. Take me through the sequence of events, Inspector, starting right at the beginning, so I have some idea what I'm talking about.'

'Ronnie Matthews and Arnie Hinksey—good pals who used to go fishing together on the river,' Bowker began. 'Both involved in criminal activities, but not together.'

'What criminal activities? Be specific, Inspector.'

'Drugs for one, pornography for the other. Besides all that, Matthews had an eye for the women, and Hinksey was married to a blonde stunner. As they say in the agony columns, Matthews had a relationship with Mrs Hinksey. And then Hinksey found out.'

'Ah, it was a case of *cherchez la femme,* was it?'

'Is that what the Frogs call getting your leg over?' Bowker asked. Billings pursed his lips, unsure whether he was being mocked. He gestured to Bowker to continue.

'Hinksey was a violent man, trained for aggressive action and sudden death by the Paratroopers. He wanted to get his own back on the pal who'd betrayed him, so he set fire to Matthews' shop one night. He didn't care if Mrs Matthews and the two kids were burnt to death with Ronnie. He may have enjoyed it all the more because of that. Real blood curdling twist-your-guts revenge of a sort you don't often come across. He was aided and abetted in the fire-raising by his cousin, Shane Hambleton—who is now in custody.'

'The fire was nothing to do with the drugs or pornography—is that what you're saying?' Billings was perplexed.

'That's what led us up the garden path. It turned out to be a case of old-fashioned sexual jealousy. After I started rattling cages around the town, Billy Swanson found out who set the fire—how, I don't know. I'd guess he tricked Shane into telling him about it. You haven't met Shane, but he's as thick as two planks nailed together. Billy was a crafty little crook.'

'This is assumption,' the Superintendent said sharply. 'Where is the proof?'

'The proof lies in what happened when Billy tried to put the black on Hinksey for a wad of money. He'd picked the wrong chap to try his scheme on—Hinksey was no soft touch. He shut Billy up forever by dropping him in front of a train. Again assisted by Cousin Shane. We've a video from Tommy Raffles' betting shop of Shane meeting Billy, just before the dire deed was done.'

'A tape!' Billings was pleased to hear there was some hard evidence at last.

'Shane met Billy in the betting shop by arrangement and told him Arnie was waiting with the money. He took him somewhere for the supposed payoff. Which never was. Instead they made Billy comatose drunk and then drove him in his own van to the railway bridge on Windmill Lane. They made an effort to fake a suicide, but it didn't fool us more than five minutes.'

'Quite so,' the Superintendent said, although he was the one who had been willing to accept Billy's nasty ending as suicide.

'Billy had confided his secret information about the Matthews murders to his wife Kitty, a foul-mouthed slattern who is known to the entire local police force for a variety of petty crimes. But she didn't deserve to die the way she did, poor bitch. She knew Billy would never commit suicide, and she carried on the grand old Swanson tradition of crime by putting the black on Hinksey herself. Or trying to.'

'Greed is the root of most crimes.' Billings commented sourly. And unnecessarily. And very likely wrongly. Bowker ignored him and got on with his explanation.

'Kitty knew Hinksey was very dangerous. Blackmailing a killer is a tricky business, so she took what she thought were sensible precautions. She came in broad daylight for her hush money. She must have thought she'd be safe here, with customers in and out of the shop to buy a crate of brown ale. Or a bag of dope.'

'Oh, dear!' Superintendent Billings said.

'You may well say that. Hinksey didn't hesitate for a minute, he did her in—and there she lies on the kitchen floor at this very moment. I came here with Knight to question Hinksey, after seeing the betting-shop video, not guessing he had a dead woman in the flat. He attacked us, Knight was injured in the scuffle, and Hinksey fell down the stairs and hurt himself fatally. End of a long and nasty story.'

'Dope, you said. Are you saying Hinksey was a dealer?'

'One of the Burtons' main outlets for the town. When we have time to search here, we'll find stacks of it. Under the counter, I wouldn't wonder. We'll pull Kitty's son Jason in. He buys his sweeties here, and when he finds out Hinksey murdered his mother and his father, he'll start talking—he's only sixteen.'

'This cousin of Hinksey's—Hambleton—can you prove that he was an accessory to the murders?'

'When we tell him his hero's dead, I think he'll crack up. It won't be all that difficult to get a confession out of him. And especially when we tell him Mrs Hinksey has made a statement in which he's named as her husband's accomplice. And she'll say it on oath on the witness stand at his trial.'

'Ah, we come to her at last! If your account of events is to be believed, she must have been fully aware of what her husband had done. How do you explain her silence?'

'What goes on in the minds of women is baffling,' Bowker said with a shrug, 'although the reason why we don't understand them is no mystery. Men and women belong to different sexes, simple as that.'

This explanation made Billings look puzzled.

Bowker went on, 'She's sure to claim she was too terrified of her husband to report her suspicions, not that I believe it. I expect she'll claim he beat her black and blue when he found out his pal Ronnie had tampered with her. That I would believe. I think she was horrified and thrilled at the same time, after she guessed Arnie had killed her boyfriend and his family. In a nasty twisted way, she might take it as proof Arnie really loved her. It's been known before.'

'Are you setting yourself up as a psychologist, Inspector?'

'No, but I can quote you precedents for silly women who found themselves all of a tremble over murderers. Wives who stay with husbands they know to be cold-blooded killers, and when we catch them insist the black-hearted creeps love them.'

'It's not unknown,' the Superintendent agreed reluctantly.

'It won't make a ha'porth of difference,' Bowker said glumly. 'When we get her to trial, she'll plead she was under duress and in fear of her life. A clever-dick lawyer will get her off with two years suspended, mark my words. At least Shane will go down for a long time. Unless he pleads he's a mental defective, that wouldn't come as a big surprise to me. If there's nothing else, I'd like to get back to the station to start the questioning of him and Mrs Hinksey.'

'Nothing else?' Billings said dramatically, 'Good God, man—you can't walk away like that! You've been in Bedlow less than a week, and you've created havoc. I can't even remember how many people you've arrested—we're having to board them out!'

'Lawbreakers, every one of them,' Bowker said morosely.

'Drug dealers, pornographers, yes—I give you full marks for bringing them in with the evidence to convict them, even though it wasn't your job. But the men and women at Davies' party were not hardened criminals. Take Sir Osbert Nunally's daughter, for example. Wild, maybe, but nothing worse. And Laurence Bicester, local director of the West Country Bank— he's a decent family man who's had to resign. His life's ruined.'

'The magistrate with his hand up a girl's skirt and a noseful of coke,' Bowker retaliated. 'It would be interesting to check through court records and see if he was on the bench when Lloyd Davies' clients got off serious charges with a few hundred quid in fines instead of being remanded to a Crown Court for trial.'

Superintendent Billings had the grace to blush.

'The same thought had occurred to me,' he said stiffly. 'I've got DI Mason looking into it now. I'm sure you realise there'll be a major scandal if he turns up anything suspicious.'

Bowker gave him his hangman's grin. 'It's not all doom and despair,' he said cheerfully. 'You can demand an apology from the editor of the *Bedlow Herald* now that the Matthews case is cleared up. He called us incompetent.'

'And hired a private detective!' Billings said. 'Incompetent my foot—I'll make him eat his words.'

'You ought to insist he prints your photo,' Bowker said. 'You look very imposing in uniform. Good for the police image.'

'Do you think so?' The Superintendent took him seriously.

'I ought to be at the station to charge Shane and Mrs Hinksey and start the questioning,' Bowker rumbled.

'I mustn't keep you any longer, Inspector. But one last thing before you go. Harry Mason will be taking early retirement this autumn, on health grounds.'

I wonder if old Harry knows that yet, Bowker thought.

'We've had our differences, you and I, in the past few days,' said Billings. 'Your methods are irregular, to say the least of it. But you get results. I want you to consider a transfer here to take complete charge of the Bedlow plainclothes branch.'

Bowker hesitated. The answer was no, but to turn the man down out of hand would be needlessly insulting, though he had little respect for Billing. And even less liking. But it appeared that Billings had developed a respect for him.

'I'll think it over.' He tried to sound truthful.

Vereker's missing wife was living in a ground-floor flat in a pleasant old house in Oxford—near the river and Christ Church Meadow. Bowker rang the bell and tried to keep an amiable look on his face while he was inspected through the spyhole. He was here unofficially—he didn't want her phoning the local police to say the Cotswold Strangler was trying to break in. He wasn't overly successful, the door opened two inches and it was on the chain.

He held his warrant card up where it could be easily read and after a while she took the chain off. Before he set a foot over the threshold he compared her with the photo of Joanne

Vereker he'd brought with him from the Missing Person file.

It was her, he decided. Pretty brown-haired woman in her late twenties. She wore a green shirt and blue jeans, white socks and no shoes. She didn't seem friendly, but he hadn't expected her to be. People who did vanishing acts were never pleased to find a copper on their doorstep.

'Will this take long?' She showed him into a sitting room with chairs and sofa upholstered in grey corduroy. 'Do you want to sit down?'

Bowker grinned at her spikiness and lowered his bulk into one of the armchairs. A furnished rental, he guessed, looking about the room. She was still in a transition stage.

'I really can't see how my life is any business of the police—I haven't committed any crime.' She wore a frown on her face as she stared at Bowker.

He was trying hard not to appear intimidating, but he was so big and broad that whatever he did, there was an air of physical menace about him—even when he sat still and said nothing. Even his nondescript grey suit couldn't make him look insignificant.

'Curiosity brought me here,' he said. 'Your husband reported you missing. And told me a fairy tale about you being murdered, because you'd got yourself involved in a murder case that I was investigating.'

'His way of getting you to take him seriously. He has a habit of dramatising himself—very boring. I haven't been murdered—you can see that for yourself. So is that the end of it?'

'It means we can close the Missing Person file. Which is only a bit of administration and doesn't mean much. But it's nice to have things tidy.' Bowker was, for him, almost suave.

'I don't understand how you got my address out of my brother. He swore he'd never tell a soul. You threatened him and bullied him, I suppose.'

'Lord love us, no!' There was a look of amazement on

Bowker's dark gypsy features, 'we don't do things like that, you must be confusing us with the KGB.'

'Why else would he tell you?'

'It was a question of conscience.' Bowker sounded very serious, 'Mr Morley is a very conscientious person. My sergeant went to talk to him to ask about you—just a routine enquiry in connection with a Bedlow murder case we were investigating. But before a word was spoken, your brother punched him in the face. He knocked him down.'

Joanne Vereker didn't sound apologetic. 'He can be short-tempered when he's provoked, but Sholto isn't really violent.'

'For a university teacher, he seems to lash out faster than he ought to. The truth is, Mrs Vereker, my sergeant is in the hospital with three broken ribs and seeing double from concussion.'

'My God—Sholto did that?'

When Bowker called on the bearded computer expert earlier, he hadn't thought it essential to tell him that somebody else had injured Jack Knight. He mentioned the injuries and waited while Morley reached the conclusion that he was responsible. He was a *Guardian* reader for sure, Bowker thought—and his sort readily accepted the blame for the world's calamities.

Starvation in Africa, massacre and rape in Bosnia, leprosy in India, sea pollution off Naples, extinction of tigers and other large wild beasts, holes in the stratosphere—a good wallow in guilt made people like Morley feel more socially aware.

Bowker didn't answer her question.

'I went to see Mr Morley this morning to inform him that Detective-Sergeant Knight was lying in hospital. He was very remorseful. He said he didn't know what came over him, he'd just struck out blindly without knowing who he was hitting.'

Joanne Vereker was looking worried by now.

Bowker continued, 'To show how sorry he was, he insisted

on telling me what he refused to tell my sergeant. And here I am.'

'Will he be sent to prison? It will ruin his career—he'll be sacked by the university.'

'That would be a great pity,' Bowker said solemnly. 'I'm sure it was a only a passing mental aberration on his part. He vowed and declared that he'd keep his fists to himself in the future, so on that assurance I agreed to take no further action.'

Joanne Vereker's attitude thawed a little. But not much—she still had a grievance against Bowker.

'Now that you know where I live, what next? Are you going to tell my husband so he'll come pestering me? I shall move again.'

'I've no reason to tell your husband your whereabouts. But he has hired a private enquiry agent to look for you—a man named Morten. Whether he's any good at his job, I don't know.'

'God, why can't he leave me alone!'

'Damaged pride,' Bowker said. 'He might even love you, how do I know? Not that it's any of my business.'

'Then what *is* your business? Why are you here?'

'I told you before—professional curiosity. Your husband and the Bedlow newspaper made a big fuss about your disappearance—Morten found your car where you left it. He was working for the paper then, but he blotted his copybook by drunken driving. The editor dumped him, and your husband hired him.'

Joanne Vereker tucked her legs underneath herself and started to look interested—as any woman would, to find herself heroine of a tangled saga.

'I've proved the newspaper's wrong,' Bowker said with a small smile. 'You're not dead or in danger. So I can forget the whole thing. Have you found a job here yet?'

'Yes, I'm teaching English to foreign students at a language school. I had the qualification before I made my big mistake of marrying Donald Vereker.'

'You don't have to answer if you don't want to—but was your leaving anything to do with Lloyd Davies the lawyer?'

'What do you mean, did I have an affair with that awful crook? Is that what you think?' She glared at him in outrage.

'Don't misunderstand me,' Bowker said hastily. 'I didn't mean that. Last Saturday I had the pleasure of arresting Davies at a party he was throwing. Prohibited substances were in use by all and sundry—and it occurred to me that your husband might have been a guest at similar parties in the past.'

'I won't drop Donald in trouble with the police, even if I've left him. If that's what you're here for, you can forget it.'

'I'm not looking for evidence against him.' Bowker was struck by what he thought of as natural female contrariness. 'He's got troubles enough as it is. If you're planning a divorce and hope to get a financial settlement, don't leave it too long. Serious problems with an insurance company are looming up. His business may slip off the edge of the world and never be seen again.'

Joanne looked at him thoughtfully. 'You've driven from Bedlow to Oxford because you're concerned about my financial prospects—is that what you're saying?'

Bowker laughed, a noise like boulders rolling down a mountain slope. At first she was startled; then she laughed with him.

'I'm a copper, not a social worker. I've told you something of interest to you, in the hope you'll tell me what I want to know. That's fair, isn't it?'

'It depends. What do you want to know?'

'Why you left Vereker.'

She sat thinking about it. Her student's clothes were just a cover while she was angry with herself for marrying the wrong man, Bowker decided. Dressed up, she'd be very attractive—when she was ready for another man, she'd know how to go about it.

'Why do you want to know that?' she asked.

'Because it's a mystery. And I can't stand mysteries.'

'I believe you.' She smiled at his intense look. 'It's simple enough, really. It wasn't Lloyd Davies in particular—he was just a part of it. It dawned on me gradually that Donald's important clients and friends were all crooked in some way. And if they were, and he knew it, what did that make him? And if I let myself be kept by him, what did that make me?'

'Thank you,' Bowker said. Words he used very seldom outside his own home. 'I'll be on my way now you've answered my question. I've a lot to do.'

He surely had. His wife and children were at his mother's, and he was going to collect them and drive them home that evening. And in one more week, he would be taking them to Spain for their summer holiday at the seaside.